The Only Time

Nicole Baker

Contents

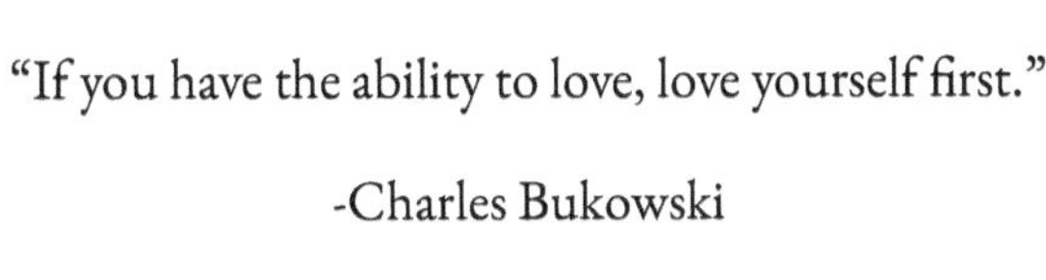

"If you have the ability to love, love yourself first."

-Charles Bukowski

Chapter One

It's nothing. It was probably just a breeze that knocked a branch against the house. There is nobody outside.

I take a shaky step towards my bed, willing myself to be strong. Then I hear another noise coming from downstairs. My heart is pounding out of my chest. It can't be him. There's no way he is in my house.

I tiptoe out of my bedroom and lean forward over the banister to look downstairs at the front door. The doorknob shakes. It hits me that he really may be more dangerous than I could have ever thought. We broke up over a month ago, and he is just getting more persistent.

It started with some threatening texts that I thought were him just trying to get me to text him back. I showed them to my sister-in-law Alexis. She freaked out and forced me to tell my brothers about them.

My brothers threatened to end his life. What can I say, they're Italian. They don't mess around with the safety of their loved ones.

Do I think they would actually do that? No.

Well...I don't think so. Honestly, they might. They are crazy protective of the women in their lives.

Another jiggle of the handle, more aggressively this time, and my stomach drops. What if this is an actual killer or burglar? Is that more or less scary than having Don at the front door? At this point, I'm not sure.

I remember my other sister-in-law Savannah had given me a blow horn after Don started sending threatening messages and showing up wherever I was. She told me if I ever think someone is in my house, don't go downstairs, just sound the horn, and I'll scare the crap out of them.

Shit, I'm sure I'm going to scare the crap out of my neighbors, but at this point, I think I want to wake people up.

I run into my room and open my nightstand drawer. Just as I grab it, I hear the door open downstairs. I don't give it a second thought; I push the button and fall back on my ass. The piercing noise blares in my ears, causing them to ring instantly. I keep it in my hands and continue to hold the button while the effect on my ears leaves me feeling disoriented.

When I stop, I look around. I don't know what I'm looking for. Maybe to see if it worked or if he's standing in the doorway, ready to hurt me. I crawl on my hands and knees out of my room and back over to the banister. I peer downstairs at the door. It's open, but I hear the sound of screeching tires as a car pulls away from the curb by my house.

Motherfucker. It's Don's car. I watch his taillights get smaller as breathing becomes more difficult. Tears begin to fall down my cheeks as I realize this has officially hit a level that I can't handle on my own anymore.

"Mia!" Mrs. Mayberry shouts from my front porch. "Are you okay? I heard a loud noise. When I came out to look, some man was running off your porch."

I look down at my hands, which are trembling, then back at her. "No, I don't think I'm okay."

"I don't think I want you leaving Cleveland. How are we supposed to protect you if you're twelve hours away from us?" my oldest brother Gabe says as he paces nervously back and forth about my parents' kitchen.

His wife, Alexis, trails behind him as she tries to get him to stand still for a second. I don't think there will be any calming him down right now.

Ma is anxiously cooking up a storm in the kitchen while we all are scattered around her. I know we're Italian and can eat a lot, but the amount of food she's made today can feed an entire homeless shelter. I'm not going to call her out, though, because I'd rather have her distracted right now.

I've never been as scared as I was last night. I called Savannah, who insisted I spend the rest of the night at their house. My second oldest brother, Lucas, is slightly less high-strung than Gabe. But even he is standing in the corner, intently biting his nails and quietly stewing with worry.

Pa is pouring a glass of whiskey. He looks up at me. "Are you sure you don't want to stay with us?" he asks.

"I think getting away from it right now feels like the best thing for me to do. He knows where all of you guys live, and I don't want to put anybody else in danger."

"Don't leave because of us," Savannah speaks up. "That's not what our concern is right now. It's about *your* safety."

Tears threaten to spill down my cheeks again. I do my best to blink them away. If I fall apart now, they won't let me leave.

"I know. I'm leaving because it's what I want right now. I feel safer taking a step back while we work with the police."

"You know, there's an easier way to fix this," Gabe says through a clenched jaw.

I roll my eyes. "I don't think going all mafia and killing him is the answer here. You have a wife and kids to worry about. You can't take care of them from jail."

"Geez, Mia," he chuckles. "I was gonna say let me beat him up, maybe put some fear in him. I wasn't talking about killing him."

Pa slams down his whiskey and then looks up. "If anyone's taking him out, it's me. No one threatens my daughter's safety like this and gets away with it."

"You guys are insane," I pause to let out a sigh. "That settles it. I'm going to go stay with Layla in Georgia."

"Didn't she just get engaged?" Ma speaks up for the first time.

"Yeah, she did. Her fiancé Josh is super nice—I've talked to him on the phone while chatting with her. I'll actually be staying with Layla's brother, Eric. I guess he has a lot of extra room at his place and I didn't want to get in the way of the newlyweds. Even though they kept on insisting that I wouldn't be."

"How long do you plan on staying?" Lucas asks as he pushes off the wall and comes further into the kitchen.

"I don't know," I answer honestly. "I guess that all depends on Don. The police said they would talk to him, but they couldn't arrest him or anything. We'll see if he follows the restraining order."

"Well, you threatened a restraining order several times," Gabe says with frustration. "I don't think that means much to the guy."

I'm afraid that he's right. That's why I want to get out of here. Last night shook me to my core. I barely slept a wink thinking about what he would have done if he got inside. Does he want to hurt me? The thought of it sends goosebumps down my spine. I never thought I'd be in a situation like this. It all feels like a terrible nightmare.—one that I'm desperate to wake up from. But this is reality, and I need to find a way to make this work. I need to leave for a while.

"That's why I think I should go away for now. I can bring my laptop and work from the house."

Lucas shakes his head back and forth. "I think you should take some time off. We could get Michelle to take over some of your urgent tasks. Right now, you just need to take a breather."

"He's right," Savannah agrees. "And I'll pitch in any way that I can. Lucas can train me on whatever he needs help with."

"You'd do that for me?" I ask with a shaky breath.

Savannah's head tilts to the side. "Of course, I would. You're my sister. I'd do anything for you."

Growing up with three brothers was great—I wouldn't change a thing. But I always wanted a sister for as long as I can remember. I never dreamed that I would be gifted with three amazing sisters. My brothers may be idiots, but they sure picked amazing women to marry. Having the love and support from them means the world to me.

"Thank you," I reply softly. "That's so sweet."

I might take the first week off to get settled in, but I'm not making Savannah learn my job so I can sit around a lone man's house all day long doing nothing. I have no interest in fighting with them right now about how long I need to rest, so I don't say anything more.

I don't want to admit this to them, but I'm nervous about staying with Eric. I don't know a thing about the guy. Just that he works long hours and generally keeps to himself. I wonder what kind of man would want a life like that. I keep picturing a tall, lanky guy with glasses and the inability to look me directly in the eyes.

Is it going to be awkward whenever we're home together? At least he doesn't sound like the type to habitually bring girls home. That eliminates having to explain why he has a random chick staying at his place.

"Are you sure this is what you want?" Gabe looks at me with concern.

He's always been the decider between me and my other brothers. Marcus is the youngest of the three boys but older than me. He lives in Chicago with his wife, Lexi. I just talked to him before I got to Ma and Pa's house and promised to call him after I left to let him know how it goes.

With him being the youngest and craziest, he is able to worry about me in a normal way.

I look around the room at everyone's unsettled faces. I know I'm going to miss them, but hopefully I won't be gone for very long. Maybe a month away will be enough time for everything to calm down.

It doesn't sound like a long time, but I've never been away from all of them for that long. We're a close family and we run a large wine distribution company together.

It took a long time to recover when Marcus moved to Chicago for Lexi. Our Sunday dinners didn't feel the same without him for a while.

"Yes," I say with as much confidence as I can muster. "This is what I want. This is what I *need*."

Gabe nods his head at Pa, as if it was somehow their decision to make and not mine. I want to tell them that I don't actually need their approval, but it's not worth it.

"When are you leaving?" Alexis asks sadly.

"Tomorrow morning."

A silence falls upon the room. I would have never thought I'd be chased out of my own home, fleeing for safety. This is so surreal. It's the kind of shit you see in the movies.

Ma wipes away a tear. She's trying to be strong in front of me, but I know she's going to break down as soon as we all leave. This is not the way I saw my life going. How could I have been so wrong about Don? What did I ever see in him in the first place?

I feel like such a failure.

My poor decisions have led to this moment where every member of the family is now affected. It's not what I'm used to. I'm the fixer in the family. I'm the one my brothers come to when they need help with a problem. They all think they take care of the family, but underneath all their macho bravado is a sister who keeps them level-headed and fixes their mistakes. I've never been the reason for the chaos in the family.

I don't like the feeling of it one bit.

I need to get home so I can pack. After I give everybody hugs, I hop into my car and do my best not to break down—that would be useless and a waste of energy. I need to be strong and resilient. Lucas insists on following me home and staying with me while I pack. I'll be spending the night at his house again.

As I drive, I take in a deep breath, my body trembling on the intake as I hold in my desire to cry, then exhale it all away.

Hopefully, everyone is just overreacting to this, and it will all blow over in a couple of weeks. I'm sure Don will stop acting so crazy once he finds out how serious I am about him staying away.

Chapter Two

Eric

"I told you she was hot," Adam jabs Jeremy as we walk back into our building after lunch.

Jeremy feigns injury. "I never said she wasn't hot. I just don't think she is *that* hot."

"She's a ten. I don't know how he gets any work done," Adam continues.

Once we're in the elevator, I press the button for our floor and try to tune out their antics.

"Come on, Eric. Tell me you don't think he's crazy for hiring an assistant like that? How does he concentrate?" Adam forces me into the conversation.

I shrug my shoulders. "He probably doesn't have the dick of a twelve-year-old who sports a boner at the sight of a pretty lady like you."

Jeremy cracks up as Adam rolls his eyes at me. "Or maybe you're just mad cuz you've become impotent at the ripe old age of thirty-two."

"Whatever. I'll catch you two later," I say as the doors open.

I try not to let his jab grate on me as I take long strides to my office. He's fucking wrong. I'm not impotent. I just don't see the value in chasing after women who have the power to destroy you for fun or because of their own selfishness.

I'm talking from experience.

I'm not saying I don't let loose once in a while with an attractive woman when I need to blow off some steam. But I'm always in control and know I won't feel anything for her. And she always knows it's just a one-night thing. I don't lead anybody on. If they get false hope, that's on them.

Just as I enter my office and sit down, my phone rings. It never ends at this job.

"Hello, Eric Williams," I answer.

"Oh, thank God. You answered."

"Layla? Is everything okay?" I ask as I sit up straight.

"No, it's not okay. Remember me telling you about my friend Mia?

I vaguely remember when Layla basically told me a friend of hers might need to get away and she'd be staying with me. I put it out of my mind, thinking nothing would come of it.

"I guess. Sort of," I say reluctantly.

"Well, she needs to come stay with you." *That was fast.*

My entire body stiffens. This is not what I need right now. Work is kicking my ass with this new acquisition I've just been assigned to. One of my sister's random friends bothering me and taking up my space in my own home isn't going to help.

"I didn't think you were entirely serious about that, Layla. I don't even know this woman."

"Of course I was serious. I already told her you were okay with it, so you can't back out now. She really needs this right now."

I push my shoulders back as I try to work out the mounting tension. "But it's weird. Why does she need a place to crash? Did she lose a job or something? Is this some crazy irresponsible chick who's going to mooch off of me?"

"Eric, your diva is showing right now. I wouldn't ask for this if it wasn't serious. The reasons are none of your business. She just needs to get away for a while."

"How long is a while?" I sigh into the phone.

She grunts in response like it's completely unreasonable for me to ask about the stranger who is going to be staying with me in my house.

"I don't know. A month, maybe two."

Fuck. That's a long time to not feel comfortable in my own home. But there's one thing you need to know about my sister Layla. She is relentless and fiercely protective of the ones she loves. She will lose her shit if I back out now.

Clearly, this chick is going through something. Since I'm the only one without a wife or kids, I get to take her in. Lucky me.

"Seriously, Lay? That's a really long time. Why can't she stay with you?"

"I tried to convince her, but she doesn't want to impose since Josh just proposed and we're still in my small two-bedroom home."

"So, it's okay to impose in my home?" I ask with annoyance.

"Well, you live in a five-bedroom freakin' mansion where you guys can avoid each other if you wanted to."

She's got me there. My house is big. Much bigger than hers. "When does she come?"

"She's driving down from Cleveland right now. She'll be there around dinner time."

"Layla! Are you kidding me?"

I now pull at my neck as the tension builds. I can't believe she's throwing this at me right now. And how is the reason she's staying with me none of my business? That seems like a reasonable question for me to ask.

"You better at least be there to help her. It'll be a little awkward if I have to welcome a complete stranger and get her settled in by myself."

"Of course, I'll be there. You think I'm gonna let her first impression of this place be you? I would never do that to her."

"Gee. What a great thank you for doing this for your friend."

"Well, it's the truth. You are literally the grumpiest person on earth. She needs a smiling face and a warm hug when she gets here. Oh, I was going to make sure one of your guest rooms is nice and cozy for her. What's the code to your garage?"

I clench my jaw in an effort to keep from going off on her. "It's my birthday," I say through gritted teeth.

"Thanks, Mr. Sunshine. Make sure to turn that frown upside down when you get home. Mia doesn't need your negative energy. See ya tonight."

She hangs up without so much as a goodbye or thanks again for doing this even though I know how much it's going to irritate you. I slam the phone down on the receiver. How is this my life? I must have the shittiest luck of anybody. Not only does my sister expect me to let her friend, whom I've never met, stay with me for two months, but she wants me to act happy about it.

That's not gonna happen.

She's probably some airhead who lost her job and wants to mooch off her friend's rich older brother for a while. Layla is too nice to see through people and their motives, but I've been burned enough times to know better.

I spend the rest of the afternoon trying not to think about what I am coming home to.

I begin researching the company that we are looking to acquire. It seems like it's going to take a ton of my time to get a handle on an acquisition this size if they want to move forward as quickly as they do. They are a massive company with two thousand employees.

I'm going to need to get Adam involved to go over who we can keep on board and who will be given severance packages.

I dial his assistant and ask for him to see me as soon as possible.

While I shuffle through more numbers, I hear a knock on my door.

"You rang?" Adam walks in casually as he plops down on the seat across from me.

I met Adam when he started at this company a couple of years after me. We both really like mountain biking, so we've taken our bikes over to Greenville, North Carolina together to bike their trails. He's a good guy.

I know he can come off like a dick but it's a front. Deep down, he would never treat anybody without the respect they deserve. He's just trying to figure out what the hell he wants out of life like all of us. At my age, I'm starting to wonder if anybody ever really figures it out or if we eventually just start pretending.

"I'm working on a new acquisition—two thousand employees. I need you to look over the numbers with me to see how many of them we can realistically keep in order to smooth over the dickhead board."

"Damn. You know whenever we acquire companies that large, there are tons of positions that get cut. Corporations always end up having positions filled where the employee doesn't have enough work to fill a full-time position."

My body suddenly feels prickly all over and I resist the urge to itch my chest. I hate this part of the job.

"I know. Based on my rough estimate of a standard company in their industry with an equivalent level of revenue, they are about thirty percent overstaffed. But I just need you to do some more digging for me."

"No problem."

I crane my neck to the side and hear a loud crack. This day sucks.

Adam looks at me funny. "You alright, man? You seem tense."

I raise an eyebrow at him. "You always tell me I look tense."

He laughs to himself. "True. But you seem tenser than usual."

I slightly recline in my chair and throw my head back as I look up at the large ceiling tiles in my office. "It's my sister. She just called me and told me one of her friends needs to stay with me for a while. She'll be there by the time I get home from work."

I can see the look of confusion on his face. He doesn't mask his feelings very well. "And you hate people, so this is equivalent to a shark attack for you?"

"I never said that. I'm not so dramatic that I'd react like that."

"Your neck just went off like a firework when you cracked it."

I resist the urge to crack it again then sit up and look him in the eyes. My shoulders deflate. "Fine. This is my own personal hell. Why does she have to stay with me?"

"Doesn't your sister live in like a tiny little house?"

"Yeah," I draw out.

"And don't you live in a five-bedroom mansion?"

"Yeah, but it only has one kitchen and one family room," I respond in defense.

"So, go watch TV in your room, or the massive basement with the huge built-in bar, or go watch it in your backyard where it's hanging above your outdoor stone fireplace."

"What about the kitchen?" I point out.

"You've got issues man. I guess you might have to risk a bit of social interaction with a woman for a little while if she happens to be in the kitchen when you are. I think you'll survive."

He clearly doesn't get it. I know it sounds crazy, but I like my space. I like coming home from work and not having to be on for anybody. I spent years with a woman who I was constantly trying to please. And she only ended up being unsatisfied with anything I ever did for her.

I'm just over all of it. "Whatever. I just like my space when I get home."

He looks at me sympathetically. "I get it. You've been burned a time or two in life. But not all women are like Kim."

"This isn't about Kim," I snap back.

"Everything is about Kim. You changed when she left you. I'm not saying what she did wasn't shitty, but you have to face the facts. You haven't resolved your shit since she left." He stands up and heads for the door. "I feel for you, I do. But maybe having someone live with you for a while will be a good thing. It might loosen you up a bit—remind you how to have some fun."

With that, he leaves. The room starts to feel like there's not enough oxygen in it. Like someone sucked it all out leaving me to die. I undo the top button of my shirt but it does nothing.

What a friend he is. The least he could have done was let me bitch and moan about it like a real friend would do. He didn't have to offer his opinion. Then he had to go and bring up my ex. Now I'm not only tense, but I'm angry. I'm sure that will be a lovely combination to bring home to this woman.

I've managed to put off leaving my office for as long as I can. It's now seven, and I'm starving.

The drive home feels like it lasts a millisecond. I drove slower than usual, trying to drag it out. I pull into my driveway and spot Josh's truck along with a black Range Rover. Not exactly the car I would think someone struggling financially would be driving.

When I step into the house, I hear laughter coming from the kitchen. It's an odd feeling to hear those sounds in my house. When Kim lived here with me, she would greet me much differently.

"Why are you so late?"

"I'm going out with my friends."

"Did you make reservations for us tonight? I told you I wanted to eat out."

"Gretchen got the new Birkin bag."

I remember the argument we got in that night when I told her that a purse that costs thirty grand is ridiculous. With my line of work, we are surrounded by wealthy people, but that doesn't mean we have to spend an inordinate amount of money on a bag just for appearances.

She told me I was being insensitive and didn't understand how it makes her look like in front of these women that she doesn't have a man who will spoil her like theirs will.

I ended up buying her the damn bag.

I take a deep breath as I prepare to walk in the room. The fact that I need to pump myself up to walk into my own home just because there is a guest sends a wave of guilt through my body. What the hell is wrong with me?

Chapter Three

Mia

If I was unsure of whether or not this would be a good place to escape to, the trees alone have sold me on it.

The live oak trees have branches so long and thick that it looks like they are trying to reach out and grab you. They stretch above the streets like a canopy covering you from the southern sun. The Spanish moss drapes off their branches like cobwebs.

It's breathtakingly beautiful and makes me instantly feel like I'm in a secret forest that only I know about. It feels magical.

I pull into the driveway and my breath is stolen from my lungs. The entire driveway is lined with these trees. The house is massive. Its low country design features white brick with large white columns that start at the front deck and rise up to the second story, anchoring a full second story porch.

The lower-level front porch is made of red brick, which contrasts nicely with the house's white brick. It's massive, with dark wood swings on each end. The porch also has expensive-looking Adirondack chairs. I can only imagine how calming it is to have a morning cup of coffee out there while taking in the enchanting trees.

After I park my car and cut the engine, the front door swings open, followed by a beaming Layla. I match her grin despite the messed-up reason for my visit.

I met Layla years ago at a wine conference in California. She was there to learn more about the wine industry for her restaurant and I was there to network. We hit it off, and the rest is history.

She's the kind of friend you want in your corner. She is fiercely loyal but will give it to you straight even if it's not what you want to hear.

She offered to get her brothers involved with Don, but I told her I have my own overprotective set of brothers and can't deal with another set. I made her promise not to tell anyone the reason I'm here. I'm still trying to come to terms with it myself and don't need the pity party that would come with some poor, helpless woman who apparently has bad judgment in men.

"You're here," Layla screams as her arms wrap around me in a giant bear hug.

I can't move my arms, so I just let her squeeze me. Her fiancé Josh joins us at my car. "Babe, I don't think she can even breathe right now."

He winks at me with a smile on his face. I've only ever met him through video chat, but he seems so genuine and in love with Layla. I'm so over the moon happy for them.

"Shut up. She can breathe," Layla replies. She pulls away and grabs my hand. "Get her bags," she calls over her shoulder to Josh. Ever the gentleman, he opens my trunk and starts pulling out my luggage.

"Are you sure we shouldn't help him?" I ask hesitantly.

"No, he's got it. You just drove over eight hours. I'm sure you're exhausted and desperately need a drink."

I shrug my shoulders and follow her up the brick steps. She isn't wrong. A drink right now would help take the edge off of my stiff muscles and creeping anxiety.

I'm running from someone who could be a killer or, at the very least, a stalker. On top of that, I'm moving in with a man I know next to nothing about. Ok. I desperately need a drink.

Stepping into the house is like stepping into my dreams. The foyer has a large light wood circle table with a vase of green and white flowers. Don't ask me the names of them—I'm terrible with flowers. The wooden floors are slightly darker than the wooden table. As we walk further into the house, I see the white brick fireplace, cream couches, and light wood end tables.

It's very country chic, though I doubt Layla's brother would appreciate me using such a feminine way of describing the place.

Everything is in neutral colors with precisely placed green plants, giving a subtle pop of color. I never considered the possibility that Eric could be gay. There's no way any straight man has this good of taste. Honestly, it would be a breath of fresh air if he were gay.

I wouldn't have to worry about walking around in my underwear if I wanted a late-night snack.

Speaking of snacks, the kitchen is unbelievable. The white brick continues throughout as the backsplash, paired with plain white cabinets, creating such a clean look. The best part, though, is a light wood treated countertop sitting on top of the island in the middle of the room. It's massive and my brain begins to think of all the meals I could cook in here.

Being Italian, and growing up in Cleveland's own Little Italy, my dishes are more Italian inspired. But I could see buying some southern cookbooks and beginning a new journey of food pairings with some of our finest wine.

"Wow," I say on a breath of awe. "This kitchen is just...wow."

Layla looks around. "I know. Eric doesn't really cook though. A shame, isn't it? What a waste."

"That's a sin of the highest order. You shouldn't be allowed to own a kitchen this nice without being required to cook in it at all times."

She smiles brightly. "I'm so glad you're here. Maybe you can talk some sense into him."

"Who are we talking sense into?" Josh joins us at the island. "I put your stuff in your room upstairs."

"That's really sweet of you," I reply graciously. "Thank you so much."

He shrugs his shoulders. "It's the least I can do since you're staying with Eric. Good luck."

My skin breaks out in goosebumps. What the hell does that mean? I look to Layla with eyes wide open.

"Josh, don't scare her." She turns to me. "He's joking. Eric is a great guy. He's just been stressed at work lately. He likes his alone time."

Yeah, that makes me feel all warm and fuzzy when I'm about to crash in this man's home. Awesome. When they described him months ago, I got the impression he was more shy and awkward. Now I don't know what to think.

Layla opens the fridge and pulls out a glass pitcher. "Want some bourbon peach iced tea?"

"Yes, I may need liquid courage now that Josh just scared the crap out of me. Plus, that sounds delicious."

Josh looks slightly embarrassed. "I'm sorry. That was supposed to come off as funny. Eric is a great guy. He's one of my best friends."

"Yeah, I think I missed the humor in that," I say as I try to force a smile.

It's not too late to just head back home. This is starting to feel like a crazy idea.

"Here," Layla slides a glass to me. "This should take the edge off. I know this is a lot for you. It would be a lot for anyone."

We all raise our glasses together. "To Josh never trying to become a comedian, since he most certainly would fail miserably," Layla says loudly.

He rolls his eyes but gives a final salute before taking a sip. I chuckle at how direct they are with each other.

I take a sip then look down at my glass in shock. "Damn, Lay. This drink is awesome. The peach is so fresh."

She smiles. "Welcome to Georgia, Mia. Where the peaches grow."

"Come on," Josh starts. "Let's give you a tour of the place before she starts on a tangent."

The house really is beautiful. There are five large bedrooms, all on the top floor. The guest bedroom, my room, is at the end of the long hall, opposite end from Eric's.

He turned one of the bedrooms into a little reading room. It overlooks the backyard which has views of the trees. I hope he isn't weird about sharing the room, because I would love to read a good book in here.

The backyard has a huge pool with a stone waterfall cascading into it. It's October, so I didn't think I'd be able to use it, but apparently, it's heated. I'm sure he won't mind if I use it. From what I hear, he is a workaholic. It's going to be like I have my own private little getaway.

Just as Layla is pouring us all another drink, I hear a car door shut outside.

"Oh, that must be Eric," Layla looks up with a smile.

My stomach does a couple of somersaults at the thought of meeting the man I'm going to be living with for a while. It just feels kind of awkward, like I'm invading his space.

The door opens and I feel my fingers clutch my drink. When he appears in the kitchen, I suck in a breath as my heart begins to race.

This is her brother?

I had pictured a tall, lanky guy with no sense in style or people skills. The man standing in front of me is certainly tall, but lanky he is not. He is wearing a blue suit that you can tell has an incredible physique underneath by the way it hugs his biceps. His brown hair is short on the sides and longer on top but looks kind of wild and messy, like he may have been pulling at it on the way home.

I smile at him, waiting for him to reciprocate the sentiment but it never happens. He pulls at the back of his neck, and I wonder if maybe he is lacking people skills despite being extremely handsome.

"Eric," Layla runs over and gives him a hug, "this is Mia."

"Hi, Mia," Eric replies flatly.

I stand up from my seat at the island and meet him at the edge of the counter   . I extend my hand. "Nice to meet you, Eric. Thank you so much for letting me stay here. I know it must be extremely inconvenient. If you need me to stay in a hotel or something just…"

"No, no, no. You're not staying in a hotel by yourself. It's safe here. And you don't need to be eating takeout for breakfast, lunch, and dinner," Layla interjects.

Eric looks at her then at me. "I have a headache. Did you give her a tour already?"

Layla seems a bit taken back but recovers with a smile. "I did. She is all set in her room."

Eric nods then turns to me. "Help yourself to anything you need. Nice to meet you."

With that, he walks away. I hear his footsteps ascend the stairs while I'm left in the kitchen trying to figure out what the hell that was about.

Josh rolls his eyes. "If we haven't explained it already, Eric is a grump. But he is a good guy. I promise that you will warm up to him or learn to ignore it."

"Um, are you sure about this?" I ask right before I chug down the rest of my drink.

"I wouldn't let you stay here if I didn't think that it was a good idea. This is about your safety. Eric has a great security system installed. No one will hurt you when you're under this roof. It's not about whether or not he's a grump, which he is, but whether or not you're safe."

I sigh as the reality of her words hit me. She's right. This is the situation I'm in. I can't be picky that the man I'm staying with isn't some warm, genuine guy. It's not about having fun and being on vacation, it's about being safe.

"You're right. I know I should be worried about my safety. I just don't want to be an inconvenience to him."

"Everything is an inconvenience to him. It's part of his charm," Josh jokes, though I find it hard to laugh at the moment. "Sorry, I suck at the humor today."

"He wasn't always like this. Once upon a time he was a happy guy," she says with sadness evident on her face.

"What happened?" I ask, curiosity getting the best of me.

"A woman," she replies. "But it's not my story to tell. He's never really opened up about it anyways, so I don't know all the details."

"I see," I reply. All of a sudden, the drive and events of the last few days seem to have caught up with me and a huge yawn takes over.

"Let's get out of her hair, babe," Josh nudges Layla. "She's tired and probably wants to settle into her room."

Layla looks over at me as she bites her bottom lip. "Are you going to be okay? I don't want to leave you here if you don't feel comfortable. I can spend a few nights here with you until you get used to Eric and your new environment."

Even though my body is slightly shaky from my nerves, I don't want to burden anyone. Of course, it would make me feel better if she stayed, but I could never ask her to do that.

"Don't be ridiculous. I'm fine," I lie. "You guys get out of here. I need to shower and go to bed. I'm beat."

I walk them to the front door where Layla proceeds to give me several hugs and tells me that she will stop over in the morning. That eases some of my anxiety…until the second they leave and the door closes.

I turn around and look at this strange place. I don't even know if I should be closing it all down before I go to bed. Should I lock up and turn off the lights? Is Eric in bed for good?

It's only seven. Does he really have a headache?

I walk up the stairs to my room, where I close the door and take a seat on my bed. It's dark and quiet, and I've never felt more alone in my life.

For the first time in years, I cry for myself. The tears spill over in quick succession as I fall back onto the comforter and let all my emotions that I've pushed down for days, weeks—even years come to the surface.

It ends up draining me to my core, where I end up falling asleep on top of the covers.

Chapter Four

Eric

I woke up extra early to get in a run before work. I didn't get great sleep last night and I needed something to wake me up.

I tossed and turned all night thinking about what the hell I'm supposed to be doing with Mia here in my home. Am I supposed to invite her to dinner even though I'm probably shit company like we're Beauty and the Beast?

I can't believe I agreed to this. Although, to be honest, I didn't really agree to this.

The morning's fall chill was exactly what I needed to wake my brain up despite its desire to go back to sleep. I walk back inside to get ready for work. My grey shirt is sticking to my body from all the sweat. I do my best to wipe the sweat pouring down my face with the bottom of my shirt as I stroll into the kitchen.

To my surprise, Layla and Mia are standing at the kitchen island clutching coffee cups. I must've missed Layla's car parked in my driveway.

My sister's face lights up when she sees me. I do my best to offer a small smile, hoping to make up for being a bit of an unwelcoming dick to her friend last night. I don't handle things being sprung on me last minute very well.

There's also the fact that I'm still questioning why a thirty something year old woman needs to stay at my place. Is there a motive? Does she know how much money I have and is looking to worm her way into my life to take advantage of it?

I wouldn't be surprised. Poor Layla is too kind to see through it.

"Morning ladies." I nod and look at Mia. "I'm sorry about last night. I was a bit worn from work. I hope your first night went alright."

There, I did it. I was nice. Layla mouths thank you to me, knowing that none of this is coming natural to me.

Mia smiles at me. "I'm sorry to be intruding in your personal space. And my first night went well. Thank you for asking."

Her response feels just as forced as mine.

As I pour my coffee, I glance over at Mia while her and Layla continue talking. She's pretty. Not the usual type I go for. Kim was blonde and stick thin with little curves.

Mia has brown hair, pulled up in a messy bun right now. She's wearing pajama shorts and a baggy t-shirt, so I can't get a read on her body.

Not that it really matters, I'm not interested.

After I take a long shower, I dress for work and grab a bar and banana for the road. Not the healthiest or most filling breakfast, but I just need to get out of the house. I heard Layla talking about wanting to taste Mia's cooking tonight.

I suppose that means I will be coming home to company again.

It's not that I don't like being around my family, because I do, but lately they have been making more and more comments about my life. Everyone wants to know when I'll get back out there and date again. It isn't that simple. I don't want to be in a relationship ever again, but I don't have the heart to tell them that. That will just invite more questions, and I don't want to talk about it. I don't want to talk about Kim.

I walk into my office and switch on the lights a little harder than necessary. Being out of my element and routine is already stressing me out.

Charlotte follows me into my office with a pad of paper and a pen. She takes a seat across from me. "Tough morning, boss?"

I fall into my chair and run a hand through my hair. "You could say that."

"Anything I can help with?" she asks.

I wish. Charlotte is an incredible assistant, and can make many of my problems go away, but this isn't one of them.

"No, I'm just having a bad morning. Didn't get much sleep. I'll get over it. Let's go over the agenda for the day."

She nods her head, thankfully not asking anymore questions. "You have a morning meeting with Adam to go over the staffing analysis for your current project. He wants to get some questions answered before he goes any further. Then you have an eleven o'clock with your team. After lunch you have a meeting with Peter."

She can't make eye contact with me when she says the last part. My hands instantly ball into fists as I try to compose myself.

"Why does Peter want a meeting with me?" I say through clenched teeth.

Peter and I generally do our best to avoid any one-on-one contact. We don't get along, but it's not something that has ever really been openly acknowledged.

"This is a big acquisition. He said he wants to make sure everything is in order to make sure it is successful."

Of course he does. While this does fall under his list of responsibilities, we've done just fine by me working with the VP of Acquisitions. Today, of all days, he wants to meet with me.

I do my best to suppress my anger under the appearance of indifference. "Fine. I'll meet with him," I say with contempt.

She nods at me, not calling me out on the fact that I have no say so in the matter. He's the COO and while I don't directly report to him, you don't get to decline a meeting with him.

After she leaves me, I kick the garbage can under my desk, knocking it over. What the hell is going on with my life? Why does it feel like I'm losing the tight grip of control that I worked so hard for? It's the only thing that's kept me together in the last couple of years. That and my hobby, which nobody else knows about. I don't know why I keep it a secret.

Yes, you do.

I look at the time and know that the next hour will be a bitch to keep my brain occupied until I meet with Ryan. I'm far too pent up to work productively. I might need a night out with the guys to find a woman to bring home. This energy needs to be released somehow.

I manage to get through most of the day, but I'm dreading this moment as I walk into Peter's corner office.

He's on the phone but holds up his finger at me to wait for him. I manage to turn around before I roll my eyes. He has pictures hanging all over his office of every important person he has ever met or done business with. It's a wall to brag about how important he thinks he is. Not a single picture in his office of family members, not even *her*.

Goes to show what he thinks is worth bragging about.

I turn around at the sound of the phone being placed on the receiver. Peter stands up and extends his hand. My body cringes at the feeling of his hand on mine.

"Thanks for meeting with me, Eric," he says as he unbuttons his jacket and sits back down. "I know I'm not your favorite person."

I feel suddenly weak and vulnerable in the face of his confidence.

"Let's just focus on the reason for this meeting," I bite.

"Fair enough," he agrees.

While he talks logistics, I can't help but take in the slight belly he seems to have acquired since I last saw him. The man is showing his age of fifty-two. It should make me feel better, but it just seems to create another surge of anger.

Peter walks me through exactly how he wants this acquisition to go, like I'm some kind of fucking moron who doesn't do this for a living. He also just proves to me how this is all about image for him, and not about making decisions based on what's best for our company and our employees.

Whether he likes it or not, the employees at this company that we are acquiring know the ins and outs of the business more than we do. I have found that listening to them and doing whatever we can to keep them on board through the transition is beneficial.

He just wants to make it as profitable as possible, whether or not that will work out well for us in the end makes no difference to him.

Instead of voicing my opinion just so he can flex his power over me and shut it down, I nod along so I can get the hell out of here as soon as possible.

By the time the meeting is over, I decide I need to get out of this office. Instead of sticking around, I head home.

All I want to do is head back to my barn to decompress, but when I pull in my driveway I realize that's not going to happen.

Before I even open my front door I hear the commotion happening inside which doubles in octave once opened. I quickly wonder if I can escape to my barn without anybody realizing that I'm home. All I need to do is sneak into my bedroom and change out of my suit.

"Uncle Eric," my niece Brielle screams as she runs up to me and wraps her arms around my leg.

She's one of the only people in my life who can still bring out the softer side of me. Her presence instantly makes me feel better.

I reach down and pick her up. She's four years old, and the best thing that has happened to our family. She lost her mom to cancer when she was an infant. It was a hard time for all of us. I didn't think I would see my brother make it out of that situation. Luckily, he met Charlotte who is now pregnant and due in a couple of months. She's the best mom to Brie and an incredibly supportive wife to Asher.

"Hi, sweetie," I say, then give her a big kiss on her chubby little cheek.

"I missed you. You didn't come to my recital. I was sad."

Shit, tear out my heart why don't you? I tried like hell to make it, but I was stuck in a meeting with executives. Needing to leave early for my niece's dance recital wouldn't have gone over well.

"I'm so sorry. I wanted to be there so badly. Did you get the cookies and flowers I sent over? Your daddy sent me the video. I watched it a hundred times. You were the best one out there."

She giggles in my arms. "You think so?"

"I know so."

We walk into the kitchen where my entire family is huddled around my large island laughing.

"Oh, Mia," my mom says with an arm around her. "This food all smells amazing. How lucky we are to be treated to your family recipes."

Ever since mom and Layla worked out their differences not too long ago, she's been so different. She shed the entitlement that came with my father's business taking off years ago, now back to the old women we once knew.

Mia smiles. "I'm so happy to cook for you guys. You're so sweet to spend the evening with me. And I'm slightly obsessed with your son's kitchen, so any excuse to use it."

Well, at least someone puts this kitchen to use. For as much time as I spend in my home, making home cooked meals hasn't been a part of my routine. It wasn't when Kim lived here, and it certainly hasn't been since she left.

It's not that I don't want to use it, but there's something about cooking for one that's depressing. With Kim, it was like cooking for one because she wouldn't eat anything but salads. It was like living with a rabbit.

"Hey, look who's home," my dad shouts over the noise.

Everybody turns to me with my niece still in my arms. I don't know why, but I focus in on Mia's reaction. I watch her eyes as they look me up and down then, as if embarrassed by something, back to the pot in front of her.

"I didn't think we would see you until after dinner," Layla says as she greets with me a kiss on the cheek then proceeds to steal Bric out of my arms.

Since she is the only kid in the family at the moment, until Charlotte has her baby, we all fight over her. I hope we don't turn her into a diva as she gets older.

"I guess it slipped your mind to tell me I was hosting a dinner at my house tonight," I mutter to her under my breath.

"Sorry. I'm trying to make Mia feel more at home here. She's going through a tough time and just really needs to feel the love."

I'll bet she's going through a tough time, and she needs a rich man to come to her rescue. I still would love to know if she even has a job.

Despite my foul mood, I walk over to my mom and give her a kiss. I know she still worries about me daily, with all her text messages and phone calls. She thinks I'm depressed and am going to do something stupid one day. She may not know that I can see through it. If I don't answer her for more than a day, she'll just *happen* to be in the neighborhood at ten o'clock at night asking me a million questions about my mental state.

I have a desk drawer filled with therapists' business cards that she hands to me like their Tic Tacs.

"I'm so happy you're home early," she says with a smile. "See, maybe Mia being here will be just what you need."

Well, that's not awkward at all to say as Mia stands right next to us. Annoyance prickles my body. I pull at the tension in my neck. I don't know how to respond.

"That smells good, Mia," I say in an effort to deflect. "What are you making?"

She bites her bottom lip. "It's cacio e pepe."

"Mia made these noodles this afternoon by hand...from scratch," Mom says proudly. "This is what you need in your life. A woman who can cook."

Mia coughs uncomfortably. I do the only thing I can think of in the moment—walk away. I find my brothers and dad who are now in the other room watching a football game.

It's some extreme nineteen fifties shit going on in my house right now. The women in the kitchen while the men watch football.

"I didn't know you got married man. Congratulations," my youngest brother Liam slaps my back.

I roll my eyes. "Fuck off."

"Seriously. Had I known Layla's friend was so hot and could cook like an eighty-year-old Italian woman, I would've offered up my place."

I don't know why that grates on me. "Well, I doubt she would want to shack up with you in your bachelor pad. She would also probably have to be okay with listening to you have sex with a different woman every weekend."

He shrugs. "If she was living with me, I could focus on just her. She's the kind of beautiful you settle down with and give up the bachelor lifestyle for."

Of course he would be pining after Mia already. Is she classically beautiful? Yes, in an effortless way. I would be lying if I said I didn't notice her full lips just now or the hint of cleavage under her top.

But all that does is stir a sense of fear and dread in me instead of arousal. Those are the dangerous ones. The ones who make you think that you could settle down with them and build a life together.

I know the reality of love. It can break you and make you second guess everything you've built in your life.

"Well, she isn't living with you," I reply coolly.

I try to focus on the game despite being fully aware of his eyes on me. "You like her or something?"

I chuckle to myself at the mere idea. "I think I've said five words to her. I don't even know her."

He shakes his head in dismay. "It wouldn't kill you to be a little more friendly to the woman staying in a stranger's house."

"Do you know why she's staying here?" I ask curiously. Maybe he knows something that I don't.

He shrugs. "No clue."

"Do you think it has anything to do with my money?"

His dark eyebrows arch at my words. "Kim really did a number on you, didn't she?"

"What does this have to do with Kim?" I bite out angrily.

"You tell me, man. You've been the leader of this anti-women campaign ever since you two broke off your engagement."

"I don't see you settling down. What are you afraid of?"

"I just haven't found the right one yet. You, on the other hand, are too afraid to find the right one."

A burning sensation spreads across my chest. "Maybe *the right one* is all a bullshit illusion we tell ourselves to justify this societal construct that we've created around the idea of love and forever."

"Dinner is ready everyone," Mom calls from the dining room.

I storm away from Liam, itching to get out of the conversation. The dining room is set up already with plates and fancy wine glasses. It's strange seeing so many of my things being put to use. We normally eat at my parents' house or Asher and Charlotte's home. I didn't even know I had this many plates.

"Take a seat gentleman," my mom instructs. "We will bring in the food."

She walks off with a big smile on her face. I don't know what she is so happy about. She's acting a little crazy if you ask me.

Josh takes a seat to my left. "You hanging in there, buddy?" he asks, sounding slightly concerned.

Good to know at least one person cares about me.

Charlotte walks in holding a big wooden bowl of salad. She places it in the middle of the table then proceeds to take a seat. "Don't look so glum brother-in-law. You get to spend an evening with family that invited themselves over."

A smirk breaks through despite my best efforts to stop it.

The rest of the women walk in carrying food, Mia last as she holds a big bowl of pasta. My stomach growls in response to the aromas that are floating in the air.

Layla sits next to Josh, seeming happy to relinquish control in the kitchen. She's a chef and owns her own restaurant here in Savannah.

Mia is the last one to take a seat, on the last empty chair directly next to me. I adjust myself in my seat, feeling claustrophobic all of a sudden as I inhale the scent of her floral perfume.

"A toast," Dad says as he holds up his glass, "to this wonderful meal cooked by an even more wonderful lady. Thank you for all the hard work you put into this."

Everyone else toasts enthusiastically, nodding in agreement. I sneak a glance at Mia who is biting her lip with a blush on her face. My eyes follow the blush that extends down to her neck and then to her chest.

My dick twitches in response. I wonder if I could get her embarrassed while fucking her, telling her how good she looks taking my cock.

Shit. What the fuck am I doing? I can't think of her like that. She is off limits.

I take a big gulp of my wine, drinking half my glass in one sip. Those thoughts are not allowed to happen. Not with someone like her, someone I'll be forced to spend time with. I can't risk it.

If I need to blow off steam, it has to be with a chick at a bar I know I'll never see again. It's safer that way.

Chapter Five

Mia

Today has been going so well, I almost forgot why I'm here. Almost. Until I got a text message from my brother Gabe telling me he talked to the cops. The restraining order is now set, but there's nothing they can do in the meantime.

Don will receive the restraining order tomorrow.

My entire body breaks out into goosebumps just thinking about it. What if it pisses him off and he tries to find me? I don't even know how easy it is for stalkers to find people. Did I need to do something to make sure I couldn't be tracked down?

I'm trying my best to act like I'm okay. Layla and her family have been so warm and welcoming. Well, all of them except for the one sitting next to me—the one I'm living with.

I can't get a read on him. I sense anger, but also sadness. With everything I'm going through, you would think it would scare me, but it doesn't. He doesn't seem crazy. He just seems like he's trying to bury emotions that he's working really hard to avoid.

"This is really good," he whispers to me like he wants it to be a secret.

I find myself smiling. "Thanks. I'm glad you're enjoying it."

"Oh my gosh. Marry me, Mia," Liam shouts from across the table. "This food is the best I've ever had."

"Excuse me?" Layla throws a roll at him. "You could at least be mindful of the fact that I'm right here."

I can't help but laugh at them. Everyone reminds me so much of my family. Now that I think about it, Eric reminds me a lot of my brother, Gabe. They share an intensity about them. Gabe was burned by his ex-wife who decided being a mother and wife wasn't for her, so she took off to California.

It messed him up for a long time.

Liam continues to flirt with me and throw compliments my way, which makes Eric shift uncomfortably in his seat. I doubt it's because he's jealous, though my heart flutters at the idea of someone like Eric being jealous over me.

He seems so...powerful. What would it be like to be the object of desire from those angry eyes?

After we finish our dinner, I convince everyone that I can handle the dishes so that they leave. I can tell Eric has reached his limit, and I kind of feel bad for being the reason his home has been invaded like this.

Josh and Layla are the last to leave. After Eric closes the door, an awkward silence instantly falls between us.

He pulls at the back of his neck. It's either a nervous habit or he is extremely tense. "Uh, thanks for dinner. I can get the dishes."

I would be shocked that he offered, but I heard his mother scold him about not helping me since I've worked on the meal all day.

I fight back a smile. "I see you listen to what your mother tells you." He looks confused. "I heard her telling you to help me with dishes."

"Oh," he smiles, "yeah, she likes to make sure I remember not to be my grumpy self sometimes. But she's right, I should do the dishes."

He's even hotter when he isn't being a complete dick. Not that I'm interested in men at the moment. In fact, I'm wondering if maybe his idea of being a loner is the route I should be taking.

"I'm not going to let you do the dishes all by yourself. How about we both do them? It'll get done faster that way."

He shrugs his shoulders. "Sounds like a good offer. I'll take it."

We walk into the kitchen where I'm all of a sudden eternally grateful for whoever invented the dishwasher.

"I rinse and you load?" he asks as we survey the damage.

"Sure. Let's start with the dinner plates and silverware. We can handwash all the big pots and pans."

We get to work quickly but spend most of the time in silence. There were a couple forced questions about the weather and his family, but I can tell he wasn't in the mood to get to know me.

I still can't figure out whether he doesn't like me or just doesn't like people. I watched him after dinner with his brothers and saw his tension ease a bit with a few laughs. Maybe it's just me. It wouldn't be the first time I had been looked over by an attractive man.

My brothers have always been oohed and aahed over, but I was just their annoying little sister who nobody really paid attention to. I went through some awkward years like most girls do, and a number of their friends weren't shy with their "jokes."

In the beginning, I really thought Don was different. He was kind, sweet, and attentive. It wasn't until he became overwhelming and controlling that I realized his level of attentiveness was odd.

"I'm gonna be outside in the barn," Eric says, pulling me out of my thoughts.

"Sounds good. I'll probably just turn in. Good night, Eric."

"Night, Mia."

I head up to my bedroom to read a book and call my parents. I don't want them to worry themselves to death over my safety so it's best to check in. I slip into my pastel-pink silk tank top and shorts then climb into bed under my fluffy comforter. Despite the awkwardness with Eric, the house is a cozy place. So much better than a hotel. Plus, Josh showed me the security system.

It's exactly like the bat cave, but it's nice. I feel safe here.

I grab my book off the nightstand when I hear a low scream come from the backyard. I jump off the bed and look out the window. I see Eric walking towards the backdoor, grabbing his arm with his hand while he lets out another scream.

Oh, shit. He's hurt.

Without another thought, I run down the stairs and outside onto the grass in my bare feet. It feels slightly wet, though I don't remember it raining, but I run as fast as I can. As soon as I get to him, he stops, bends over, and grunts.

"Oh my god!" I scream. "What happened?"

"My arm," he says through the pain with clenched teeth. "I was in the barn. Shelf broke. Everything fell on me."

He's in so much pain he can't even speak in complete sentences. His hand is holding his arm over his blood-soaked shirt. I don't know much, but I think I need to tie it off to stop the bleeding.

My knowledge of this is coming from movies, so there may not be any accuracy to it. I look around, fearing we're too far away from the house to grab a towel.

I rip off my top. "Move your hand. I'm going to tie this around your wound. I think we need to stop the bleeding."

He lets go of the wound and I work so quickly I don't even get a good look at it. It's probably for the better because my specialty is wine, and if I'm being honest, blood makes me a bit woozy.

After I tie it, we both look down at his arm. There doesn't seem to be any blood soaking through, at least not at a quick rate that is noticeable.

Eric's eyes meet mine, only for a second, then they look down. I see his throat bob as he gulps. "You don't have a bra on."

I look down at my breasts which are on full display. "Yeah," I whisper, "I was just getting in bed."

Another moment of silence passes between us, our eyes latched on to each other's, before he groans again in pain.

"Come on. We need to get you to the hospital. Let's get you in my car," I tell him.

I wrap my arm around his waist and try to let him lean some weight on me.

"I think you need to get clothes on before we go," he croaks.

"Shit. I do. Let me get you set up in the car and I'll run inside and change."

I manage to get him in the car and change into jeans and a sweatshirt before we head to the hospital. I have no idea where I'm going so Eric has to navigate for us.

My hands tremble on the steering wheel as I drive. I don't think I'm good in emergency situations. I can feel my leg shake on the pedals, making my driving feel erratic.

I drop him off at the emergency entrance and promise to come in and find him after I park.

Why the hell aren't there like valets or something at the emergency room? I don't need someone to park my car ten feet away for me when I'm going to a restaurant. What I do need is someone to park it so I don't have to leave a man who's bleeding and in pain alone.

I sprint inside directly to the front desk. "Hi," I smile at the blonde woman behind the desk. "My friend just came in here. His arm is cut, I think pretty badly, and I was hoping to make sure he's in a room and doing okay. I want him to know I can be there if he needs me."

She returns my smile calmly. "The gentleman with the arm injury is sitting over there. We will call him back shortly."

I turn around to see Eric sitting next to some patient blowing his nose. His face is pale and there's blood all over his white t-shirt. An odd sense of rage bubbles out of me as he looks at me.

I cannot believe they didn't take him back immediately.

"Excuse me," I turn back to the woman. "I'm sorry, but my friend is badly injured. He needs to be taken back immediately."

Her eyebrows turn up at me, which for some reason pisses me off.

"Your friend has been evaluated by our staff. He will be brought back by priority," she says sternly.

I don't accept that. He is bleeding and obviously in an immense amount of pain. What kind of hospital doesn't see that as a priority? "He clearly should be top priority. I was there when it happened. There was a lot of blood. Just look at him." I turn back to him and see a slight smirk on his lips which is not helping my argument right now, but I'm invested. "His face is pale, and his shirt is soaked with blood. Tell me how that doesn't take top priority?"

Just then a nurse comes up to the desk and looks at her colleague. "I'm sorry, is there a problem?"

"Yes," I interject. "My friend sliced his arm open, has lost a lot of blood, and currently looks like he could lose consciousness at any second. He needs to be seen now."

The nurse turns towards Eric and her eyes open widely. "I see. We can take him back now. Sir, would you follow me?"

I turn to the blonde and give her a smug look. I knew I was right. I walk quickly over to Eric and give him my arm. We follow the nurse back to a room where she immediately lies him down on the bed. After she asks a couple of questions, she tells us the doctor will be in shortly.

The room falls silent as we wait.

"That was quite the outburst you had out there," he says, breaking the silence.

I look over at him. There's no hint of a smirk now. He's just stating a fact, and I can't tell if he's judging me or not.

"First of all, you're welcome. You could've been waiting there for God knows how long. Second of all, I'm Italian and we're known to be loud and opinionated. I'm proud of that, and you aren't going to make me feel like shit because I care enough to fix a wrong."

His eyes bore into mine with such intensity that I find myself needing to look away.

"I never said it was a bad thing. I was just stating my observation. Thank you for doing that. My arm hurts like a motherfucker. I was thinking the same thing."

"Why didn't you speak up?" I ask him.

He shrugs his shoulders. "Didn't seem worth it to me I guess."

"Mr. Williams." An older doctor with grey hair walks in holding a clipboard. "It looks like you had quite the accident. How much pain are you in?"

Eric rolls his eyes and it's my turn to smirk. "A lot. My arm was sliced into while being hit by large falling objects."

"Let's take a look." The doctor walks over and unties my silky tank top, then holds it up. "Interesting choice."

I slide down my chair, completely mortified. My cheeks feel like they just got scorched with boiling water.

"Yeah, it offered a nice distraction from the pain," he says as he looks at me.

My legs squeeze together from the intensity of his burning eyes. I still can't tell if he's complimenting me or insulting me. He's such a mix of emotions. I can't get a read on him. But all I know is my body has never felt this aroused from a simple look before.

I don't know why I'm reacting like this to him.

"Well, you do have quite a deep cut there. And I can tell with the bruising already forming around the cut that there will be a significant amount of swelling. Other than that, I think I can just stitch you up, get you cleaned up, and you will be good to go home. You will have to wear a sling for a little bit to let the wound heal."

He groans. "How long will it take to heal?"

The doctor mindlessly gathers materials and starts cleaning the wound as Eric winces from the pain. "You need to rest. No lifting anything with this arm for at least a week. Then you can start gradually with objects no more than five pounds."

I can tell where this is going. Eric starts to argue with the doctor about going back to work on Monday. In the end, Eric is stitched up and now sporting a scowl as he accepts his fate of resting at home for a week.

Chapter Six

Eric

I cannot believe this happened. I go out to the barn to relieve stress only to destroy my arm and any chance of using it for the near future.

The second we get into the car, my head falls back onto the headrest.

"How is your arm feeling? Does it hurt?" Mia asks as she pulls out of the parking lot.

I take a deep breath, trying to control the rage that I feel inside. I know I can't take it out on her. She helped me out and basically threw a tantrum so I could be seen immediately, which I found oddly hilarious. It was a nice distraction from the throbbing pain in my arm.

"It hurts pretty bad. I don't think the over-the-counter pain meds are going to help all that much."

She sighs. "I'm sorry. If you want, I can go back in there and try to convince the doctor to give you something stronger."

I find myself smiling. "You know, I don't doubt that you could do that, but I'm alright. I just want to get home, shower, then get some sleep. I'm still impressed with how you handled the lady at the front desk."

Her shoulder lifts like it were nothing. "I have three older brothers. Sometimes it felt like I took on second mother duty with them. I'm used to taking care of people. God knows my brothers needed the help."

Interesting. She has three older brothers. I don't know why I pegged her as the oldest sibling. Weird dynamic where the youngest is taking care of the older ones.

I lean my head back again and close my eyes. I'm hoping the pain relievers will work enough for me to get some rest tonight.

When we walk back into the house, Mia turns to me. "What can I do for you?"

I'm a little thrown off by the question. It's like she isn't even feeling inconvenienced at all by this entire evening turning into a hospital run.

"Um, I think I just want a shower and bed. Thanks again for taking me to the hospital."

"Of course. Are you going to call your family to tell them what happened?"

"I think I'd rather save that for the morning. I'm sure that'll only be an open invitation for everyone to barge in here."

She smiles and shakes her head. "True. Let me know if you need anything."

She walks away in her jeans and for the second time tonight, I find myself staring at a forbidden body part. The first time it was her naked breasts in my face, now it's the sway of her ass.

I walk away shaking my head. She has the type of breasts that can make a man lose his mind. For a brief second, I thought I was going to sport a hard-on right in front of her while I bled to death.

Talk about a humiliating way to go.

I grab a garbage bag and some painters tape and head upstairs into my bathroom. How hard can it be to tape this bag over my arm so I can shower?

Thirty fucking minutes later, I'm leaning against the sink in my bathroom sweating. I've tried every possible way to get this arm taped, but it's impossible to do with only one hand.

Not showering isn't an option. I have blood and dirt all over my skin.

I could call one of my brothers, but it's late. I'm sure if I called Liam, he would just point out the fact that I have another person in my house that's a couple of doors down from my bedroom.

Dammit.

I grab my phone and text Mia.

Me: Umm I have an odd favor to ask.

She texts back within seconds.

Mia: What can I do?

Me: I'm trying to get the plastic bag taped over my arm so I can shower. It's proving to be rather difficult.

Mia: I'll be right there

Before I can respond, she's knocking on the bathroom door. I open it, standing in my t-shirt and boxers, suddenly feeling exposed. Mia is in another silky pajama set. I have to force my eyes to remain above her neck at all times.

I run a hand through my hair as she studies me.

"First of all, why are you still in your shirt?" she asks.

My shoulders sink. "Because I couldn't get my shirt off either. If I move this arm even an inch, it's throbbing in pain."

"I think we need to start with that. It's steamy in here. How long has the water been running?"

She approaches me and I sense a slight amount of hesitancy in her steps. Her hand reaches for the bottom of my shirt. I keep my eyes on hers as she glides my shirt up my chest. It feels extremely intimate, like she's taking my shirt off for an entirely different reason.

I can't help but stare into her eyes, noticing the beautiful light brown color with specks of gold.

The air in the room becomes thick. I try to swallow back this feeling settling in my throat, but it feels like it gets stuck. It must be all the steam in here.

"It's probably been thirty minutes. I've been struggling for a while," I admit.

"Ok, slip your good arm out of the sleeve." I follow her instructions as she holds the sleeve for me to do so. "I think that gives us enough slack to get it over your head. Then we can maneuver it down your other arm so you don't have to move it."

I bend my head to help her as she pulls the material up. As soon as my head is out, she slowly lets the shirt fall down my arm. I catch her looking at my stomach as my shirt falls to the floor. Her tongue slips out and licks her bottom lip.

Now it definitely doesn't feel like the steam making it hard to breathe.

She grabs the bag and makes quick work as she wraps my arm up to my shoulder.

"How does that look?" she asks as she places the final piece of tape on my shoulder.

"Better than I could have done. Thanks for helping. I realize this isn't what you signed up for when you decided to stay here."

"I don't mind. Consider it a thank you for letting me crash at your place. I'm sensing Layla pushed this on you rather than you offering it up willingly."

Is that true? Yes. So why do I feel like a dick for being so transparent and that she noticed? It's been years since I've even given a second thought to what a woman thinks about me. Why do I care now?

I'm probably just tired from the events of the night. I'll feel better tomorrow when I get some sleep.

I turn towards the shower, realizing she's watching me and not leaving.

"Are you going to be able to...umm...shower," she asks as I notice her cheeks blush. It's a good look on her.

I don't think it will be easy, but I can get it done. "I think I've got it from here."

She nods her head then starts to back away. "Just holler if you need anything. I'll leave our doors open so I can hear you."

When I step in the shower, I wince at the pain as the hard droplets hit the plastic bag over my stitches. It's extremely sensitive. This needs to be done quickly. I just want to go to bed.

Once I finally dry off, I only manage to get on sweatpants, deciding against the hassle of putting on a shirt. I get my sling back on and fall into bed. Despite my best efforts not to, I fall asleep picturing Mia's breasts.

I never claimed to be a saint.

Chapter Seven

Mia

Okay, so I'm attracted to the man I'm staying with while I'm hiding out from my crazy ex who may or may not be trying to kill me.

It's okay. That says nothing about me or the choices that I make. Plus, I don't really think you can choose who you are attracted to. And I just saw him with no shirt on. He looks like an athlete who is training for the freaking Olympics. It's not like I'm attracted to his personality. That I can say for sure.

Good. That makes me feel better.

Now I can go downstairs and not feel bad about the fact that I couldn't stop picturing his shirtless body.

I look down at my pajamas and am brought back to the doctor's comment last night. It was so humiliating. I felt like I was in high school and the teacher caught me giving my boyfriend sexy lingerie.

I was surprised by the look Eric gave me when the Doctor joked about it. It felt like a mixture of anger and interest. I didn't think

I would like the combination, but my body proved me wrong on that account.

After I get ready, I feel a bit better. I think I will explore a little bit of the town today. Maybe find a good bookstore that I can peruse with an iced coffee. I'm in my jean shorts and a V-neck shirt. The fall weather down here isn't exactly what Ohio sees. It dips a bit lower at night but gets up to the mid-seventies.

Before I do anything, I need to call my brother back. He was texting me last night, but I was so drained I couldn't find the energy to respond.

I grab my phone and lower into the chair in my room. It's angled to overlook the backyard.

"Finally," Gabe's voice sounds in my ear. "I was texting you last night."

"I'm sorry. Eric cut his arm last night. I had to take him to the hospital. He needed stitches. It was a whole thing."

"I talked to Mrs. Mayberry," he says, ignoring my statement about Eric.

"You talked to my neighbor? Why exactly did you do that?"

"I got a call from the police station. Mrs. Mayberry saw Don's car two nights in a row sitting at the end of the street. She called the cops. They called me. So, I paid her a little visit to get more information."

I suddenly get a strange sensation all over my body—like someone is watching me, even though no one is around. Is Don crazier than I thought? Did I leave any clues behind as to where I was going?

"I thought he was given the restraining order," my voice cracks with fear.

"Well, the motherfucker didn't see it as a real threat. But she told me she thinks she saw him peeking into your windows one of the nights. By the time the police came, he was gone."

Oh my god. This can't be happening to me.

"Did the police contact him?" I ask.

"They did. He denies that he was anywhere near your house. Without proof, there's pretty much nothing that they can do."

"How is that possible? They can't, like, scare him or warn him off?"

Gabe sighs. "Crazy people don't care about what an officer says. If he thinks he can get away with it, or rationalizes what he's doing in his head, he won't listen to anyone. I think you should come home."

"Why on earth would I come home now? It sounds like the worst time to come home," I argue.

"Because I don't trust this guy. I had someone go check his place out—try to see what he was up to—and it has been empty since the cops showed up at his place yesterday morning. I don't know where he is."

Tears prick the corners of my eyes, but I do my best to hold them in.

"Gabe, I'm not coming home. This was the plan the entire time. The reason why I left. If he's looking for me, it's better that I'm hiding."

"I don't like not having you here for us to protect."

"I'm not coming home and risking something happening. Right now, there's no reason to assume that he knows where I am."

Gabe argues with me for another ten minutes, but finally he agrees to give it another week before we make any rash decisions.

When I walk downstairs, I'm greeted with Eric's bare chest. His grey sweatpants are hanging low on his hips, and I feel my muscles tighten with appreciation. I walk closer and watch him try to open the new coffee bag with one hand.

"Stupid fucking coffee. Open," he curses under his breath.

"Need some help?" I ask as I walk up to the counter.

He grunts. "It shouldn't be this hard to open this with one hand. But it hurts to grip anything with my other hand right now."

I reach over and grab the bag from him, desperately trying to keep my eyes off of his chest. His body is a nice distraction from the shit news I just received.

"Well, the doctor said you sliced into your muscle, so it's going to hurt for a while. You should be resting it for the first couple days. Do you always go against doctors' orders?"

"When I want coffee, yes."

I smile. "Alright, I'll give you a pass on that one. Let me make this for you. You just sit down."

He lets out a long sigh then backs away, taking a seat at the island. I feel his eyes on me and for some reason, his attention makes my body burn.

Mia, just put the damn coffee beans in the coffee machine. There is no reason to pay any attention to your body, it doesn't know what it's doing.

"How did you sleep?" I ask in an effort   to distract myself.

Once the machine is grinding the beans, I turn around and see him biting his bottom lip. He has really nice lips. Perfect size, not too big or small. They look really soft.

"Like shit," he says roughly.

"I'm sorry about that. Maybe you can get a good nap today."

"Hopefully," he says to the counter, avoiding my eyes.

Well, isn't he charming this morning. He seemed nicer last night—must have just been the adrenaline.

Once I pour our coffees, I escape to his front porch. As soon as I sit on one of the swings, I hear a rustling come from behind me.

I fly out of the swing as images of Don jumping out flood my brain. My eyes search anxiously for the source of the noise as my body begins to shake. Then, I see a squirrel run out of the bushes and dart up the nearest tree.

I try to take a deep breath and shake the feeling, but I can't get myself to sit back down in the swing. What if it's not safe? Instead, I sit down on one of the rocking chairs against the wall, leaving no room for anything to jump out from behind me. The coffee cup, now only half full from my jump, shakes as I bring it to my mouth.

There's no way I'm going out today. It doesn't feel safe to leave his house when we don't know where Don is. Just the thought of him searching for me brings tears to my eyes. I don't know how to live like this. It's like my entire life is put on hold, and I just have to sit here in this stranger's house and wait.

Wait for what though? For him to find me and hurt me? Until he attempts or even succeeds, there's nothing the police can do.

My tears finally break free from their prison and cascade down my cheeks one by one. They continue to fall while I drink my coffee, not knowing what to do or who to talk to.

Chapter Eight

Eric

This is so damn awkward. I've been walking around without a shirt on all day because I can't get it on. There's no way I'm going into work tomorrow. Unless I ask Jeremy or Adam to help me get my pants back up and in place after I go to the bathroom, which I'm not doing, there's no way. I'll just have to stay home in my sweatpants.

I don't know where Mia is. She's been missing ever since she helped me get undressed last night.

Although she's been helpful with all of this, I still don't trust her.

I hear a sudden noise echo in the kitchen. Instead of ignoring it and focusing on my rest like I should, I get up from the chair in my room and walk downstairs to check it out.

I walk into the kitchen, my eyes immediately drawn to the sight before me. Mia is rummaging through a lower cabinet, her back to me as she is bent over, her curves accentuated by her fitted denim shorts. Her legs stretch gracefully, the smooth lines and tanned skin drawing my gaze, making it hard to look away. She hasn't noticed me yet, and I find myself holding my breath, caught with desire.

"Can I help you find anything?" I ask and she lets out a shriek.

She stands up and the first thing I notice is her hair up in a loose bun, messy and wild on her head, but effortlessly beautiful. Her cheeks are stained a pink hue.

"Oh my god. You scared me," she says with a hand over her heart.

I walk into the kitchen, slightly amused. "I can see that. Just trying to offer help where I can."

She smiles shyly. "I was just looking for a strainer."

"Ah. I can't say I've used it, but it's in that cabinet up there. I think."

I try to walk over to retrieve it for her, but she beats me to it. "No need to reach for it. You need to rest."

That's what I've been trying to do all day, but it's been driving me mad. I'm used to being busy with work. I don't like having down time. It allows me to think, and that hasn't been something I've liked to do in the last couple of years.

"Are you hungry? I'm making dinner."

Do I want to sit around and have forced conversation with a woman I find far too attractive? Absolutely not. "I could eat," my mouth replies despite my brain telling me no.

"Good. I'm making plenty."

I take a seat at the island and watch her work effortlessly in my kitchen like she's lived here longer than I have. Everything is already smelling amazing.

"What are you making?" I ask with genuine curiosity.

She doesn't turn around, just continues to dice an onion on the island right in front of me. "A chicken pot pie with an arugula and peach salad—cobbler for dessert."

My entire mouth fills with saliva. "Is it all homemade?"

She chuckles as she throws the onions into the skillet with peas and carrots. "Where I come from, you don't eat anything unless it's homemade."

"Interesting choices. A bit different from your Italian meal the other night."

"Layla made this amazing peach cocktail the night I got here with peaches from Georgia. I was inspired to learn some southern cooking and take advantage of the peaches while I'm down here."

A thought occurs to me. "I didn't see you leave at all today. When did you get groceries?"

A strange look appears on her face. "I didn't leave the house. I had the groceries delivered."

Interesting. I wonder why she hasn't wanted to go anywhere. Maybe she's a homebody. I remember I still don't know why she is staying with me and it's odd it hasn't come up yet.

Once everything is thrown into the oven, she turns to me. "That needs to bake for an hour. I already have the salad in the fridge and the cobbler ready to bake later. I was going to go read in my room for a bit. Can I help you with anything first?"

"Um, now that you mention it, I haven't been able to change all day."

"Oh, is that why you haven't been wearing a shirt all day?"

How? I don't remember seeing her at all today. Has she been hiding?

"Yeah, I mean, it's just hard to move my arm right now. And...you've noticed me not wearing a shirt?"

I don't know why I said that. I want to take it back until I notice that damn blush of hers spreading down her chest. Fuck me, why do I find that so sexy? I want to explore how far down it goes. Does it reach her nipples? I've pictured taking those into my mouth ever since I saw them the other night.

"I mean, sorry. Yes, that's why I haven't put a shirt on. Any chance you could help me?" I change course, and wonder why I just asked her if she's been checking me out. I don't want her to check me out.

We walk into my bedroom to grab a clean shirt and I hand it to her. She throws it on the bed.

"First, let's take this sling off," she tells me.

I've been reluctant today—it hurts to use my arm muscle right now. But I know it needs to be done. She lifts the strap of my sling over my head. The weight that was taken off immediately forces my arm down to my side. I wince at the pain and she mirrors my reaction.

"I'm so sorry. Are you okay?"

I nod my head as I allow the throbbing to settle. "I'm fine."

"Okay, you just stand there. I'm going to do this so you don't have to move your arm at all."

She puts my hand hanging at my side through the sleeve and slowly slides the shirt up my arm. I watch her forehead scrunch in concentration as she's trying not to hurt me. Once my head and other arm are in, she grabs the bottom of my shirt and slowly pulls it down my body. Her fingers glide against my chest down to my abs, leaving my skin scorching from the heat of the moment.

Both of our breathing appears labored as she looks up and our eyes meet. She shakes her head and steps away from me.

Shit, what the hell was that? If she hadn't pulled away, I don't know what I would have done. The way I react to her presence, to her touch, is terrifying. I need a drink to take the edge off.

"Okay, let's get this back on," she says, grabbing the sling.

She is gentle but works quickly to help me get back in, with only slightly throbbing pain this time around. Her nearness is both exciting and disturbing. Luckily, the second I'm in the sling, she backs away. "Alright, I'm going to go read. I'll let you know when dinner is ready."

With the much-needed space, I lie on my bed and close my eyes, hoping to get some rest before dinner.

"Eric," a soft voice echoes in my room, making me feel calm and at peace. When I open my eyes, Mia is standing over me.

I look up at her, feeling slightly disoriented. "What time is it?"

"It's just after six. Dinner is ready if you'd like to eat. If you want to rest more, I can put the leftovers in the fridge for you."

She's twiddling her fingers together in front of her like she's nervous. "I'm sorry. I shouldn't have interrupted your nap. I don't know what I was thinking."

"No," I groan as I rub my eyes. "I shouldn't be sleeping all day. I won't get good sleep tonight if I do. Plus, I'm starving. Thanks. I'll be right there."

"Oh, ok. Well, I'll go set the table."

I nod my head and wait until she walks out. I probably should trade out my sweatpants for a pair of jeans for dinner. Might be the least I can do to not show up like a slob after all the work she put into it. Call it my southern manners, but it just seems rude. Not sure when the last time was that I worried about my rudeness.

It's a struggle to get the damn jeans on and zipped. I quickly remember why I was walking around in sweatpants. Whatever, I'll just have to leave them unbuttoned. My shirt will cover it.

When I walk into the kitchen, everything smells incredible. Mia is filling up two wine glasses as I meet her at the table. It feels kind of weird and—romantic. But she does seem to be knowledgeable about wine based on the dinner she prepared the other night. I'm getting in my head. This isn't some kind of date. We live together right now. Having wine with dinner is perfectly normal.

"Thanks for letting me eat your food. It smells really good."

We both take our seats. I feel like I should be helpful in some way around here, so I grab the pie cutter.

"Can I cut you a piece?" I offer.

She smiles. "Sure. Thank you."

With my one good hand, I start to cut into the pie. The dish moves an inch, but without another hand, I can't hold it down. I try again, but it keeps sliding around the table. "Dammit," I mutter to myself. I try again but to no avail.

Mia sucks in her lips, trying to hide her smile. "Um, how about I do it?"

I drop the cutter. "I'm sorry. I'm fucking useless right now."

"Don't worry about it. Like I said, you're allowing me to stay here, it's the least I can do."

She stands up and cuts each of us a slice, then scoops the salad.

"Thank you," I manage to grind out though still irked by my inability to do the simplest of tasks.

"So, what did your family say when you told them about the accident?" she asks after she takes a bite.

I do the same and have to stop myself from moaning. This woman can cook. The pie crust is so crispy and yet the chicken and vegetables in the cream sauce are the perfect offset to the crust.

"I haven't told them yet actually."

She stops her spoon midway to her mouth. "You didn't tell them yet?"

It kind of takes me by surprise—the guilt her reaction garners from me. I'm sure I should've told them first thing in the morning, probably even last night.

"I know. I'm a horrible son and brother," I say then take a bite of my pie. It's good enough to make me feel slightly less of a prick. I think I'll be eating another slice, see if it can make me like myself. Maybe it's magic pie.

"I never said that you were a horrible son or brother. I'm just surprised. You guys all seem close."

It's an interesting observation, and, to some extent, it's true. We are close. But sometimes being too close to your family isn't always a good thing. It's times like these, when you are in a rut or just trying to figure yourself out that makes it hard when there don't seem to be any boundaries.

"We're close. To be honest, I'm just tired. Once I tell them, there's going to be a crowded house of worried faces all not only wondering how I'm doing physically, but they will use it as an emotional intervention."

She lets out a heavy sigh. "I understand that."

I look at her, my head leaning to one side. "You do?"

"Yeah, I'm close with my family too. Three older brothers and my parents. All three brothers are married. Everyone seems to treat me like I'm fragile or damaged."

"Hmm."

Her eyebrows pinch together. "What does hmm mean?"

I can't help but laugh at how defensive she became by a simple noise. "Nothing. I was just thinking. Why is it that someone being single means they are subject to a massive amount of scrutiny from their family members?"

She rolls her eyes. "If you ever figure it out, let me know."

A smirk stretches across my face. I'm actually enjoying our dinner together. It's nice to have someone to talk to. And it's a relief that she isn't judging me for taking some time before I tell my family. I'll call them and tell them after we eat, but it's still nice that she gets it.

Hours later, I'm lying in bed trying to sleep but it doesn't come. My arm hurts like a motherfucker and my family finally stopped messaging an hour ago once I threatened to block all of them.

I didn't even ask Mia to help me with anything, I just stayed in my shirt and threw on a new pair of sweatpants. Maybe a late-night snack will help. Mia and I both ate too much of the pot pie to have room for the cobbler.

Would it be rude to have a piece before her?

Before I can make it to the fridge, I notice the pool lights on and a figure swimming in the water. I walk outside, surprised that the October chill isn't too bad tonight. Instead of going back inside like I should, letting her enjoy her swim alone, I feel compelled to sit on one of the lounge chairs and lean back.

It's peaceful out here. She continues to swim laps while I watch. When she stops to take a breath, I figure it's a good time to announce my presence.

"You always swim by yourself in the middle of the night?"

The scream that escapes her is piercing, filled with pure, raw emotion. Once she sees my face, her body settles and her hand lands on her heart. "Eric! Oh my gosh. You keep scaring me."

"I'm sorry. I guess I shouldn't have snuck up like that."

Although, I don't feel like I snuck up. I'm not sure what I should've done, but she's been very jumpy around me. A simple noise can throw her into a panic and now this. She also never leaves the house. It seems strange.

"No, no it's fine. I'm sorry, I'm just a little jumpy lately," she says, seeming   embarrassed. "I was just finishing up here. I wanted to get in a little exercise, work off some of those dinner calories."

"There's a gym in the basement. I'm sorry I never gave you an official tour. I'll give you one tomorrow."

"Sounds great. Thanks."

She begins to climb the stairs out of the pool. With each step, more of her body emerges. She's wearing a black two piece and once her ass is above water, my dick instantly takes notice. She turns around and walks towards me, giving me the view of her front.

It's like someone climbed inside my brain and found what I think the perfect body is and made her just for me. That's a fucked-up thought, but it's how I feel as I watch her.

The water droplets glide down her slender stomach making their way down to the edge of her bikini bottoms. I'm suddenly thirsty and want to lick the water off her. Her wet hair sticks to her body, adding to her effortless allure.

The world around me fades away, leaving Mia in sharp, stunning focus. She grabs her towel, which I now notice is sitting on the chair next to me, and wraps it around her body.

"Can I join you?"

"Of course," I reply.

She takes a seat on the chair next to me and we both lay back in silence for a minute.

"It's a beautiful backyard. I love the trees here," she says into the night.

"Thank you. I love the trees too. It's what has always sold me on this house. Plus, the privacy it creates is nice." I look over at her, noticing she doesn't have a drop of makeup on. Her skin is perfect. "What made you want to get in your workout this late at night?"

Her lips press together tightly—a troubled look on her face. "I just felt like my body had a ton of stored energy when I laid down. I knew I needed to get rid of some if I was ever going to sleep. I think I'm just used to working a ton of hours. It's been slow here."

"You lost your job?" I ask, suddenly remembering why it was I didn't trust her in the first place.

"What? No. I didn't lose my job."

"You didn't? Don't you need to head back soon or risk actually losing that job?" I ask, now more confused.

"No, my job is waiting for me."

She's not very forthcoming with information. "What do you do for a living, Mia?"

"I own a wine distribution company with my brothers. I'm the head of marketing and deal with all of our branding."

That, I wasn't expecting. Suddenly, her expensive car pops into my mind. "How long has your company been around?"

Maybe the car is an expense on the company, something to help with lowering taxes. A lot of startups do that to try and lower their taxes at the end of the year.

"About eight years. We do about a billion in revenue a year now."

If I was drinking something, I would've choked on it. That's no startup. That's a well-established, successful company. And she owns it. Her bank account must put mine to shame. I don't know what to do with that information.

Here I thought she was using me—interested in my money.

"Well, I think that swim actually did me in. I'm gonna go shower and try to sleep. I'll see you tomorrow, Eric. Let me know if I can help you with anything."

She gets up and walks away, but I'm too speechless to offer a goodnight.

Okay, so she isn't using me for my money, but that doesn't change anything. I still can't trust my attraction to her. I have to stay strong and remember why touching her would be a very bad idea.

Chapter Nine

Mia

Okay, I'm bored. I've been here for a week now. My brothers still insist that I take more time off work, but since I'm too afraid to leave the house, there's nothing for me to do.

I really should get over my fear and go to the grocery store today. It's a good first step in getting out. I mean, honestly, is Don really going to be able to find me? Maybe I'm blowing this entire thing out of proportion. Even if he found me, he'd probably just beg to get back together, not kill me or anything.

Okay, good. It's settled. I'll go to the store and buy some food. I wonder what Eric would want for dinner. I should go ask him. I just hope he's wearing a shirt this time. I swear I can't even close my eyes now without seeing an image of his topless figure. It's burned into my retinas.

I head downstairs and search the house. He must be in his bedroom and I am not about to barge in.

When I was in my room looking out the window, I saw a gazebo at the edge of his property by the woods. I pour a glass of iced tea and start to walk through the grass to see what's inside of it.

It could be another nice place to read or eventually pull out my laptop to work.

Maybe I could work without telling my brothers.

I start to walk past Eric's large two-story barn when I hear a noise. The barn door is open and curiosity gets the best of me. I walk in and find Eric picking things up off the ground with his good arm and placing them back on a shelf.

I look around and my jaw hits the floor. The barn is covered with incredible woodwork, from long farm tables to rocking chairs. There are large circles made of wood with, what appears to be, last names burnt on the surface.

I'm stunned. I look up to the second story of the barn and it's filled with unused wood.

It looks like a factory in here.

I look back over at Eric whose eyes are fixed on me, filled with anger. He takes a step closer to me, he stands over me, but I'm not scared. I stand my ground, refusing to back away.

"What are you doing in here?" he bites out.

I look him up and down, his jeans and black t-shirt cling to his muscles. His anger is doing something to my body, making it respond again in a way that is totally inappropriate for the circumstances of the moment.

"I was walking over to look at the gazebo and heard some noise coming from in here. This is amazing stuff. Do you make all of this?"

I see a moment of appreciation on his face before he goes back to glaring at me. "I do. But I don't tell anybody about it. So do me a favor and keep your mouth shut. Don't tell Layla."

As much as I want to know why he would keep this art a secret, I know now is not the time to ask. He turns away from me and begins picking up nails and tools from the ground.

Instead of talking, I decide I can work with him in silence. I begin to pick up a bunch of nails and place them in the box lying next to them.

"How long have you been doing this?" I dare to ask, expecting him to blow a gasket.

"Four years," he answers, continuing to clean.

Maybe if we just don't make eye contact and work together on this, he's okay with talking to me.

"I started out wanting a big table for my backyard. Couldn't find the size I wanted anywhere. Then I just kind of kept going."

I'm shocked he divulged that information without having to pull it out of him.

"It must come naturally to you. Your work looks like you've been doing it for much longer than four years."

"Thanks. My ex hated it."

"Why in the world would she hate it?"

He shrugs before picking up a nail gun. "She said the work was beneath me. She said carpentry is for poor people."

What a bitch. I can't believe those words could ever come out of someone's mouth.

"Well, it's a good thing she's an ex because she's wrong."

I hear a strange sound coming from just outside the barn door.

"What the fuck is that?" I whisper as I drop the nails in my hands and run further into the barn.

In the process of it all, I trip and fall onto my hands and knees. What could that have been? Is it Don? Did he find me? Terror takes over my body and the room begins to spin.

Eric looks at me then at the door until a dog comes into view. "Um, that's my neighbor's dog, Max. He likes to walk around the property sometimes." He crouches down. "Are you okay, Mia?"

I feel like I've reached a new low point. The reality finally hits me. I feel the sadness come in waves, the weight of it all pressing down on my chest until I can't take it anymore. My breathing hitches and my vision blurs as tears spill over.

I'm here in this man's house, who doesn't want me here, and I'm scared of random noises because I don't know if my ex is trying to hurt me.

Eric seems skittish and slightly alarmed. "Look, you've been acting strange and a little on edge at times. I'm just going to come out and ask. Is there something I need to know? Why exactly are you staying at my place? Are you in some kind of trouble? Drugs or something?"

I wipe the tears with the back of my hands. "No," I say through an inhale, "not drugs."

"What has you on edge?"

I look him in the eyes. "My ex."

"Your ex?"

I nod. "He was stalking me for a while then I caught him trying to break into my house at night."

His body visibly stiffens. "Where is this man now?"

I shrug my shoulders. "My brothers have the cops involved. He hasn't been home in days. We don't know where he is."

Eric stands up. "You're here hiding out."

I stand up to meet him. "Yes. I'm so sorry. I should've told you, I just...it's embarrassing."

His head turns to the side. "Why is it embarrassing?"

"Because," I throw my hands up in the air, "I thought he was normal. I thought he was a good guy. I didn't see anything wrong with him. I liked him! Clearly something is wrong with me."

"And you're saying this guy could be out looking for you right now for all you know?"

"Yes," I say through a shuttered breath.

He shakes his head and then turns around mumbling something to himself, walking out of the barn toward the house.

I feel awful. He should have known what he was getting himself into before he agreed to let me stay here. Now he's involved in this mess when I know that's the last thing he would want to be a part of.

I turn and walk back to the house as well, wondering if I should pack my things and leave. That's probably the right thing to do. When I get back, he is standing outside on his porch pacing back and forth while he yells something into the phone.

That's it, I'm leaving. I can't be living under the same roof as someone who clearly wants nothing to do with me or my drama.

I walk upstairs through the blur of my tears and pull out my suitcase.

I open a drawer full of shirts and scoop them up against my chest.

"What the hell are you doing?" a voice startles me.

Eric is standing in the doorway. "Umm, I'm packing. You were so mad. I figured you didn't want me here."

"You're not going anywhere, Mia. Put those clothes down."

"But…" I start but he storms into the room and grabs clothes out of my suitcase and tosses them in a drawer.

"But nothing. You just told me there is a psycho out on the loose possibly looking for you. Do you really think I am letting you get in that car and leave?"

I don't know what to say. But the doorbell rings before I can think of anything. Without another word, he stomps out of my room, down the stairs, and answers his door. Layla's voice rings throughout the house.

I close my door for a second. I need to gather myself and apply some makeup, so I don't look like I've been crying. By the time I go downstairs, his entire family is standing in the kitchen.

"Mia! Thank God you were here," his mother wraps me in her arms. "Who knows if something worse would have happened to him if you weren't here to get him help."

She pulls away and I realize he finally told his family he got hurt. Just as he suspected, they are all here and freaking out. I smile to myself.

I spend almost an hour listening to their questions about what happened. They all want to know what he was doing in the shed. He looks over at me as if to see if I'll call him out on his secret. The power of his eyes on me is staggering. I have to look away.

"Well, I brought dinner from the restaurant," Layla says. "Let's sit down and eat. We can talk about why he is such a dick and didn't call us right away later."

Everyone starts to walk into the dining room, but Eric trails behind.

"You okay?" he asks.

"Me? I'm alright. What about you?"

He looks over at his family then shrugs. "I'm alright."

We both smile at each other then join everyone in the dining room. Everyone eats, talks, and laughs, but my eyes are drawn to Eric. Every time I look, his eyes are on me. He doesn't make any effort to pretend like he's not looking at me. It makes my body temperature spike with each lingered stare.

I feel like I'm getting whiplash. He was angry when I told him about my ex, but then seemed equally pissed at the idea of me leaving. I don't know what to expect. His behavior is erratic, and I should be scared. I should still leave. But as weird as it may sound, I don't want to.

Eric finishes his beer and then looks up at his brothers. "Are you guys ready?" he asks.

They all nod and get up from their seats, his father and Josh included. That leaves me with the women. His mom, Layla, Charlotte, and his niece Brie. I don't know what is going on, but no one else at the table seems curious as to what is going on.

"Do you know what they're up to?" I ask Layla.

"It sounded like Eric was trying to turn his house into the latest CIA center."

I don't know what the hell that means, but Brie jumps up and asks all of us to play Uno, so I let it go. After she whips our butts, only because we all clearly didn't play to win, I hear power tools just outside the front door followed by Eric barking orders.

I open the door, the cool autumn breeze sending shivers all over my body, and I see Eric walking up and down the front lawn yelling at the guys.

"I want them everywhere. Every single point of entry. Every window, every door. Asher, you make sure to check Liam's work. I don't want anyone slacking."

"Fuck off, man. I'm not gonna slack," Liam yells back.

What is going on? I run out to the front yard and look up to see all the guys on the roof.

I gasp. "What are they doing?"

He looks my body up and down which makes me visibly shiver, then he shakes his head. "I'm installing more security."

"What? Why? I thought you already had a great security system?"

"I have a *basic* security system. Layla doesn't know what she's talking about. She thinks her dog is a form of security, but I can promise you, he's not."

I bite my lip as I try not to smile, but that sounds like Layla. "What are they putting up there?"

"Flood lights with motion sensors."

"At every window?" I ask.

He looks at me intensely. "At every single point of entry."

"You don't have to do all of this. I understand if my being here isn't worth the risk for you. I don't want to make you feel unsafe in your own home."

Instead of answering, he continues to bark orders at the guys. I do my best to avoid everybody for the next hour. I start cleaning and doing the dishes while the girls play another round of Uno. I'm just too distracted to participate.

I don't know what's gotten into Eric, but he's acting insane. I'm relieved once everybody has left. But then it's just the two of us standing awkwardly at the front entrance once it's closed. I shift my weight back and forth from one foot to the other, finding it impossible to stay still.

He steps closer then reaches out and tucks a stray piece of hair behind my ear. The gesture is small, but it steals my breath away.

"How are you doing?" he asks.

I'm thrown by his question. I don't know what he means by it. "I'm confused. I feel like I'm turning your life upside down. I really should leave."

He shakes his head back and forth disapprovingly. "You aren't going anywhere, Mia. Not with that man out there looking for you. If that motherfucker ever tries to lay a hand on you, he's gonna wish he was never born. Now go get some rest. The place is safe."

He walks away like he didn't just say the sexiest thing any man has ever said in my lifetime. For the first time since I've been here, I truly do feel safe walking up to my room. Although, safe from Don, the feelings brewing for the man I'm living with are anything but safe.

Chapter Ten

Eric

"So, you seriously sliced your arm open?" Adam's voice asks with disgust.

I adjust my phone on my shoulder. "Yeah, it was pretty brutal. The pain isn't nearly as bad now, but it's still hard to move my arm."

"And you're out for the entire week?"

I sigh, knowing that's not realistic. "I'm supposed to relax and let it heal. I'm just going to work from home, though. I don't have the time to take a week off. Not with this acquisition."

"Alright, man. Let me know if I can do anything to help."

"Will do. I'll talk to you later."

I put the phone down and try to type out an email with one hand. It's been impossible to get shit done this morning with one hand, but I'm not going to be useless all week. There's far too much work to get done, and my bosses would lose their shit if I told them I needed to rest for a week. I called my assistant

Charlotte and let her know that I'll be working from home for the week and she nearly choked on her coffee.

When lunch time hits, I make a sandwich and decide to take it outside onto the patio to enjoy some sunlight.

As soon as I sit down, I notice Mia on the far side of the patio in a sports bra and spandex leggings. She's bending over, stretching. Her body is far better than I had realized. There's something about it that is unlike what I'm used to, but makes my hands twitch with eagerness to touch her. Her cleavage is popping out of her bra. A groan escapes my throat, and she turns around.

"Oh, hey," she stands up and walks over to me. "I didn't see you there."

Now I'm inches from her ample cleavage and round ass, both secure in her tight-fitting clothes. It should be illegal for her to wear those. At least for someone with her curves and snatched waist.

"What are you up to?" I ask as I grab my chips as a distraction.

"I'm just trying to keep myself busy. I think I want to try to get out of the house today."

I sit up straight. "You think it's safe to leave?"

She looks so fragile standing in front of me, worry etched on her face. "I don't know, but I can't just hide away my whole life. I don't even know for sure if he's out to get me. Maybe it's all in my head."

"Where do you want to go?"

"I was hoping a grocery store. I'd like to cook tonight."

"I'll go with you." The words are out before I can take them back.

Spending any more time with her than necessary isn't something I should be doing, not with how my body itches to have her. But I'm also damn sure I'm not going to let her go out alone.

"You will?" she asks. "Are you sure?"

I shrug my shoulders like it's no big deal. "I've got nothing else to do."

That's a lie. I have a ton of work to get done. But I suddenly feel the need to make her feel safe...to make her smile. If that's not a red flag that I'm walking into dangerous territory, I don't know what is.

"Okay. Thank you."

Without any permission from my brain, my eyes drag up her body as I appreciate every single inch of what I see. When I reach her eyes, I notice her throat bob as if she's affected by my reaction.

"I'm ready whenever you are."

"Okay," she smiles. "I'm just going to go get a quick shower."

She walks away and I'm left wondering how I got myself in this situation. I'm supposed to be in control of myself here. She isn't the money grabbing opportunist that I thought she was, but that doesn't mean that she can't destroy my heart.

There's always an ulterior motive. I'm only going with her because it's my responsibility to keep her safe. It has nothing to do with my attraction to her, which is only physical anyways.

I'm sitting outside on the porch waiting for her when she comes outside in tight jeans and a cream sweater. She has sunglasses on and somehow manages to look sexy but sweet. I don't know how she pulls it off.

My heart does something weird in my chest. I think the stress of all of this is getting to me.

"I'll drive," she smiles as she looks at my arm.

I nod my head and stand up. At least I know I'm not looking much like a man these days with my injured arm. Not sure how attractive it is that she's had to help me change clothes and open jars like a child.

The car ride to the store is quiet, but I find that neither of us feel the need to fill the silence. It's quite relaxing. She grabs a cart, and I follow her around as she picks things up.

"What are you thinking of making tonight?" I ask curiously.

"Gnocchi in a cream sauce."

I hold my stomach. "Woman. You're gonna make me fat with your cooking."

"I highly doubt that's going to happen. I've seen you without a shirt."

I smile, then notice a blush that creeps over her face and goes all the way down her neck. She reaches for some potatoes, but I'm too transfixed on her reaction.

"Did you know that when you blush," the back of my finger touches her cheek "it goes all the way down to here," I say until my finger is resting at the top of her cleavage.

Her chest is rising and falling rapidly as she looks up at me with wide eyes. We're both rooted in our place, unable to break away from the hold that this attraction seems to have on us. She shakes her head back and forth.

"It's distracting," my voice says with anger. Because that's how I feel right now. Angry. Angry that she does this to me. That I can't stop myself from wanting her this way.

"I'm sorry," she whispers delicately.

What would it feel like to have those lips wrapped around my cock. My dick hardens in my jeans at the thought. I move my hand down to adjust myself in my pants, her eyes following my movement. She looks shocked, and I'm too full of rage to behave.

"That's right, Mia. That's what your blushing does to me. It makes my dick hard."

Without another word, I grab the cart and start pushing it away.

Chapter Eleven

Mia

My body has been tense all day. Ever since he said those words to me at the grocery store. I'm ashamed to admit that it instantly made my panties wet. He was so crass, and I should be offended. For all women, I should have smacked him and told him to get his finger off me.

But instead, I stood in place, my body scorching as I almost begged for him to put that finger to work somewhere else.

I haven't been able to shake it since. Dinner was torture. It was like every move he made, every muscle in his arm was amplified by my desire for him.

I'm going to need to take care of myself when I get in bed to get my body under control. I can't go walking around here panting at the very sight of him. Though I'm starting to doubt an orgasm is going to turn down the flames.

I look outside the window as the wind starts to pick up speed. The trees are blowing wildly in the night as a loud boom of thunder shakes the house. It's an eerie feeling out there. I'm not used to these southern storms. They feel more intense than the ones we get up north.

I grab my book and pull back the covers of the bed to get in.

My phone goes off and I see a text from Savannah.

Savannah: How are you doing?

I think about it for a second before I text back.

Me: I'm hanging in there. It's weird to be away from you guys. How are things going over there?

I watch the three dots appear and disappear repetitively. I almost give up on a message coming through when my phone beeps.

Savannah: I've debated on whether or not to tell you, but your brothers have been working with the cops. They tracked down his recent credit card activity to North Carolina. We don't know if he's on vacation or just getting close to you. Just be careful.

I put my phone down on the nightstand. Fear feels like it is gripping me by the throat, making it impossible to breathe. My entire body is trembling. A crack of lightning makes me jump followed by the wind blowing a large tree branch onto the side of the house. The scratching and banging is about all I can take.

I run out of my room and begin pacing back and forth in the hallway. I try to reason with myself that I'm safe, that he isn't here, but I can't stop from panicking at the thought that this isn't over. Will it ever be over?

Does over mean I'm dead?

I start to cry as my thoughts take over until I'm startled by a voice.

"Mia?" Eric stands in his doorway with messy hair and a sleepy face.

He's only wearing black boxer briefs and his sling. Even through my panic, my body still has a slight reaction. I'm messed up.

"What's going on?" he asks, voice etched with concern.

My body keeps propelling me back and forth. "Just my ex. His credit card is showing him in North Carolina. It's fine. I'm fine. He's probably just on vacation and we're all blowing this totally out of proportion."

He takes me by the arms and stops me. "Are you sure about that? Why are you outside my door pacing back and forth?"

Tears continue to spill down my cheeks. I can't look him in the eyes. "It's just the storm. Every noise creeps me out. My brain keeps conjuring up images of him outside the house trying to get in."

He takes my hand and pulls me into his room. "Come on."

"Where are we going?" I ask reluctantly.

He doesn't answer. He just brings me to his bed and pulls the covers back. I look down at his bed and up at him.

"Just get in, Mia. We don't have to make a big deal about it. It'll make you feel safer. I promise I won't let anything happen to you."

I'm too drained to fight him on it. All the years that I've tried to take care of everyone else, it feels nice to hear those words spoken to me. Just for tonight.

I climb under the covers and roll onto my side facing away from the middle of the bed. I can feel him slide in next to me but it's a king size bed, so there's plenty of room. A part of me wants him to roll to my side and wrap his arms around me. To tell me again that I'm safe with him.

Every time I close my eyes, I picture it. My body can almost feel what his warmth would be like.

After tossing and turning for a while, I end up facing him. I steal a glance and notice he is lying on his back, his eyes open.

"You're awake?" I whisper in the dark.

His chest rises and falls with a deep breath. "Yes."

"Why?"

"Because my dick is hard as a rock knowing that you're under the covers with me right now in only a t-shirt and underwear."

My entire body shudders at his words. I want to reach out and feel the evidence of his arousal. Liquid pools in my underwear as I picture what it looks like.

I wait for him to say something else. To look at me or maybe even touch me, but it never comes. He turns away, making it glaringly obvious that whatever he's feeling at the moment isn't something he plans on acting on.

The rejection stings.

I came into his bed to feel protected and safe, but somehow end up feeling hurt and dejected. The story of my life.

Chapter Twelve

Eric

This is absolute fucking torture. I'm living in my own night-mare. I barely slept last night knowing she was inches away from me and all I needed to do was pull her underwear to the side and I would find sweet relief.

What is it about her that has me reacting like this? I've never been so crazy over a woman before. I've been attracted to them, wanted to sleep with them, but it was never such an out of control, all-consuming feeling. Not like what I'm experiencing now.

This is terrifying.

I walk into the kitchen and she's on her phone. She's holding a cup of coffee in her hand and laughing at something. She hasn't noticed me yet, so I just stand here watching her. She's effortlessly beautiful.

Not an ounce of makeup on, hair a mess, but still the most beautiful woman I have ever seen.

I try to work out what draws me to her like this, but it's impossi-ble to calculate. She just seems different from any of the women

I've been around. Kindness radiates from her, touching anyone who is in her path.

She's dangerous. She has the power to break me, which is why I cannot let myself give in. I have to be strong and resist.

I take confident strides directly to the coffee machine. This is ridiculous. No woman has that kind of power over me anymore, not again. I start to pour my coffee and she reaches around me to grab the creamer.

Her arm brushes my stomach, causing the hairs all over my body to stand. She just goes about refilling her coffee like she didn't just turn me upside down with a simple touch.

It pisses me off. I wonder how she would like it if I did the same to her.

Fuck it. If she wants to drive me crazy, let's see how she feels. I've seen the way she looks at me, I know she likes what she sees.

I can tell she's talking to Layla. I hear my sister's loud voice through the speaker as she rambles on about God knows what. She has her elbows on the counter as she continues to talk like I'm not here.

She's bent over the counter, ass sticking out. I decide I definitely need something from the drawer she is standing in front of. I can't even remember what's in that drawer at the moment, but that doesn't matter.

I step behind her, my body a breath away from hers. I place my hand on her hip and give it a gentle squeeze. She stands up straight and turns to look at me. I step closer until my body is flush against hers.

Her eyes open wide. I let time stand still as we both stare at each other, our breaths mix together. I get lost in her reaction, noticing her cleavage that is now rising and falling rapidly. Then I remember what I'm supposed to be doing.

I reach for the drawer, pushing my body further onto hers. I open it and grab the first thing my hand touches, never letting my eyes leave hers. Retreating back a couple of steps, I raise my hand.

A small smirk creeps across her mouth. I'm holding my niece's miniature doll. I don't know how the damn thing got in there, but here I am, a grown man trying to play tricks on the woman who is driving him crazy, holding up a damn doll.

I feel my face turn down in anger as she bites her curved lip.

"Dammit," I growl as I throw the doll on the ground and storm off.

That is not what was supposed to happen. My hand grips my hair as I pace in my bedroom. If I didn't have this fucking sling on, I could at least lift some weights to blow off some steam.

I don't know what the hell I'm doing anymore.

I want to tell her to leave, that this is starting to fuck with my head, but with her ex out there, I can't imagine letting her leave. She's only been here for a week, and I'm already worried about her like she means something to me. It's crazy.

I need to figure out a way to release some energy in this damn sling. I have some large logs that need to be cut for my outdoor fireplace. I can cut through all of it if I use the electric chainsaw.

Fuck it. I don't care if it's annoying or how long it takes, I need to get out of here. I'll get some work done later.

My arm is doing better anyway. With the ibuprofen, it only hurts when I move it. I slide my sling off and whip my shirt over my head with my good arm, then put the sling back on.

It's sunny out and probably in the seventies, I don't need a shirt while I'm working out there. We're most likely on our last few days of getting some good vitamin D before the colder weather starts to gray the sky.

The sun beats down on my back as I cut the final piece of wood. I've been at it for hours, but it's been worth it. I'm drenched in sweat. I wish I could go jump in the pool, but my stitches won't allow for that. I'm stuck with only a shower to cool me off.

On my way back to the house, I spot movement by the pool. Mia is resting on one of the chairs in a red two-piece bikini.

Avoid her, you fool.

Instead of listening to my inner voice, my feet start taking me directly to the pool. I stand at the end of her chair as I wait for her to notice me. I cough, impatient with her complete disregard of my presence.

"Oh, hey," she smiles up at me.

Her eyes drink me in, fixated on the sweat dripping down my chest. I notice her squeeze her thighs together, and my dick starts to harden in my jeans.

"Enjoying a little sun this afternoon?" I ask.

"Yeah, figured I'd get some sun in before the cold weather sticks. Are you done playing with your doll?"

She can't even keep a straight face. She thinks she's so funny. I'll show her.

"As a matter of fact," I rip my belt buckle open then push down my jeans until I'm standing in only my black boxer briefs. Her eyes are staring at my bulge, which is substantial, if I do say so myself. "I'm exhausted from playing with my dolls. I think I'll dip in the pool to cool off."

I kick my jeans to the side and walk over to the pool's entrance.

She can't hide her reaction to me.

I see it.

I feel it.

And she is lucky that I'm so fucked in the head, or I'd be balls deep inside of her by now.

I walk down the steps, the warm water not doing much to relieve my aching muscles. I step down until I get waist-deep, then stop.

"What are you doing? You can't get your arm wet?" she says, trying to act indifferent but I can sense her concern.

I turn to her and smile. "Just going to walk around this end of the pool for a while. Not going any further? Why? Are you worried about me, Mia?"

She rolls her eyes. If only I could slap that luscious ass of hers to teach her poor attitude a lesson.

"Not worried. But don't expect me to keep changing your clothes like a child if it gets worse."

I chuckle to myself. She's got a fire in her. It's fun messing with her. Maybe that can be my new strategy to deal with my attraction. If she thinks she got an eyeful of me before, just wait until I walk out of this pool with my briefs molded to my dick. That'll teach her.

But before I get a chance, she stands up from her chair. "I think I'll go change, maybe get started on dinner. Enjoy."

When her ass comes into view, I nearly lose my footing. My fingers coil by my sides with the desire to squeeze, to fucking mark those cheeks. Cheeks that are on full display to me. Her skin is tan, which must mean she wears a two-piece often.

Why does that piss me off? And who the fuck does she think she is walking around my house like that? Is she trying to torture me? Now she's leaving me with a raging hard on and no outlet.

I stomp up the steps of the pool and through the kitchen, leaving water in my tracks. Once inside my bathroom, I rip off my briefs and get into the shower. I move the spray to my right, keeping my left arm out of the direct stream of water.

I grab my dick, stiff and thick, and start to stroke it. My grip is hard and punishing while I chase relief. My eyes close as I picture her perfect body, the sexy blush that drives me wild, and that ass. I'm coming hard within minutes as I picture painting her ass with my cum.

After the final jolt of pleasure is released, I let my head hang down under the water as I try to compose myself. This is not who I am. I don't get so crazy for someone that I have to jack off in the shower like a teenager. I don't even feel satisfied, not even close. This woman is turning my world upside down.

When did this happen? How did this happen?

While I get dressed, I try to pinpoint the time that I lost control of the situation, but I keep coming up short.

It wasn't instant lust. Sure, I noticed she was beautiful, but I didn't immediately lose myself over her beauty. So how did it get to this so quickly? There's just something about her movements, the way she carries herself. It's all so different, so confident without being arrogant.

When I walk into the kitchen, she's standing over the stove with a glass of wine in her hands.

She looks up at me and smiles.

I groan and walk over to the fridge. I'm not going to have dinner with her tonight. I'm sick of feeling like this in my own home. I need some space.

As I look up and down the shelves, the aroma from her chicken parmesan drifts past me. Motherfucker, she's a good cook. Maybe that's what's going on, she's putting me under a spell with her food.

I shake my head. Clearly, I'm losing my mind. Now I think the woman staying with me is magically controlling my mind. Maybe I got an infection from my cut. Do I have a fever? I feel my forehead like it's going to solve everything.

"Are you hungry?" she asks.

I turn around and see her grabbing two plates. "I am. But I'm not eating with you," I grind out.

"Oh, ok. I can just put this in the fridge for whenever you're ready."

I take a step closer. "Maybe I don't want to eat your food, Mia. Maybe I just want to be left alone."

"What's gotten into you?" She slams the plate down.

I take another step closer. "What's gotten into me? You walking around my place in next to nothing, cooking me food like you're my girlfriend. I don't need this right now."

"Fine! I was just trying to be nice!" She takes an abrupt step toward me, her body only inches away. "But I'll stop it. I'll leave if I'm too much of an inconvenience."

She turns to storm away, but I catch her by the arm and spin her toward me. "You can't leave. It's not safe."

She looks me up and down. "I'm not staying here if I'm not wanted, Eric."

She pulls her arm away, and takes off again, her footsteps thundering down the hall. I try to talk myself out of chasing after her, but I lose.

"Well, that's tough shit," I scream as I jog to catch up with her. She turns around at the bottom of the stairs and I continue toward her. "You're staying."

"No, I'm not. You don't want me here."

"I never said that!"

She laughs bitterly. "You just said it!"

"No! What I said was I don't need this." I point back and forth between us. "This fucking attraction!"

Her jaw drops. "Are you kidding me? That's why you're throwing a tantrum? Because you're attracted to me? Well, I'm not attracted to you, so problem solved."

She starts up the stairs. "Bull shit," I call as I follow her. "I see the way you look at me. You can't stop drooling over my body."

We're at her door. Before she opens it, she looks me up and down again. "It's not that impressive. I've seen better."

I slam my hands on either side of the door frame and cage her in. "I don't believe you for a second. You can't hide the way those thighs squeeze together when you see me half-naked. I know you're just trying to ease the throbbing between your legs. I bet I made you so fucking wet downstairs when you were eyeing my dick by the pool."

"Oh, please. Your dick isn't even that impressi…" I don't give her the chance to finish her lie. My lips capture hers, swallowing her words.

I can't control the fire inside of me that has been stoked by her presence. The world outside disappears as we fight with our mouths. Every move of our lips is another effort to prove a point.

I slide my tongue into her mouth, and she responds with a moan. She reaches around my back, sliding her fingertips up. My hand grips her jaw as our tongues work together in a brutal attempt for control.

My dick begs for some relief, breaking me from the spell. I pull away quickly, my breath is ragged as I take her in. Swollen lips, chest rapidly rising and falling, intoxicating big beautiful brown eyes.

I'm such an idiot. I can't believe I lost control.

"Fuck," I yell as I hurry down the hallway to my bedroom.

I slam my door and begin to pace back and forth. That wasn't supposed to happen. How did it happen? One second, we're yelling at each other, the next, my tongue is in her mouth and I'm kissing her with everything I have.

Okay, it's fine. It was one slip up. I won't let it happen again. I just have to be more careful. Apparently, fighting with her gets me going. Not sure what the hell that's about.

Despite everything, my dick is still hard after that kiss. But I refuse to jerk off again to the thought of Mia. My attraction to her seems to be a slippery slope, and I need to resist these temptations.

After hiding out in my room for an hour, my stomach growls for the hundredth time. I go back downstairs for dinner, and see that Mia cleaned up, but left a plate for me in the fridge with plastic wrap over it. Even though I want to prove a point that I don't need her or her cooking, I can't resist it. I warm it up and sit by myself while I try to pretend it's not even that good.

I end up going to bed early but can't seem to wind down enough to fall asleep. I toss and turn for hours when I hear my door crack open.

Her silhouette appears in my doorway, and even a darkened shadow of hers manages to make my heart beat faster. I watch her walk further into my room, her fingers playing with the bottom of her long t-shirt.

"I'm sorry," she whispers. "I shouldn't be in here. I just...it's dark and I can't stop thinking about him. Wondering where he is."

I don't know this motherfucker, but what he's doing to her causes this rage inside of me unlike one I've ever felt before. She is too perfect, too kind to be afraid to sleep alone.

"Come on in," I tell her, knowing there is no world in which this all ends well, but not wanting her to feel unsafe.

She crawls under the covers. We lie awake in silence for a moment.

"I'm sorry about the kiss. It shouldn't have happened," I admit, needing to get the words out.

She sighs. "It's alright."

"I don't want you to leave, Mia. I want you to stay here. I want you to be safe. I'm just...I'm messed up in the head. We can't let that happen again."

She turns away from me. "Got it. Goodnight."

This is good. It's how it should be. But I already hate the distance I feel from her and the sadness in her voice.

"Goodnight, Mia."

Chapter Thirteen

Mia

My body has been on edge all day. That kiss last night—it shook me. Never have I had such an explosive feeling before like I did when he claimed my mouth.

Fuck, he knows how to kiss a woman.

But he stormed off like a mad man, regretting the best thirty seconds of my life. I can't lie, it hurt. He clearly doesn't want to want me. Is it because I'm his sister's friend? And what does he mean he's messed up in the head?

I shouldn't care. I should just move on and forget it, but I'm drawn to him. I want to know more about him. I want to know what made him this way.

A knock from the front door pulls me out of my thoughts.

"Hello!" Layla's voice echoes in the foyer.

Relief floods me that I don't have to be in this house alone with Eric for a couple of hours. I think we both need some other people here to cut the sexual tension between us.

"Hey big brother. Look at you. No more sling!" I hear her say.

Her and Eric walk into the kitchen while I pour myself a glass of wine. Two other people that I've never seen before trail behind them. I'm loving the idea of more people here tonight.

"Yeah, I just talked to a physical therapist. He told me as long as the pain is tolerable, I can stop using the sling."

I didn't realize he was going to be out of the sling so quickly. It's only been four days. A weird sense of disappointment hits. Is he going to go back to work tomorrow? I guess this also means that he doesn't need my help changing.

Shit. I need to get a hold of myself. I'm upset that I don't have an excuse to change the shirt of a grown man.

"Well, I'm glad to see you're recovering quickly," Josh hits his back. "It's nice to see you on a Tuesday night. You're normally claiming to be too busy at work to get out on time."

Eric smiles and rolls his eyes. He seems to have a playful relationship with Josh. I'm glad Layla found someone who seems to fit in so well with her family.

"Nice to see you again, Mia," Josh says as he gives me a big hug. "How has it been living with this man?"

"Eh, pretty uneventful," I lie as I steal a glance Eric's way.

His brows knit together in a tight, hostile line. He doesn't approve of my remark, but I don't care. Am I supposed to tell everyone how close I came to having sex with him last night? Or how much I still want to despite his grouchy demeanor.

"Pretty uneventful, huh?" Eric crosses his arms across his chest. "Was last night uneventful?"

"What happened last night?" Layla asks.

I shoot him a look that could cut glass.

"Nothing happened," I interject before he can talk any further. "Your brother and I were watching a chick flick, and he started crying. It was very entertaining. Hi, I'm Mia," I extend my hand to the woman standing across from me, trying to contain the smile that wants to break free. Eric is giving me a death stare right now.

That'll teach him to mess with me.

"Hi, I'm Avery," she smiles kindly. "I've heard so much about you. Layla's pretty excited to have you here."

"It's nice to meet you. I've definitely heard your name over the years."

"And this is Ryder," Layla says, pointing to the tall, handsome man standing next to her. "He's a friend of Josh's."

Oh, so this is not Avery's boyfriend. Interesting. He's extremely good-looking.

"Nice to meet you, Mia," he says, his eyes travel my body's height.

"Nice to meet you," I shake his hand.

"Well, let's go outside and have some dinner." Layla leads the way. "I hope everyone has a sweater, it's kind of chilly out tonight, but it's perfect sweater weather!"

I'm so excited to try some more of the food she brought from her restaurant. I'm also feeling horrible that I haven't stopped in yet, but I know she understands. I've already told her I'm working up the courage to leave the house. It's still scary with no more news on Don's whereabouts. My brother assures me they are all over it, but they haven't come up with any solid leads yet.

We all take a seat outside around the large table. Ryder sits next to me while Avery and Eric sit across from us. I suddenly wonder if there has ever been anything between the two of them. A sharp pain of jealousy stabs me in the chest.

"Thanks so much for bringing food," I tell Layla as she sets it out for us. "I'm excited to eventually check out the restaurant.

I fidget in my seat, uncomfortable with even having to navigate around this subject of me not being able to leave the house. She must sense my feelings.

"You take as long as you need," she says with an understanding smile.

"So, Mia," Ryder turns to me, "what can I plate you with?"

"Oh, umm, thanks. I think I want to try a little of everything," I admit shyly.

Ryder smirks. "Not afraid to eat. That's my kind of woman."

Eric coughs loudly and I think I catch a roll of his eyes. That can't be jealousy coming from him, can it? The idea that a man like him could be jealous over me sparks a bit of excitement.

After everyone has their food, Josh holds up his glass of wine. "A toast," he begins, "to finally getting to know Mia, a longtime friend of Layla's. To all our health, especially Eric's close call the other night, and to my amazing fiancée and her skills in the kitchen. Which I can tell you is not the only place she is skilled."

I chuckle while Layla gasps.

"Seriously, dude," Eric cringes. "That's my sister. You gotta stop with that shit in front of me."

"Oh, please. You all seem to fall in love with each other's friends then cry about it later like you can't believe that means they have sex," Avery rolls her eyes then takes a sip of wine.

I smile at her. I think I like her. She's the type to speak her mind. Still—she better not have slept with Eric.

"Mia, what brings you to Isle of Hope?" Ryder asks.

My spine goes rigid. My mouth falls open as I try to speak, but nothing comes out.

"Umm," I stutter, wondering why I can't come up with a simple lie as those around me who know the truth sit in silence.

"She's just taking a much-deserved vacation from her job," Eric cuts in. "She wanted to spend some time with Layla, but I offered up my place since I have the extra space."

There was a depth in his expression, a quiet assurance that conveyed empathy without words. His eyes hold mine, making me feel seen and valued in ways I've never felt.

"That's cool," Ryder responds, clueless to the interaction I'm having with the man opposite me, "what do you do for a living?"

My eyes break away from Eric's. "I own a wine distribution company with my brothers."

"She's being modest," Layla says. "She owns an extremely successful wine distribution company."

Ryder's eyebrows raise. "I'm impressed. Beautiful and successful."

I smile to myself, slightly embarrassed by the attention. "It's no big deal. It's a joint effort with me and my brothers."

Sometime after dinner when we're enjoying our drinks, Ryder's arm rests on the back of my chair. He keeps it there the rest of the evening, leaning toward me when he talks. Eric has had a scowl on his face throughout most of the dinner, his eyes bouncing between me and Ryder.

I may have flirted back with Ryder a lot during dinner, knowing it was getting to Eric. He doesn't get to push me away then be furious when I have another man's attention.

At the end of the night, we're saying goodbye to everyone and Ryder leans in to give me a kiss on the cheek.

"I'd love to take you out sometime while you're in town," he says. "Can I get your number?"

"Oh, um, sure," I hesitate. He's a very nice guy, and definitely attractive. But I can't lie and say I wasn't thinking about the grump across the table all night. But I don't want to hurt Ryder's feelings or make this awkward by saying no in front of everybody. So, I rattle off my number and say goodbye.

The door closes and Eric disappears before I have a chance to say anything to him. I'm tired and don't feel like chasing him around the house trying to gauge how pissed off he actually is.

I'm in my room stepping out of my jeans when my door opens. "What the hell, Eric?" I scream.

He doesn't answer and strides further into my room until he is inches away from me. His presence is palpable, his breathing mingles with mine in the centimeters that now separates us.

"You have fun trying to make me jealous all night?" His fingers play with a strand of my hair, then quickly drops it.

I can't believe he's storming into my room without knocking and accusing me of this. He's got some nerve.

"Why? Are you saying that you *were* jealous tonight?"

"Be careful, Mia. I only have so much self-control," he threatens before he walks away.

Damn him and his sexy words that should scare me off but only seem to turn me on. This is not what I need to feel right before I go to sleep. As soon as I throw on my t-shirt, I walk over to my bed, look down at it, then over to the window.

What's the point of even trying tonight? I know I'm going to end up in his bed. I keep telling myself it's only because I'm afraid. That there's no other reason my body keeps pulling me in there every night.

I take small, quiet steps out of my bedroom into the hallway. Tonight he left his bedroom door wide open, like he knew I was coming. It feels like an open invitation even though he's pissed at me right now. I follow the same path I have for the past couple of nights, then pull back the covers.

Once I'm under, I close my eyes, but his angry words have my body reeling, wanting more of them—wanting more of him.

He hasn't said anything to me which is getting under my skin. Is he mad at me for flirting with Ryder? After several minutes of silence, I can't take it anymore.

"Fine. You're right," I confess. "I was flirting with Ryder to make you jealous. Are you happy? I admit it. I've been so worked up lately. No release of mine seems to satisfy me. You walk around here like Jekyll and Hyde, making me feel all—ugh whatever—then storm away."

I hear the shuffling of sheets and look over. Eric is now resting on his side looking over at me.

"How do I make you feel, Mia?" he asks, voice deep with gravel.

"It doesn't matter," I whisper.

I don't know why he is focusing on that part when I'm admitting that I tried to make him jealous.

"Tell me how I make you feel," he demands.

I swallow. He sounds angry and it just makes me feel more aroused. "You make me feel...," I struggle to find the words, "'hot."

"Go on. Tell me more."

I take a deep breath. "You make my body feel like all the blood is rushing down..."

"Down where?" he asks on a whisper.

"You know where," I respond.

"I want to hear you say it. I *need* to hear you say it."

"My...," my voice lowers to a soft whisper, "pussy."

He groans then scoots closer to me. "Do I make your pussy wet, Mia?"

I can't help but look into his deep blue eyes and nod my head up and down.

"Fuck," he utters with frustration. Then I feel the warmth of his fingers on my inner thigh. I gasp at the sensation it evokes. "Maybe," he says as his fingers slide up my thigh then back down, making my underwear soak with excitement. "Maybe here in the darkness, it doesn't count. If I lick this sweet pussy of yours, giving you some relief, we pretend like it never happened in the morning."

Right now, I'd agree to be his slave in excuse for his mouth on me. I can almost feel the hint of an orgasm starting just by the thought of it. That's how primed he has me from just his words.

"Do you want me to taste your pussy, Mia?" he asks while his fingers move higher up my thigh.

"Yes," I manage to whisper. "Please."

"Just for tonight. Just here in the darkness where it doesn't count. Right?" he says with a plea.

It really seems to matter to him that this be considered *nothing*, whatever that means. That's fine. I'm in no emotional state at the moment to need a complicated long-distance relationship.

"Yes. Just for tonight," I agree.

I barely get the words out before his mouth is on mine. My lips open instantly and our tongues swirl together. His hands work to rid me of my t-shirt before he rolls in between my legs.

"Fuck," he winces.

"What? Are you okay?" I ask.

"I'm fine. My arm just hurts a little when I put my weight on it."

I try to sit up, but he pushes me down. "Eric, I don't want you to hurt your arm."

"I don't give a fuck about my arm. I can deal with the pain. What I can't deal with is not getting a taste of your pussy when you just admitted to me how wet I make you. Tell me, Mia...are you wet right now?"

His hands grab my breasts and start to massage them as his eyes remain on mine. I can't think enough to respond, and he doesn't seem to care. He keeps playing with my breasts and squeezes each nipple between his finger and thumb.

He kisses the top of my stomach and starts to make his way down past my belly button all while still playing with my nipples. "Your breasts are fucking perfect."

His mouth continues until it reaches just above my clit, where he gives a featherlike kiss just centimeters above where I need it.

"Eric," I pant as my body squirms beneath him.

His hands move from my breasts then slide underneath me on the bed and grip my ass. "And this ass. You fucking teased me with it in your bathing suit the other night. I didn't know whether to spank you or cover you up."

I let out a moan just thinking about the idea of him spanking me.

He starts to knead my ass. "Do you like the idea of that, Mia? You want me to punish you for teasing me?"

"I never thought I would, but with you—you make it all sound so sexy. It's like your anger just turns me on and makes me—curious."

"Fuck, Mia. Don't say things like that to me. This is only for tonight. Just one taste."

With that, his tongue comes out and ever so gently swipes across my clit. My hips buck up, but his hands grab them and push me back down into place as his tongue moves faster and harder.

His lips press against my skin while his tongue dives deep into my pussy then moves back up to circle my clit. His face is buried in me, and I can barely breathe from the sensations it evokes.

"Shit!" I scream as he begins to suck my clit.

"Mmmm," he moans into my sex. "You like that baby? You want me to suck on that clit some more?"

I don't answer. I can't. Not while his mouth ravishes me so perfectly. I close my eyes, basking in the sensations when a hard slap hits my clit.

"Answer me when I fucking talk to you, Mia," he says, eyes dark with lust.

"Yes!" I scream. "Yes, I like it when you suck my clit. So much. It's so fucking good."

"Good girl," he growls then slams his mouth back on my pussy.

Never would I think that would be something that turns me on, but oh my god! How do I tell him that I want him to do that again? I think I want it harder next time. I want him to spank me. Oh my god, I want him to fucking lose control on me.

No one has ever eaten me with such visceral desire. It feels like this is the one thing he's wanted his entire life and is finally getting. It's overwhelming.

His final groan onto my clit does me in. I come on a scream as my fingers clutch the sheets below me, desperately trying to hang onto this world, afraid I'm being transported to another universe with my earth-shattering orgasm.

When he pulls away, he wipes his mouth with the back of his hand as a tortured look crosses his face. Before I can even offer to return the favor, he gets out of bed and walks into his bathroom. Not even a minute later, I hear a groan come from the bathroom.

I don't know how to take it that he didn't want me to touch him. But I can feel that his wall is back up when he comes back into bed, so I don't press him on it. I turn to face the window, knowing it'll be impossible to calm my racing thoughts and get to sleep.

Chapter Fourteen

Eric

I'm screwed. I'll never be the same after tasting Mia last night. I could've come from just the pleasure of watching her take what I was giving her. She was one hundred percent in the moment, unafraid to show exactly how turned on she was. I love it when a woman expresses herself freely during sex, and Mia did just that.

I didn't mean to slap her pussy, but she just pissed me off. I don't like feeling so out of control with desire. But what I didn't expect was for her to be so turned on by it. I can't imagine what it would be like to sink myself into her. To play out my darkest fantasies.

And that's exactly why I can't go down that path. It will lead to my heart getting involved. One thing that I haven't done since Mia has come around is think about my ex. This is the longest I've gone without her crossing my mind.

But is it really an accomplishment when my mind trades in one woman for another? It's not like Mia doesn't have the same capability as Kim did to break me.

Instead of letting either girl occupy my brain, I decide to throw myself back into work. I don't even stop for lunch. I don't want to risk walking out of my office and getting distracted. I manage to get on the phone with Peter without wanting to kill him, which in of itself is a miracle.

The acquisition is still on schedule, even with my injury taking up a lot of my time. I'm still going to wait until Monday to go back into the office.

After I feel like I can't look at a screen for a minute longer, I slam my laptop down. I get up and walk into the kitchen where Mia stands, talking on the phone.

Judging by the voice I can hear when I walk past—I know it's Layla. Her ability to not scream into the phone is non-existent. I've tried to tell her she does it, but she tells me I'm being dramatic.

"Oh, he wants to take me there tonight. That's nice," Mia says halfheartedly.

I stop in my tracks and turn back around, leaning closer to hear what they're talking about.

"Yes, you should come. I'll be there all night. Ryder will keep you safe, I'll make sure of it," I hear Layla say.

No fucking way. There is no way she is going to my sister's restaurant with Ryder. That man is a douche. Okay, fine—he's a nice guy. But I don't like the idea of him taking Mia there. She'd be more comfortable with me. She'd be safer with me. I know what's going on, I know to be on the lookout. He doesn't know about her ex, so he can't keep her safe.

I grab the phone out of Mia's hand. "I'll take her to your restaurant."

"Eric?" she questions. "You want to take Mia out tonight?"

"Yes. She'll be safer with me."

"Oh, I didn't know that you knew. Umm, what does Mia want to do?"

I hand the phone back to Mia. "Tell her I'm taking you."

"Layla?" Mia says while glaring at me. "Yeah, I told him. Uh huh. No, I suppose it would be safer with someone who knows. Okay. I'll see you tonight."

She hangs up the phone and slams it on the counter then comes after me. She pushes my chest, and I actually fall backward, needing to catch myself with my foot. Shit, she's strong. It's kind of hot. I have to try not to smirk at her after she pushes me again.

"What the hell was that for?" she demands. "You don't get to make decisions for me. I'm a grown woman. I can make those on my own. And based on the way you ran away like a scared little boy last night— I wouldn't think you would want to have dinner with me."

My face falls at her words but I do my best to recover quickly. "I'm just trying to protect you. You know as well as I do it's safer with me there. I'll be hyper-aware of our surroundings. That way, you can just relax and enjoy Layla's restaurant. I'm trying to help you, and here you are coming at me. Now, I'm going to go get ready for dinner. I *suggest* you do the same."

I walk away feeling butthurt—feeling like a child. I don't like her calling me scared. And I didn't run away last night. I chose not to put myself in a situation that could end in disaster. It's called self-preservation.

After I spend far too much time picking out what to wear. I settle on a black button down and dark jeans. It doesn't mean anything that I do my hair or that I opt to spray a bit of cologne on before I leave the bathroom. That means nothing.

I'm sitting at my kitchen island when I hear Mia walk downstairs. As she steps into the room, I feel my breath catch. Everything else seems to fade. My pulse quickens and I can't help the smile that tugs at my lips, feeling a little dazed, as if seeing her for the first time.

She's in a red dress that hugs her breasts perfectly and flows loosely below her small waist. Her dark hair is down in waves and she's wearing red lipstick to match her dress.

Fuck. She looks hot. This is going to be a long night.

An hour later, we're seated at the restaurant waiting for my sister to come by.

"Do you know what you want to drink?" Mia asks as she looks over the menu.

I shrug. "I'll probably order a beer."

Her eyebrows turn up. "Just a beer?"

"I'm sorry. Would you like me to order some fruity pink drink? Is that what kind of men you're used to dating?"

"Are you saying this is a date?" she asks with a smirk.

"What? No! That's not what I meant."

Her head falls back as she laughs at my defensive response.

"What's so funny?" Layla asks, her presence startling me.

"Oh, Eric was telling me how he always wanted to try your fruitiest pink drink but has been too afraid to ask."

My cheeks feel hot as a wave of embarrassment hits me.

"Oh, um, ok. You could've asked me for...that," Layla replies awkwardly then turns to Mia. "And what can I get you?"

She taps at her chin with her finger while thinking. "I'll take whatever foreign beer you have on tap," she says then winks at me.

"Got it. One beer and one fruity pink drink coming up."

Layla walks away before I can get my shit together enough to change my drink order.

She smiles proudly as she rests her chin on her hand. "So, tell me more about your woodworking. I can't stop thinking about it. When do you think you'll be healed enough to work again?"

Her question takes me by surprise. "I was thinking about starting back this weekend. I can move my arm with only slight pain now, so I think by the weekend, I should be in a good spot. What do you want to know about it?"

"What's your favorite piece so far?" she asks.

I lean forward and rest my chin on my hand mirroring her. "That's easy. My second piece."

"What was it?" she whispers with an edge of excitement.

I can't help but smile. "A rocking chair. My grandpa used to sit on this old rocking chair all the time sipping his coffee or bourbon as he watched the sunrise or sunset. I would sit on the steps of the porch with him whenever I could. They were the most peaceful times of my life."

Her head tilts to the side as she looks at me strangely. "That's really sweet. Is your grandpa still alive?"

I shake my head. "No, he died about ten years ago. None of my grandparents are alive, actually."

"I'm sorry to hear that," she reaches across the table and squeezes my hand. "I'm guessing you and your grandpa were close."

I nod my head. "He was my hero. Before my dad's company took off, I would've said my dad was my hero, but money changed my family. My grandpa, though, he just lived a simple life. He never seemed to care about money or status."

"Here you go," Layla interrupts, making me realize I've shared more with Mia just now than anyone in the last decade of my life. "One beer and one pink fruity drink. What can I get you guys to eat?"

"I think I'm going to try the shrimp and grits," Mia says.

"Nice choice. And for you, big brother?"

"I'll have the salmon."

"Okay. I'll be back soon. I'm so glad you could make it out," Layla says to Mia.

Once my sister walks away, I look down at my drink. Mia grabs it and slides her beer across the table to my side. "I wasn't really going to make you drink that. I wanted it. I just thought it'd be funny to see you sweat."

I find myself laughing. "Good one, Mia. You're a funny lady."

She shrugs. "I know you're saying that sarcastically right now. But I would like to point out that you are actually laughing, so it worked."

I ponder that. "I suppose you're right."

The rest of the night is surprisingly easy. I laugh more than I have in a long time, forgetting to put my guard up. I just had fun. Every man who even looked in her direction was on my radar. No one was coming within five feet of her without my permission.

Once we get back to my house, I breathe a sigh of relief as I set the security system.

"Thanks for taking me out tonight. I had a lot of fun. I even managed to forget about the whole crazy ex thing," she says softly as we reach the top of my steps.

"I'm glad. Layla was thrilled you were able to make it out."

We stand in the middle of the hallway. She looks so beautiful it's hard to look directly at her. Everything about tonight has felt like a date. I wish I could lean in and take those lips against mine.

"The food was delicious. I'm so proud of her," she says with a smile.

"You're a good friend to her."

"Only because she's a good one to me."

We stand in silence for a minute. I'm not sure how to end the evening, but I know I can't end it the way I would like to.

"Well, I'm gonna go get in bed. I need to get in a full day of work tomorrow," I eventually say.

She nods her head but doesn't make any effort to move. I pull at the tension at the back of my neck.

"Goodnight, Mia." I walk away before I do something stupid. Something my body is begging me to do, but my brain is screaming it's a bad idea.

"Goodnight," I hear her whisper behind me.

I still leave my door open, knowing if she is scared, I want her to come into my bed. Once I'm under the covers, my brain can't think of anything else but the way she tasted last night. The way she came so loudly and uninhibited.

This time when she walks in, my dick instantly gets hard as I watch her climb into my bed. The way her shirt rides up, showing me her black satin panties.

I'm not going to do it. I'm not going to touch her. It cannot happen again.

I don't know how many times I repeat these words to myself in the silence of the night. My hands are clutched into tight fists, as I continue my chant to myself.

"Eric," she says in a silky voice.

Fuck. "Yeah?" I respond roughly.

"Do you think..." she starts but the silence fills the room again.

I'm in no mood for her hesitation. Whatever it is that she needs to say, just say it. That way I can go back to talking myself off of this ledge.

"Spit it out, Mia. Do I think what?"

She huffs her frustration then rolls away from me. "Forget it."

That won't do. I roll onto my elbow ignoring the pain as I grab her shoulder and roll her onto her back. I look down at her eyes, shining in the moonlight and creating a pain in my chest. My reaction to her beauty only fuels my anger.

"Don't be childish. If you have something to ask me, ask it."

Her mouth trembles as I see the conflicting emotions she's battling in her mind. I hold my breath, terrified she's going to ask for something I don't want. Even more terrified she's going to ask me for something I desperately want.

"Do you think tonight in the darkness, it won't count again?"

My dick goes rock hard against her stomach. I know I need to tell her no. The words are on the tip of my tongue, but then I watch the rise and fall of her chest against her white shirt and see the dark outlines of her nipples.

"What exactly are you asking for?" I ask as I try to find the strength within me to turn her down.

She rolls her eyes. "I think you know."

She tries to roll over again, but I grip her wrist and pin it above her head. That's it. Her beneath me, bound to the bed by my strength. There's no way I'm not taking her as mine tonight.

"You should know me better than that, Mia. I like to hear the words. Do you feel my dick?" I press my body against hers. "It loves to hear those dirty words out of your mouth. Tell me exactly what doesn't count here in the darkness."

She exhales on a shaky breath. "I was thinking—I wanted to feel your tongue on me again."

"Anything else?" I groan as my lips drop to her neck and run along the delicate curve.

Her body squirms beneath me. "I want to taste you."

"You want my big cock in your mouth?" I ask as I can feel pre-cum drip from my tip. Just the thought of her mouth around my dick makes me feel like I might explode.

She nods. That's about all the restraint I have in me. I capture her lips with mine in a punishing kiss. My firm mouth demands a response from hers, and she obeys. She matches my hunger with her own.

Raising my mouth from hers, I gaze into her eyes. "Get on your hands and knees."

Her eyes open wide with both surprise but also excitement. She flips over, obeying my command quickly. My dick strains in my briefs, begging to be released, but right now I want to worship every inch of her. I want to make this last forever. I wish the sun would stay on the other side of the world forever, so this will never end.

I reach for her silky underwear and pull them down. She lifts each leg so I can pull them all the way off. Now, she's bared to me, and I feel a ripple of excitement that she is mine tonight.

My thumbs spread her lips apart as I take in her pink pussy.

"Such a perfect pussy," I tell her as I ease one thumb into her entrance. "Nice and wet, just for me."

"Please," she whispers. I think her begging is my new favorite sound.

"What do you want, Mia?"

I push in both thumbs, spreading her apart. She's dripping wet, and I can barely resist.

"Your tongue," she breathes out.

She doesn't need to ask twice. I lean down and lick her from clit to ass. My tongue slides against her puckered hole, teasing her at the taboo spot. I pull away just enough to spit and then slide a thumb inside.

She turns her head around and looks me in the eyes, jaw slack as I push in further. Her moan vibrates through her body.

"Do you like me playing with your ass?" I growl, not willing to break our stare.

She nods her head quickly. "Yes."

"Fuck, you look so sexy right now. I'm barely hanging on, baby."

I keep my thumb inside of her and lean down to lick her clit. She pushes her ass up, my thumb slipping all the way in, as I bury my mouth in her pussy. I moan my approval, loving how she is taking what she wants from me. As I continue to lick and suck, she moves while my thumb slips in and out of her ass.

Before I can get her off, she flips over. She sits down in front of me while I'm on my knees and grabs my dick through my briefs.

The contact, even through a layer of fabric, feels incredible. She grabs my briefs and tugs them down my hips. My dick springs forward right in front of her face.

Her eyes open wide. "Surprised by something?" I ask with interest.

She bites her lip as her eyes take me in. "You're so big."

She looks at my dick like she's considering whether it'll fit inside of her mouth. When she wraps her delicate fingers around me and gives my dick a tug, I let out a deep moan. Everything with this woman is magnified by a hundred. Then she opens her mouth and closes it around my tip and my head falls back in ecstasy. I gasp like a fucking chump, but dammit, I can't help it.

I look down at her and watch her eagerly take me to the back of her throat. When she's gotten my dick all good and wet, she starts to slide up and down quickly, letting out her own moans along the way.

"Do you like having my dick in your mouth?" I ask as I pull her hair out of her face.

She looks up at me, mouth filled with me inside of it and hums her agreement. That alone almost makes me embarrass myself and come in her mouth sooner than I had planned.

Her eagerness to suck me off is sexy as hell. I hold her hair up on top of her head while she bobs up and down like a champ. Her eyes keep looking up at me, and I swear I see a smirk on those lips.

She knows she's rocking my world right now. Then she pulls off me and leans back on her hands.

"Fuck me, Eric," she demands, looking boldly into my eyes. "Please."

She starts to rub her clit in front of me. Why haven't I been with a woman who so clearly knows what she wants and asks for it before? My dick throbs at the thought, but I wasn't planning on letting myself go that far with her.

But looking at her begging for it while touching herself, there's no way in hell I can deny her.

I grab my dick and play with it while she rubs herself. "You want my dick to stretch that tight cunt of yours?"

She bites her lip and nods at me. "Do you have a condom?"

Fuck it. I open the drawer of my nightstand and pull one out then toss it at her.

"You asked for it. You can wrap it up, baby."

She rips open the condom faster than I've ever seen. She's just as desperate for this as I am, and somehow that makes my dick harder. I stay on my knees and watch as she slowly rolls the condom down my shaft, giving it a few jerks once it's on.

"Get back on those hands and knees," I demand. When she flips back over, I slap her ass. "That's for making me so damn crazy for you."

She lets out a groan. "Again," she whispers, almost shyly.

"What did you say?" I ask while holding my dick at her entrance, about to push in.

She turns her head. "There's something about your anger. I like it. And the thought of a bit of pain mixed with pleasure. I've never tried it before."

My head falls back. "Mia, I'm going to lose my mind with you."

I've never done more than a little slap before. I once asked Kim, and she told me that I was depraved for wanting to hurt her. I tried to explain that I didn't want to hurt her, I wanted to make her feel good. Either way, I've never brought it up with another woman since.

"Tell me if it's too much," I tell her right before my hand whips her ass cheek, this time with more force.

Just as she screams in response, I slam into her pussy from behind which only elevates her scream. But what I don't expect is the absolute feeling of contentment when I slide into her.

"Dammit!" I cry as I bottom out. "Your pussy was made for me."

I pull out and slap her cheek again, this time harder. I can already see my handprint take shape on her skin.

It brings out a primal animalistic feeling. I just marked her as mine, and now I'm going to fuck her like she's mine, too.

I grab her hair and wrap it around my fist then start to thrust harder than I thought was possible. Each time I pull out, I slap her ass which is now pink with my handprints. My dick tightens at the sight of it. When I start to feel her walls tightening around me, I grab each side of her waist and pound my dick inside of her until she screams her release and her walls have my dick in a vice, making holding out impossible. I spill my own release into the condom, both of us grunting and moaning together.

I slide in and out slowly until her muscles relax then I fall on top of her.

We both struggle to catch our breath as we lie next to each other.

"That was…" she starts but doesn't seem to have a word to explain what just happened.

"I know," I agree. There isn't any word in the dictionary that can adequately describe how that felt. I'm addicted already, I know it. "Let's get cleaned up."

After we both clean ourselves up, we crawl back into my bed. Despite my best efforts to keep my distance, I end up pulling her into me, as I fall asleep with my arm wrapped around her.

Chapter Fifteen

Mia

"How are you holding up?" Ma asks as I start to shuffle through missed emails from work.

I opted to set my laptop up on the front porch and enjoy some of the crisp morning air while I get back to work.

"I'm doing really good. It's peaceful out here," I tell her as I look around at the trees. "You should see the trees. I'll have to take a picture and send it to you."

"I'm so glad you found somewhere to go where you feel safe during all of this," she chokes on her words. I know Ma is having a hard time with this. I wish I had something more optimistic to say.

"I'm safe here, Ma. Eric paid for his place to be set up with the top security system."

"That's so sweet. I'm forever grateful to him for protecting my baby girl. I'm just sorry we weren't able to do it."

"Ma, don't do that to yourself. This is just for a little while. Just think of it as your daughter on a little vacation."

I eventually have to end the phone call, feeling like it's almost too hard for her to talk about my predicament.

I throw myself back into work, despite the massive amounts of texts from my brothers telling me I don't need to be working right now. I don't care. If I don't work, all I'm going to do is replay last night's events in my mind.

If I do that with Eric still in the house, I seriously might wind up begging him to take me again. I've never been so thoroughly fucked as I was last night. It felt like we were both not holding anything back from each other.

When I go in for lunch, I happen to see him sitting in his office right off of the foyer. He looks so handsome in his white t-shirt and jeans. He has such a ruffled look with a little stubble on his face. My heart beats faster just looking at him. I swear, my panties are a little wet. It's embarrassing the effect he has on me.

"Like what you see?" his voice pulls me out of my gawking.

There's something about that cocky smirk he has on his face right now. He knows exactly what he caught me doing, and he loves that he caught me.

I want to rip that smirk away. I want to do what he does to me. But it's not dark out. Will he push me away? Will it be too real for him? My feet seem to make up my mind for me as they start into his office until I'm right in front of him. He swings his chair so it's facing me.

"Something I can help you with?" he asks as he folds his arms across his chest.

His muscles flex in that position, showing me exactly how strong he is.

"Yeah, I was just thinking about something."

His eyebrows raise with interest. "What's that?"

"Last night you didn't let me finish."

"Finish what?" he asks, voice gruff now.

I sink to my knees and look at him with seductive eyes. He swallows slowly as he watches me.

"Last night," I say as a hand reaches up and grips him through his jeans, "I told you I wanted to taste you. You never let me."

I massage his dick as it grows hard under my palm.

"You—" his voice gets stuck, and he clears his throat. "You want to suck my dick right now?"

I nod my head and unbutton his jeans then pull down the zipper. I reach in and pull his dick out. It's thick and hard with a big vein running down the shaft. I can't help it, I lean down and run the tip of my tongue from the bottom to the top of the vein.

He groans and bites his bottom lip as he watches. "You want to taste my cum, Mia?"

I give him a devilish smile then wrap my lips around him. For a while, I tease him as I only suck on the tip. I move my tongue around it, getting it nice and wet then I pull away just enough to give the tip a kiss when a bit of precum gets on my lips.

He makes a low guttural noise. "Lick your lips, baby. That'll be your first little taste of me. But don't worry, I've got more."

I turn my head to the side. "You know, for a man with few words, you sure are a talker during sex."

He laughs loud and unashamedly. I realize I want to see more of that from him. He's truly something when he lets loose. I smile up at him, but the moment doesn't last for long. His eyes are hooded with arousal as he watches me take him back into my mouth.

I bob up and down his dick, using my hand on the part of it that can't fit in my mouth, which is a lot. He's bigger than any man I've ever been with. He starts cussing and groaning as I continue to take him, hollowing out my cheeks to make sure I suck him hard.

When I pop off of him, I grab his dick and push it up towards his stomach then start to lick the base of him where it meets his balls. Then I start to lick those as well.

"Fuck, Mia," he says as he grips the bun on top of my head. "Keep doing that."

I look up at him and slowly let my tongue run down his balls then lifting them and licking underneath. I'm so close to that forbidden area and he gasps with surprise, but doesn't stop me.

I start to stroke his dick while I run my tongue up and down, back and forth. His dick starts to twitch in my hands, letting me know that he's close. I adjust myself, rising up and put his dick back in my mouth.

I increase my speed until he is groaning his release into my mouth. His hands in my hair while he lifts himself off the chair, fucking my mouth until he's emptied himself out entirely

There's so much cum that it starts spilling out of my mouth. I pull off of him and his release is dripping down my chin. The look on his face tells me he likes the sight. I wipe it off with the back of my hand as we both continue to stare at each other. Our breaths mix together in the space between us.

"Let's get you cleaned up," he whispers, then takes my hand and walks me into the kitchen.

We stop at the sink, and he grabs a paper towel then wets it. He starts to wipe my face and chin softly, not saying a word while he does it. It feels like an oddly sweet gesture, as weird as that sounds. Then he cleans up my hands that have also managed to get a bit messy.

"There," he says softly.

I don't know what else to say in the moment. We broke the rule he set. We touched each other in the daylight outside of the bounds of his bed. Is he going to freak out? Are we going to keep doing it?

Instead of asking these questions I go with something light. "Are you hungry for lunch?" I ask.

He laughs again, in that way that makes my heart flutter. "Am I hungry for lunch? That's your response to me cleaning my cum off of you."

I shrug my shoulders. "We gotta eat."

"Yes," he nods with a grin, "I am hungry, Mia."

"Okay. Take a seat and relax that arm. I'll make us something."

And that's how we end up eating lunch together while talking about our childhood. He tells me about the kind of trouble he and his brothers used to get into while I tell him about the trouble I   used to watch my brothers get into.

Our family dynamic is very similar. We have a lot in common, and I get the sense that our brothers would get along. Not that there's any world in which our families would meet.

Chapter Sixteen

Eric

Layla has insisted that she come spend the weekend with Mia at my house. Josh is out of town meeting with a developer that wants to build in Savannah, and she wants to keep Mia company. That shouldn't piss me off, but it does. I go back to work on Monday, and that doesn't give me much time left alone with Mia.

No, this is good. I shouldn't be getting used to the idea of spending my time with her, or even sleeping with her. This weekend will be like a cleanse. No more touching Mia.

I'll keep my distance and let them have their fun. Maybe I'll slowly start back up on my work in the barn starting with a small project that won't put too much stress on my arm. Although, I'll be risking my secret getting out to Layla if I spend too much time out there while she's here. She'll ask questions.

I don't know why I've insisted on not telling my family about my hobby. I think I've been so used to the persona that I hide behind that I'd feel too raw exposing them to this. It's an emotional side of me and I'm not good at showing my emotions.

Mia and Layla decide to cook dinner together in my kitchen and get drunk off several bottles of wine that Mia brought with her. I've decided to call up the guys and get the hell out of here. Every time I turn the corner, Mia is there. I can't even look at her without my body reacting.

It's pathetic.

I'm at the bar with my brothers an hour later. The music is loud, the people are annoying, and I try to remember why I thought this was a better option.

"So," Asher says as he wipes his face with a napkin, pushing his plate aside, "are you going to tell us what's going on with you?"

I take a big sip of my beer before I respond. "What do you mean?"

Asher looks over at Liam and they both smile. "*You* asked *us* to go out. We're normally dragging your lame ass out of the house. Something's up if you're initiating it," Liam says.

"I just felt like getting out of the house. That's all," I lie, avoiding their eyes.

Asher doesn't miss a beat. "What's at your house that you're avoiding? Is there something going on with you and Mia?"

That makes me look up. Him and Liam are smiling. "What makes you say that?"

"Well, for one, you freaked out and made us secure your place like you're protecting the queen when you found out about Mia's ex. Add in the fact that you two were making googly eyes at dinner that night. I felt something brewing."

It's scary how on the money he is. I don't say anything back, which in of itself feels like an admission.

"I knew it," Asher chuckles. "Looks like you missed your chance with her," he swats Liam on the back of the head, "unless this chump is too chicken shit to actually seal the deal with her."

Pure hot rage pounds in my chest. "Over my fucking dead body will you ever touch Mia."

Liam smiles. "Tell me this. Why do you need to escape her company and get out of your house tonight?"

"That is none of your business."

"Isn't Layla spending the weekend there to keep her company?" Asher asks.

Liam gives me a pouty lip. "Aw, are you jealous that your sister is stealing time away from your crush?"

I roll my eyes at my brothers, who are both laughing like they made some hilarious joke, which they did not. "At least you make each other laugh," I mutter to myself then finish the last of my beer.

"All jokes aside," Asher's face goes serious. "Are you doing okay?"

For the first time in a long time, I feel this slight urge to talk. To tell them what's really going on in my head, but I stop myself. I'm not even sure I know the answer to that.

Instead, I shrug my shoulders and pretend like everything is fine.

By the time I get home, I'm worn out from the day. I walk into the kitchen to take some pain medicine for my arm and this throbbing headache that has come on, and am greeted by Mia and Layla who are deep into their second bottle of wine hanging over the counter laughing.

"Hey, you're back," Layla pops up enthusiastically. "We were just wondering when you would be back."

"Oh, yeah? Here I am," I say as I pop open the bottle.

"You feeling alright?" Mia's voice echoes behind me etched with concern.

I don't turn around to answer. Hoping that not looking directly at her will help even though all I want to do at the moment is bury my face into her chest and have her rub my head. It scares the shit out of me that that's what would make me feel better in this moment.

"I'm fine. Just a headache. I'm gonna turn in early."

I walk out of the room to Layla shouting at me to feel better. Just as I'm getting to the bottom of the stairs, I feel a warm hand grab mine.

"Hey," Mia looks at me with concern. "Are you sure you're okay? You were acting kind of weird all day today. Kind of seemed distant. Is it okay that Layla is spending the weekend?"

"Yeah, it's fine. Actually, it probably works out for the best."

Her head falls to the side. "What do you mean?"

"I just think we were heading into dangerous territory. Maybe with my sister here, it can be like a reset button. You can spend the nights with her, and we can go back to having a more platonic relationship."

Her shoulders sink and she looks away from me, clearing her throat. "I see," she says as her eyes meet mine again, now filled with moisture. "A platonic relationship. Got it. I hope you feel better, Eric."

She backs away from me, giving me the space I wanted. But for some reason, I don't feel relieved. The breath I thought would come easier with the distance is now becoming harder to take.

Chapter Seventeen

Mia

My head is pounding. I roll over in my bed where Layla and I both ended up passing out last night. I told her how I'm not sleeping too well on my own lately, so she agreed to spend the night with me.

Despite the pounding in my head, my brain brings me right back to the moment at the bottom of the stairs with Eric last night. It was like a punch to the gut. I didn't see it coming. Here I thought we were finally letting go and enjoying each other's company. We literally just had sex the night before and he already called it off not even twenty-four hours later.

What does that say about me? Is that all I'm worth to him—to all men?

Aside from my psychotic ex who wants to control me, all the men I've been with have found very little reason to stay with me. I want what my brothers have with their wives. I want someone who will fight like hell to be with me. To stand up to the world and tell them that I'm the one they love.

But my brothers were morons at first. It always took some convincing on my part to make them see the light and chase after the women they love. Who's going to be there to convince a man to do that for me?

More importantly, why would someone need convincing?

"Ugh, my throat is so dry," Layla whines next to me.

At least I have her here to distract me from her idiot brother. Maybe I can ask her some questions about him. Find out more about why he's so afraid of commitment.

"I think that's a wine hangover," I croak. "Did we drink any water with dinner last night?"

"Is there water in wine?" she asks.

I chuckle slightly. "Yes, I think there is."

"Then yes, we drank water, but I need real water right now."

We somehow manage to drag ourselves out of bed and downstairs. I catch a glimpse of Eric in his office but have no interest in saying anything to him. Maybe it's the wine hangover, but I'm feeling pissed at the world right now.

"I think we should order breakfast," Layla suggests in the kitchen as we both gulp down water like we've been lost in the desert. "We could have biscuits and gravy, pancakes, cheesy grits."

"Mmm, I think I'd like some biscuits and gravy."

"Biscuits and gravy it is."

An hour later, we are curled up on the lounge chairs by the pool in our sweatshirts as we devour our breakfast. With the food in my system, the sunlight, and the slightly cool breeze—I'm starting to feel slightly better.

"So, how is the wedding planning going?" I ask over a big bite of my biscuit.

"It's going. My mom is starting to get a little obsessed. She keeps going on and on about how I'm her only daughter and this is the only time she'll get to experience what it's like to see me try on a dress for the first time."

I smile. "That's sweet. I'm glad you and your mom are doing so much better. Have you tried any dresses on yet?"

"No. Oh, come with me!" she exclaims excitedly.

"What? Me?" I ask, feeling slightly uncomfortable.

"Of course! We are going to go next weekend. It would be so much fun!" she smiles brightly.

"That's so sweet of you to ask." I love Layla, but it's not like we've been able to spend a ton of time together with the distance between us. This feels like a lot for me to be a part of such an intimate event.

"It's settled. You are coming. That way if my mom has some god-awful taste, you can step in and be the tie breaker."

Later that night we are snuggled up on the couch about to watch a scary movie. Layla wants to get in the Halloween spirit. Eric walks in from outside, looking a little rough around the edges. It looks like he has saw dust on him.

"Where were you? What is all over you?" she asks absentmindedly, clicking through movie options.

His eyes meet mine. "I was just going for a walk and some of the moss from the trees fell all over me."

"Huh, weird," she says, barely listening. "Go get cleaned up and watch a movie with us."

"I'm not really in the mood."

"Come on. We never get to do these things with each other anymore. Pleeeease."

He rolls his eyes while his head falls back. "Fine. I'll be right back."

He's always acting annoyed by his family, but for a man who claims to want to be alone he gives in awfully quickly.

When he comes back downstairs, he's in black sweatpants and a white t-shirt. My body suddenly feels hot as my heart starts to pound against my chest. I despise this reaction my body has to him.

The way he touched me the other night. No man has ever fucked me like he did. But I was a fool to think that there was something different about him.

He sits on the chair diagonal from the couch that Layla and I are on. I do my best to get into the movie, but I'm too aware of his presence. Every time I steal a glance at him, his eyes are on me. He's not even trying to hide the fact that he's watching me.

I try my best to ignore him, but somewhere in the middle of the movie my eyes find him again. That's it. I'm not going to look at him again for the rest of the movie.

Only my eyes disobey me. Even when I tell them don't look, they do. The last time I looked, I saw the beginning of a smirk play on his lips before he remembered he's a dick, then he was back to acting broody and sad.

"What the hell? Why would they go further inside? It's clearly a setup. Why is it always the women they make do the idiotic things in scary movies? It's so insulting," Layla says while throwing her hands in the air. "My niece could make smarter decisions than them and she's five."

Layla manages to break the tension that was building. Enough for me to at least get back into the movie with her. We pop some popcorn and make fun of the decisions of the characters for the remainder of the movie.

Eric remains quiet, though Layla doesn't seem to think that is cause for concern. Once the movie is over, he stands up.

"I'm going to try and get some extra sleep. It's my last night before I go back into work."

"You have to go to work on Monday?" Layla asks sadly. "Boo, that sucks. Who will keep Mia company?"

I shift uncomfortably in my seat. I don't like being pitied.

Eric looks at me then back to his sister. "Mia is a strong woman. I think she'll appreciate me out of the house during the day. She can do whatever she wants here."

"Do you feel safe enough?" Layla continues. "I can try to take some time off at work."

"That's not necessary," Eric interjects. "I have surveillance all over the house. I will be monitoring it while I'm away. I'll make sure she's safe."

"Monitoring it?" I interject. "Like spying on me? Where are these cameras? They aren't in my room, are they?"

His eyes dance with mischief. "Why? Doing anything in there you don't want me to see?"

"Eeww! Gross. Get out of here," Layla cringes.

Eric looks amused as he walks away from us. He still didn't answer my question. Where are all of these cameras? And why does he still care so much about my safety if he only wants us to be platonic with each other?

Chapter Eighteen

Eric

"Nice to have you back," Jeremy says to me as he walks into my office. "How's the arm doing?"

I move it around like I need to check before I respond. "It's good. Still have some minor pain as I move it, but nothing I can't deal with."

He takes a seat in the chair in front of my desk. "I heard the acquisition is moving along nicely."

"Yeah, I managed to keep it afloat somehow while I was out."

"Word around the office is that you slacked off a bit on your week at home," he says as he scratches his chin.

I sit up straight in my chair, not sure I heard him correctly. "Excuse me? Who the fuck said that?"

He shrugs his shoulders. "I don't know. Just word around the office. Apparently, they said you should've been pulling twelve hour days at home to accelerate the process."

I don't know who is talking like that, but I'm not at all surprised. It's a cutthroat business. Every man for himself. If there's a way to make someone else look bad to get ahead, you take it. Only, I've never felt the need to play it that way.

"Whatever. Let them talk. They're going to anyway," I grit through clenched teeth.

"What did you do with your time off? Got some rest in hopefully. That text you showed me of the stitches was brutal. Almost passed out when I saw it."

That makes me laugh. "You're such a wuss."

"Dude, that cut was fucking deep. You're gonna have a nasty scar once it heals. Were you home alone when it happened? I probably would've fainted and bled out."

"You're quite the drama queen. No, I wasn't alone. My sister's friend was there. She drove me to the emergency room."

"I guess there was a silver lining to her staying with you after all." Voices outside my office break his attention. "I should get back to work before I'm tagged as the guy who talks and never works. Lunch today?"

"I think I'm gonna have to work through lunch. Apparently, I'm slacking."

He rolls his eyes. "Ignore the comments. I shouldn't have said anything. We'll catch up soon."

By Wednesday, I'm exhausted. I've spent all of my time at the office trying to get this acquisition ahead of schedule. I know I shouldn't let someone else's words get to me like this, but I can't help it.

To make matters worse, I discovered there are going to be more layoffs than I had initially anticipated once we acquire the company. It's not because I want to be a dick, but the company overstaffed in every department. No wonder they are struggling so much.

When I start to look at the amount of people I have to fire, I slam my laptop shut. This is the worst part of my job. I loathe it. I've been told to get over it, that it's part of the job. Or that these people will just go out and find another job and it's not that big of a deal, but they're wrong.

Some of these people have worked at the company for more than fifteen years. They've accumulated a lot of raises in those   years for their commitment to the company. Starting over somewhere else at their age could be the difference   between being able to send their kids to college or retire on time.

Unfortunately, my coworkers   don't think about things like that. They're only worried about making more money to maximize they're bonuses at the end of the fiscal year. But once upon a time, my family was that broke family. I was the boy with the old hand me down clothing from my brother and not the one with the latest Nike's.

I had always told myself I would never be in that position again. One where I struggled financially. But sometimes the thought crosses my mind that I was happier back then.

By the time I get home, the stress has mounted, and I need a drink. A strong one.

I open the door and there's silence. Mia has been distant ever since I pushed her away Saturday night. She didn't come to my bedroom last night, even though Layla was gone. I can't stop thinking about her which makes me miserable. And I'm angry that I'm the reason I'm miserable. I got spooked that night from my feelings and made a rash decision.

Now I have to feel her in my home without being able to touch her or even talk to her.

I go straight to the bourbon and pour myself a glass, not even making it to my office. I fall onto the chair in my living room and work my tie open as I take a sip of the auburn liquid, hoping it relieves the tension that's building.

"Long day?" Mia's voice startles me from behind.

I crane my neck to see her leaning against the large white column. I shrug my shoulders, not sure how to answer or maybe unwilling to. Either way she takes the hint.

She laughs sarcastically. "Whatever. Just thought I'd ask."

She begins to walk away, and I start to panic. "Yes, it was a long day."

When I no longer hear her walking away, a soothing feeling takes over my body. I don't know what makes me do it, but I start to talk. "I have an acquisition that I'm working on. Not only did I hear that people were criticizing my work ethic for not pulling twelve hour days while I was recovering, but I just found out that we're going to have to lay a lot more people off in this company than I had originally anticipated."

She appears in front of me, silent at first as she pulls out the ottoman and sits between my legs. "I can't believe they think you need to work twelve-hour days in general, but to expect it out of you when you clearly were injured and took your sick days. That's ridiculous."

Rather than look at her, I keep my eyes focused on the glass in my hand resting on my thigh. "The other men in the office probably would've done it. It's how you make the company money."

"That's bullshit. I run a successful company, and we treat our employees with respect. If you use your time off, you are entitled to actually take the time off. Life is too short to be married to your job."

I don't know what to say back to that. If she's right, then what the hell am I doing at this company?

I shake my head. That's ridiculous. I'm not leaving the company.

"How many more people do you have to lay off?" she asks, resting her elbows on her knees. Something I notice from the corner of my eye. I risk a glance at her and see concern in her eyes.

"About one hundred more people."

"That's a lot of people."

I nod my head. "That's a lot of families I could be destroying."

"That must be a really tough part of the job. I'm sure most people feel this way when it comes to these layoffs."

A bitter laugh escapes me. "Nobody else gives a fuck about the people they layoff. I'm looked down upon for caring. I've been told it's what makes me weaker than my other colleagues."

"That's gross. I think it's the other way around."

That makes me look back up at her. "What do you mean?"

"Only a weak man with a big ego would be unaffected by ruining lives. Someone like you, someone who cares about those people, that's a strong man."

I don't know what to say back to that. She thinks I'm strong. I care way more about that than I should. I'm not sure how long we look at each other, but it feels like she is looking into my soul. A loud sound coming from my stomach pulls us out of the moment.

She looks at her watch. "Did you eat dinner yet?"

I shake my head back and forth. "I didn't really have time to. I skipped lunch as well."

She sighs. "Eric, it's eight thirty. Come on, I'll warm something up."

When we get into the kitchen, she pulls out a plate that looks like it was already ready for me and pops it into the microwave.

She stands in front of the microwave while the food she prepared for me, despite me being a complete dick, warms up.

My body moves to her like we're magnets that are being pulled together. I stand right behind her, our bodies just barely touching then whisper in her ear. "Thank you for dinner."

The goosebumps on her skin are evidence that, in spite of my pushing her away, her body still reacts to me. I know I shouldn't, but I can't not touch her. I pull her hair off her neck and kiss her just above where her shoulder and neck meet.

"I'm sorry," I whisper.

Her body is still as I pepper her neck with another kiss. "For what?" she whispers.

"For pushing you away the other night."

I rest one hand on her hip and the other on the counter.

"Why did you do it?" she asks softly.

I turn her around until she's facing me, ignoring the beep of the microwave. I don't care about food right now. I think my body has been starving for her.

"I got spooked. I realized when my sister was going to spend the weekend, that meant I couldn't touch you or be with you all weekend. I didn't like it, and I didn't like that I didn't like it."

She smiles. "You are one with words."

"I never claimed to be a poet. I'm just trying to be honest."

"I appreciate honesty, but what I don't appreciate is being tossed around."

I tuck a stray piece of hair behind her ear. "I'll try my best. I just need you to know that I'm not looking for a relationship right now or ever really."

She bites her bottom lip as she looks up at me. "I'm just trying to find out if my ex is trying to kill me or not, and my life is back in Cleveland. I don't know what I'm looking for right now."

"One thing I can promise you. I may not ever be boyfriend material, but I can make you feel good, and I can protect you."

She sucks in a shaky breath. "I think I can handle that right now."

"Good," I spin her off of the counter and lift her on top of the island, "because I've decided what I need to eat right now isn't sitting in the microwave."

She throws her head back laughing. "Oh, no? Where is it?"

My hand moves between her thighs. "It's right here, and I can tell it's begging for me to taste it."

In the light of day, I can see her blush. I groan and my head falls to her chest. "Do you have any idea what your blush does to me?"

I look up and she shakes her head back and forth shyly.

"It starts here," I point to her cheek with my finger, "and it travels all the way down your neck." My finger drags from her face down to her neck until it reaches the top of her breasts, "and it ends right here on your chest. It was one of the first things I noticed about you, and it has driven me crazy."

I lean forward and gently kiss her lips, letting the kiss start slow and controlled. It doesn't take long before I slide my tongue into her mouth. She meets me with her own hunger, her hands grabbing the back of my neck as she increases the tempo of the kiss.

I pull away and grab her shirt. She raises her arms, and I slowly pull it over her head, throwing it on the floor then seal my mouth back to hers.

"Lift your ass for me," I say against her mouth.

She obeys my command. I rid her of her jeans and underwear then grab one of her legs and lift it up until her foot rests on the edge of the counter, opening herself up to me.

My thumb begins to rub circles around her clit. Her jaw falls slack as she watches. We both watch as I insert two fingers into her pussy, twisting my hand so my fingers can move along her g-spot.

There's something so hot about going slow while both of our eyes are locked on my hand. When I pull my fingers out, they are coated in her arousal. I drag them up and down her pussy before pushing them in her again.

This time I lean down and suck on her clit as my fingers push up against her walls.

"Oh, fuck," she exhales.

I moan into her pussy, letting her know how much tasting her turns me on. I lick her up and down as I suck on her clit, and then flick my tongue until she is grabbing my hair and screaming through her orgasm.

When I pull away and stand up straight, her eyes are hooded, and her chest is rising and falling.

I grab her leg and pull her towards me until her body is against mine and cover her mouth hungrily. I want her to taste herself on me. She reaches down and grabs my shirt and helps me get it off. Her eyes drink me in, dragging up and down my chest and abs.

"Do you like what you see?" I ask, loving the attention she's giving me.

She bites her lip and smiles. "I don't understand how you look like that. I haven't seen you work out once since I've been here."

"Not sure if you remember, but I sliced my arm open. Working out hasn't been possible."

"Oh, right," she laughs.

My dick is uncomfortably hard. Never have I felt like I would die if I didn't have someone, but it's starting to feel like that. I rub my hand against myself through my pants, hoping for some relief. She presses her lips against mine. Our tongues tangle together while her hand reaches down and grabs my dick. I groan as I push my hips forward into her hands. I need more.

Luckily, she starts to unbuckle my belt and I'm kicking off my pants and boxers within seconds.

"Spread those legs again for me, baby," I tell her as I push both feet to the counter this time. "I need to take you right here, right now before I lose it."

I grab the wallet out of my pants and take the condom I stash in there out. As soon as I'm covered, I stand between her legs.

She's leaning back on her hands, her slick pussy proudly on display. My heart beats erratically in my chest as I swallow slowly.

I line my dick up and slowly push inside of her. My eyes struggle to stay open, but I don't want to tear them away from where we are connected. When I bottom out, I steal a glance at her. Her face takes my breath away.

My hands grip each of her knees and push her legs up to her chest as I pull out then push back in a bit faster this time. I build up a rhythm until I have a good pace, slowly pulling out and then slamming back in.

I can feel her walls start to squeeze my dick, and I know we're both close.

"That's it. I feel that pussy ready to explode. You gonna come all over my dick, Mia?" I ask as I pick up the pace.

"Ahhh," she yells, "yes, I'm coming!"

I push her knees out and fuck her hard, her hands on the counter behind her needing to catch the force of my thrusts. "Fuck, that's right. I feel it. I'm right there with you."

I let myself go inside of her all the while feeling her own orgasm come down. I keep moving inside of her until her pussy stops convulsing completely then I drop her knees and fall forward, my head leaning on her shoulder as I try to catch my breath.

We don't move for a minute as we both work to even out our breathing.

"I think we need to reheat your food again," she finally says.

I laugh then pick my head off of her shoulder. "Now I'm officially starved. I didn't eat lunch or dinner."

Her eyes open wide while she shakes her head. I can tell she wants to say something, but just pushes herself off of the counter and goes straight for the microwave.

"I'm going to go get cleaned up. You better be eating when I come back down."

"Yes, ma'am," I say with a smirk as I take her in, scolding me while naked.

She rolls her eyes, but I catch her own smile before she turns around and walks upstairs. I throw on my boxers and pull the plate out of the microwave. It's a big plate of lasagna with some steamed vegetables on the side.

I decide to sit at the island and eat, not bothering to put on more clothes.

The bourbon bottle is sitting on the edge of the counter, reminding me how badly I felt that I needed it when I got home. Now I can't even remember feeling stressed. I just feel—satisfied. Relaxed.

I normally have to work out or go to my barn to get this kind of feeling after work. Fear grips me again at the thought of being this affected by someone.

But then she comes downstairs with a big smile on her face, and I realize there's no way I can push her away again.

Chapter Nineteen

Mia

It's Friday and I'm waiting around for Eric to get home from work. Since we had sex in his kitchen, he's more relaxed around me. It's like he's finally willing to accept that there's something between us.

It's nice to be open about our attraction to each other in the daylight and not have to hide it away until night time.

We did manage to wait until we were in his bed last night to have sex, but he did invite me to sleep in his bed at dinner. No sneaking into his room anymore.

I'm starting to feel happier and less afraid to sleep at night. I talked to my brothers. It seems as if Don is back in Cleveland. The police have confirmed it, and Gabe even stalked out his house to confirm it for himself.

They still want me to give it some time before I come home to make sure he doesn't leave again. But Gabe thinks I should be able to come back in the next couple of weeks.

That's good news. It's great news. I can go home and have my life back. So, why am I not excited about the idea of going back home?

Before I have time to analyze it, the door opens. Eric places his briefcase at the front entryway and kicks off his shoes.

He's been back to work for five days, and every day he comes home with a frown on his face. I don't want to say anything, but I don't understand why he stays at his job. Sure, he clearly makes a good living there based on his house, but it can't be worth it if he's miserable.

I now have a mission every day he gets home to put a smile on his face or at least relieve his stress somehow.

I have dinner ready on the table with wine already poured. It takes a little while to get him loosened up, but I eventually see the tension in his shoulders begin to fade.

After we eat, we're sitting on the couch with our wine when I spot the game of twister.

I laugh. "Playing Twister in your spare time?" I point.

He looks over and shrugs. "My niece brought it over one time."

I can't help the surprised look on my face. "And did you play it?"

He smiles. "Of course I played it. I can't say no to her."

That makes me laugh.

"What's so funny?" he asks.

"I just can't picture you playing twister.

"Pfft...I'm amazing at Twister."

"Too bad we don't have a third person here to be the spinner, because I'd love to see you try to beat me."

"Well, there just happens to be an app for that," he says as he pulls his phone out. "Go get the mat and set it up. Also, be prepared to lose."

"An app?" I ask as I get up.

He proceeds to connect his phone to the surround sound speakers, where there is indeed an app that will call out the colors and body parts for us.

Once the mat is spread out on the floor, we both stand on each end of it. He's ditched his work shirt for just his white undershirt and black slacks. He looks incredibly handsome.

The sound of a wheel spinning echoes through the speakers until it starts to slow down. His eyebrows raise at me with a smirk on his face as we wait.

"Left foot, red," the lady tells us.

I put my left foot on the red circle right in front of me. Eric walks onto the mat and places his foot on the circle next to mine instead of on the other end of the mat. I look up at him as he invades my space.

"What are you doing?" I ask.

He smiles down at me. "It's called strategy, Mia."

The wheel spins again, and we wait. This time I'm trying to figure out what my next move can be to mess with him. The next move is right hand green. Before he can do anything, I place my right hand on the circles that would be easiest for him.

I think I've won, but it is equally as awkward for me, and he ends up leaning over my entire body to get to his circle.

"Right foot, yellow."

We both manage to get our right feet on yellow, but my ass is in the air, and he is standing over me like he's about to fuck me from behind.

"Was this your strategy?" I ask as I look over my head. "To get me in this position so you could fuck me?"

He chuckles. "It wasn't, but I'm thinking this is ending up better than I had originally planned."

"Left hand, blue."

Fuck, our hands and feet are spread out on opposite ends of the mat. I'm already sweating. Our limbs are already a tangled mess, and it seems this was exactly what he was going for. While I already feel my arms tiring, showing my poor upper body strength, he feels sturdy as a tree above me.

A couple more moves and I have my left arm woven under my right, and my legs crossed giving me little balance from my lower body. I'm relying heavily on my arms to hold me up, and I feel my body start to shake from the strain of it.

He's laughing above me. "Are you having a seizure down there?"

"Fuck you. This is your fault, you got me all tangled up too quickly," I say through panted breath just before my arms give out and fall onto my stomach.

I roll onto my back and Eric is standing up with his arms in the air. "Victory is mine."

My eyebrows draw together as I watch him gloat. "I still feel like you did that to get me into a compromising position. Was this all about sex to you?"

He steps onto the mat until he's towering over me. "I was playing to win. If I wanted it to be about sex, I would've made it about sex."

My eyes open wide. "That kind of feels like a threat."

"Stand up and find out for yourself."

I don't know what the hell he's talking about, but the wheel starts to spin again so I think we are about to play another round. As soon as I stand up, he grabs his phone and pauses the spinner.

"I think I can call these next few on my own," he says as he looks my body up and down in the way that makes me break out into goosebumps.

"Turn around," he demands.

I'm not sure why he wants me to do that, but I also can tell by the look on his face that he'll get angrier by the second if I don't listen. I may also really want to find out what he's intending on doing.

"Left hand blue," he calls out standing behind me.

I place my left hand on the circle then wait for another command.

"Right hand yellow," he says as he takes a step closer to me.

I'm now standing with both hands on the mat, my knees bent slightly with my ass in the air. I watch him with my head upside down. He kneels right behind me.

"There it is. I think I like this position. Let's see how long you last here," he says, then I feel his hands at the top of my yoga pants.

Next thing I know, air hits my bottom when he pulls them down quickly with my underwear. His hands grip my ass and spread me apart. I don't think I've ever felt this on display for someone. But the guttural groan that reverberates from him makes me feel slightly more confident.

"This pussy, Mia. I think about it every second of the day. I dream about it. I swear, I live for it right now."

Those are his words before his mouth closes over my clit and sucks.

I moan instantly at the sensations it evokes. It feels like he has a roadmap to my body, knowing exactly which turns to take to make me come or how to draw it out. It's overwhelming.

His tongue drags long licks from my clit to my pussy as he spreads me wider with his thumbs. He makes his own sounds of pleasure like I'm the one doing it to him.

His tongue moves further until it hits my back entrance where his hands then grip my ass. His tongue continues circles at my hole which makes me let out a loud moan. It feels so good that my legs begin to shake. He starts to push his tongue inside then pull out, repeating this process as he fucks me with his tongue. He continues this while his thumb rubs my clit.

I'm panting and swearing as I'm on the edge, so close but just not there.

"You need more, Mia?" he says against my clit. "I can give you more."

He stands up and drops his pants, pulling a condom out of nowhere. Next thing I know, his thick dick pushes into me so slowly I want to scream at him. But with his hands on my hips, he takes his time until he's all the way in.

"Is that enough for you? You think you can come with my cock deep inside you now?" he asks then pulls out and pushes into me a bit harder this time.

He picks up speed, fucking me harder while keeping me upright with his hands on my hips. I'm begging for more, pleading for him to make me come when he sticks his thumb in my ass, and I go off. I can barely keep myself up, but I wait until I hear him come then my arms give out.

We both fall to the ground, laughing on our way down as we hit the mat.

I look over at him and witness him in hysterics, laughing without a care in the world. My heart suddenly beats off tempo, as I realize I've never felt more gratified in my life than watching this man break free from his own head, knowing I had something to do with it.

"I like playing Twister with you," I smile as I watch him.

His eyes have a twinkle in them when he looks at me. "I think I like everything more when it's with you."

And that's the moment I realize that I am falling in love with this man. Because no words have ever felt more right or more accurate. Everything feels better with him around, even if he's being a grump.

Chapter Twenty

Eric

I wake up in the morning to the smell of something incredible. I move my hand around the other side of the bed but don't feel Mia.

What is that smell?

I roll out of bed and stumble down the stairs to find Mia in nothing but one of my grey t-shirts standing in front of my stove. She has a spatula in one hand and a coffee cup in the other while she dances around to the music.

The sight of her in my clothes while dancing in my kitchen terrifies me, but only because of how much I like it.

I walk towards her and wrap my arms around her waist then nuzzle my head in her neck.

"Morning," I whisper. "I think this is my new favorite outfit for you." I lift it up until her cheeks come into view which makes me groan. "And no underwear. You're killing me."

She giggles then flips a pancake. "Not right now you animal. After we eat."

"Then let's hurry up and eat. This smells amazing by the way. The scent woke me up."

"Thanks," she smiles as she plates the last pancake. It's pumpkin spice pancakes with a cinnamon swirl on them topped with cinnamon butter."

"I see what you're doing," I cross my arms over my chest. "You want me to get fat. You're jealous of my abs that you keep commenting on and this is your plan all along."

She laughs. "You caught me. I'd rather be physically un-attracted to the man I'm sleeping with."

"I'm on to you," I say with a smile. "Seriously though, this looks and smells incredible. I feel like I should do something in return for all of this cooking you're doing. Maybe I can," I start, but quickly wish I can take it back.

I don't know why I thought it would be something she would like.

"Maybe you can what?" she asks curiously.

I shrug my shoulders feeling the heat in my face. I wish I never said anything, but it's too late. "I was going to say maybe I could make you something in my barn, but that's stupid. You have enough money. If you wanted something you would just buy it from a professional."

She places our plates down and wraps her arms around my neck then presses her lips to mine. She kisses me long and slow, making me savor each second of it until she pulls away.

Her hands slide to my neck, and she holds me in place while she looks up at me. "I would absolutely love you to make me something. That's so sweet of you to offer that. Can we go out to your barn so I can look around, maybe get some ideas?"

My throat bobs as I swallow, not able to speak. I nod my head up and down. I can't believe she actually wants me to make her something.

I have to look away, afraid I might just fall in love with her right here.

She turns around and grabs our plates then brings them to the island. We sit there and have a nice, casual breakfast. I ask more about her company, learning about all of the traveling she has done over the years. She has been to Italy more times than I could have ever dreamed. There's no way my work would allow me to be gone for long enough to do a trip to Europe.

It's incredible that she has been able to accomplish this success at such a young age with her brothers. And it sounds like they all love what they do.

After we eat, I insist on doing the dishes so she can go take a shower. Eventually, we end up walking back to my barn. The walk back to it is silent, but I feel at peace for the first time in ages.

Once we get into the barn, I turn on the light and the familiar feeling that washes over me whenever I step in hits me. Everything feels simple and easy in here.

I know that when I get to work, my mind will settle in ways that it can't anywhere else in my life, minus when I spend time with Mia, and that's a terrifying realization.

I follow her around as she looks at everything I have in here. I've sold some items to random people online, but I am constantly working in here, so I have an entire wall filled with my work.

Her hands slide gently over my art as she studies everything. I can't take my eyes off of her. The way she purses her lips while she thinks, how her eyes open wider when she likes something, I'm drawn to every movement.

"You really are talented. Why aren't you doing this for a living?" she asks as she continues down the line.

"It's not a career. It's a hobby."

"Who said woodworking isn't a career? There's plenty of people who do this for a living."

I kick the dirt below me as I avoid looking at her. "People would think I'm crazy if I left my career to do something that pays less, like a lot less."

"Why do you care what people think? Isn't it more important for you to be happy?" she says like it's so simple.

"Who said I wasn't happy? You've known me for a couple of weeks. If you're implying that I'm not happy," I reply, slightly annoyed that she is seeing right through the walls I put up.

"Forget I said anything," she says quickly. "I'm sorry."

I don't know why she thinks I'm not happy. So, I don't wake up every day excited to go to work, but—does anybody? It's called being an adult. We can't all love our job and make the kind of money that she makes. She's living in a fantasy world if she thinks that happiness in a career should be everyone's goal.

"Okay. I think I know what I want you to make me," she stops and faces me with a smile.

In an instant, I forget that I'm mad at her. I raise my eyebrows. "What would you like?"

"I want a porch swing like the one you have on your front porch. I've been too afraid to sit on yours because there's no wall behind it, and I keep picturing my ex in the bushes, but I would love one for my house."

My jaw tightens as she tells me about her latest fear. Just the thought of anyone making her feel afraid sparks a fire in my chest. I hate that her ex has any kind of hold on her.

"A porch swing it is," I say through my unyielding anger in hopes to distract her from her fear. "Let's go pick out the wood and stain you want."

Later that day, I'm sitting in my office trying to catch up on some work when I get a text message from my mom reminding me that we are having a family dinner at my parents' house tonight.

The first thing I think is that I don't want Mia spending the evening alone, but that's not all of it. I don't want to spend the evening away from her.

I stand up out of my chair and find her reading a book in the reading room I have upstairs.

"Reading anything interesting?" I ask as I lean against the door frame with my hands tucked into my pockets.

She looks up at me as a hint of red stains her cheeks. "Probably nothing you would be interested in."

Now, I'm curious. I push off the frame and sit on the side of the lounge chair that she's lying in. I grab the book from her hands and start to read. My eyebrows shoot up when I read the words, a bit taken aback.

"Why Miss Giannelli," my voice mutters deeply, "these are some dirty words."

She worries her lip which makes my dick slightly hard knowing what those lips can do. "I've never read a book quite this—graphic before."

"Oh really? Might I ask what has inspired this upgrade in your smut reading?" I ask as I hand the book back to her.

Her lips turn up slightly. "It may or may not have something to do with this guy. He's a big grump, but kinda phenomenal in bed."

Her words hit me like a knife in the chest. "Maybe he's not such a bad guy under the surface."

She turns her head to the side, analyzing me curiously. "I never said he was a bad guy. From what I can tell, he's pretty fantastic."

Why does it feel like someone sucked the oxygen out of the room? I try to breathe but it feels impossible. I grab her book out of her hand and place it on the table next to my chair.

"What are you doing?" she asks defensively.

I place my hands by her ears, caging her in. "Mia, you are all flushed right now. I bet your pussy is wet from your dirty book. But I think I can help you with that."

"What if I was going to use my fingers to take care of myself?"

A groan leaves my chest. "If you want to touch yourself in my house, you have to do it in front of me."

I push off of the back of the lounge chair and scoot all the way to the opposite end of it. She's in a green cotton dress that brings out the color of her eyes. I'm temporarily stunned by her beauty.

"What?" she asks hesitantly.

"Lift your dress and spread your legs for me," I growl as I lean back on the other end of the lounge chair.

She delicately moves her legs until they are spread right in front of me. Her legs are so toned and fit, it makes me want to run my hands along them. Then she slowly lifts her dress like she's revealing a secret to me. My throat bobs as I wait with baited breath. Her white lace underwear makes her look innocent. The sight of it makes my dick grow uncomfortably hard in my pants.

"That's it, baby," I praise. "Now pull those panties to the side. Show me that pussy." She obeys my command and I'm rewarded with the sweetest pussy I've ever tasted. "There you go. You are already so wet. Go ahead and spread it around your pussy. I want to see all of you glistening down there."

She uses all of her fingers as she moves her arousal from her entrance and up to her clit. Fuck, I'm going to explode in my pants. No one has ever made me feel this turned on without even touching each other. She starts to move her fingers over her clit slowly as her jaw falls.

"Do you like how that feels, baby?" I ask.

She nods her head up and down quickly.

"Good girl. Keep going. Move your fingers faster."

A delicate moan escapes her as she starts to move faster circles.

"Pull those lips apart for me," I demand. Wetness drips out of her when she pulls them apart. "Fuck, baby. Don't waste your juices. Use your fingers and push it back inside of you."

"Oh, god," she screams as she fingers herself.

Her eyes are hooded as she watches me. "I want to see you do it."

"What?" I ask hoarsely, still mesmerized by her fingers moving inside of her.

"I want to watch you touch yourself," she breathes heavily. My eyebrows pull together as I watch her thoughtfully, not sure how to respond. "Please," she begs.

I don't think any woman has ever wanted to watch me touch myself. This woman in front of me is so confident in asking for what she wants. I could never deny her. I let my legs fall over each side of the chair and unbuckle my belt then pull down my zipper. My dick approves of this new turn of events as it is already begging to break free. I pull it out and give it a nice hard tug.

"Yes," she says on a loud exhale.

"Oh, you like that baby? You like watching me stroke my cock?" I growl as my hand moves up and down my shaft.

She nods her head then moves her fingers back up to her clit. Our eyes are everywhere, not sure whether we want to hold eye contact or watch the other one touch themselves. I start to grip my dick tighter and work him harder which makes me release a groan. But I don't want to come this way, this far apart from each other.

"Come here," I tell her as I reach into my back pocket for a condom.

She doesn't hesitate and is on her hands and knees crawling to me before I can get the condom on. "Turn around. I want you facing the other way," I demand.

I want her reverse cowgirl for this so I can watch my thick cock stretch her tight cunt. She remains on her hands and knees but turns until her beautiful ass is in my face, slightly covered by her lacy underwear.

Fuck, I want to eat that ass. I smack a cheek and only faintly hear her scream because I'm so damn entranced by her. Then I grab her thighs and pull her ass up to my face. I pull her panties out of the way and stick my tongue into her back entrance as I squeeze each of her cheeks tightly. I lick and play with her ass until she's begging me to fuck her, which is music to my ears.

"You are doing the fucking, baby," I tell her as I lead her back down to my dick, her wet ass in perfect view.

She places one knee on each side of my thigh then I slowly guide my tip into her pussy. Before I tell her to, she pushes her ass down until I'm seated all the way into her.

"Fuck," I moan as my head falls back and my eyes almost roll into the back of my head.

It's pure ecstasy. But I don't want to miss the view so I pull my head back up. She starts to bounce on top of my dick like she's done this a million times, but for the sake of my sanity I tell myself she's only ever done this with me.

I grab her hips and help her up and down my dick. Her pussy is squeezing my dick already. Each time she pulls away, my dick is wetter than it was before.

"You look so hot taking my dick, Mia. Keep going like a good girl. Fuck me until you make me come."

She picks up the pace and starts moaning her own pleasure. I smack her ass again and her pussy instantly spasms around my cock as she comes all over me. Her juices start to drip out of her which is enough to send me over the edge into my own mind blowing orgasm.

We both are gasping for air even though I didn't even do any of the work. She slides off of me and adjusts her panties then falls onto her back on the other side of the chair.

"Do you want to come to dinner with me at my parents tonight?" The words are out before I have time to process what I'm asking.

Her eyes open wide in shock. "What?"

"My parents are having everyone over for dinner. I want you to come."

I'm not sure what has come over me, but it's true. I want her there with me tonight, and I'm in no mood to analyze why or come up with an excuse.

"Oh, okay. Um, yeah if you don't think I'd be imposing."

"Of course not. Layla and my mom would be thrilled. I'll let my mom know to set an extra plate before we go if it makes you feel better."

She smiles and nods. "Okay. I'd be happy to go with you."

I smile across the chair. "Good. I'm gonna go grab a shower. We're supposed to be there around five."

As I walk back to my room, I know I'm fucked. I'm on a train with no guardrails, but I can't seem to slow it down.

Chapter Twenty-One

Mia

I'm trying not to read into why he wants me to go with him to dinner at his parents. It's probably just because he feels bad that I'd be all alone here. There is no reason to pretend like it's something more than it is.

But it sure does feel like it.

No, I'm not going to do this to myself. We are just two adults having some fun and getting to know each other while he helps me through this crisis in my life.

Even so, I take extra time getting ready. I choose a caramel-colored cashmere sweater with black jeans and brown boots. The caramel brings out the natural caramel highlights from the summer in my long brown hair. I tease the top to bring a little body to my hair and put on some subtle looking makeup.

Then I spray myself with my favorite perfume.

When we walk into his parents house, his warm hand rests on my lower back the entire time like he's telling me he's got me. It's comforting and confusing as hell.

"I'm so glad he brought you," Layla bounces up and down. "Come on, Brie and I are playing store."

That instantly makes me feel at home. I love playing with my niece Sienna. I walk into the room off the kitchen which has random items from around the house displayed all over it, and a small pink toy register.

"I invited my friend Mia to play with us," Layla says to Brie.

Brie smiles at me. "You can be the register worker."

"Wow," I say as I join her. "That's a pretty big honor. Thank you."

I've played this with my niece, so I know how coveted the clerk position is to kids. Layla and I play several rounds of store with her until Layla manages to get Liam and Josh in the room. Brie convinces them to play, and we sneak away for a drink.

"So, how have you been? Any word about Don and his whereabouts?" she asks as she pours us a glass of wine.

I take my glass. "Thanks. Actually, the police have confirmed he's back in Cleveland. My brothers just want to give it another couple of weeks to settle down and have him followed before I go back home."

A hint of sadness crosses her face. "That soon?"

I smile. "It'll be a little over a month by then."

She sighs. "I know. It just feels like you got here yesterday. I've really liked having you here. And I think Eric has too."

Before I can ask her what that means, Josh comes in and grabs her hand. "You don't get to escape that easily. Brie has insisted that Auntie Laylay and Uncle Josh shop as a family."

They both walk away laughing together hand in hand. I watch them in envy, wishing I had someone that loved me that way.

"They're annoyingly cute, aren't they?" Eric startles me.

I turn around and lose my breath again just like I did when he walked downstairs tonight before we left. He looks so damn handsome with his cream sweater which has a zipper that goes down about a fourth of the way, paired with dark jeans and brown shoes.

"I don't know that I'd say annoyingly," I say standing beside him.

"Trust me, it's annoying. They make it look easy."

I look up at him and once again want to know more about him. I want to know about his past relationships. Was he ever in love? Did she hurt him like I suspect?

"Maybe it's easy when you find the right person," I whisper as I watch him.

He doesn't respond, just looks deep in thought. I don't know if he's going down a dark path of memories or not, but I suddenly feel the urge to change the topic.

"Your parents' home is beautiful. It's what I would have pictured a large southern home to look like, but it's somehow even more beautiful in person."

When he looks back at me this time, he appears more laid back. Like whatever was on his mind is now a distant memory. He smiles. "Care for a tour?"

I smile in return. "I'd love one."

He grabs my hand and pulls me away from the kitchen. "I think you've seen most of the first floor, but we can do a general recap."

He never lets my hand go all through the tour of the basement, backyard, and first floor. As he leads me up the stairs, I start to wonder what his family must think if they spot us holding hands.

"Is this the house you grew up in?" I ask once we make it to the top of the steps.

"I guess you could say that. We moved into this house when I was eleven. Before that, we didn't have much money. It was a bit of a culture shock for me."

"Sometimes money makes things complicated."

He doesn't respond to me but opens the first door on the left. "This was my room. Not much to look at."

"Wait," I stop him before he can close the door. "It looks like your parents haven't done much with the room. Is this all of your stuff?" I ask as I walk into the room.

"They haven't changed much in all of our rooms. A fresh coat of paint and some new bedding, but other than that it's all the same."

The colors are just what I would have guessed for a teenage boys room with blues and greys. There's dark wooden furniture that shows its age, but is still expensive looking. There's some Green Day and New Found Glory posters hanging on the walls above the desk.

"You listened to punk rock?" I turn and smile.

He chuckles. "Yeah, I still find myself listening to that music in the car."

"Does it feel weird when you come in here?" I ask him, opening a drawer in his desk.

He takes a seat on his bed then lies back. "Not really. I don't really think about it. I'm usually in here just to crash for the night. I don't really look at anything."

Nothing but old school notebooks and pens. I open the next drawer.

"You being a little snoop over there?" he asks.

"I'm curious to know more about teenage Eric. You're not much of a talker. That means I have to resort to snooping to figure you out. Plus, is it really considered snooping if you're sitting right there watching me?"

Another smile from him. I feel like I've won the lottery tonight. He's starting to loosen up around me, and my heart explodes with joy every time he does.

"Oh, jackpot," I exclaim as I pull out the contents of the last drawer. "Yearbooks."

I grab a stack of them and run over to the bed to join him. We both sit up and lean our backs against the headboard.

"Is this high school?" I ask as I open the top one.

He nods. "Looks like my senior year."

I flip through the pages until I find the senior photos then skim the names until I find him. "Dang, you were sexy even at eighteen. I bet you got any woman you wanted back then."

He shrugs his shoulders. "I did okay."

"When did you lose your virginity?" I ask curiously.

"Fifteen."

"Someone in this yearbook?" I ask, feeling jealous all of a sudden of someone that got to have that special moment with him.

"Leah Pearce," he says. "She was in my grade."

I scan the pictures until I find her. Long blonde hair, blue eyes, high cheekbones. Why am I not surprised? She's in a cheer uniform. The picture is only from the shoulders up, but I see the uniform.

"She's pretty." My words are sullen and bitter, even I can hear it.

I see his chest reverberate as he laughs. "Are you jealous of a high school girlfriend of mine?"

My jaw drops. I don't know if it's from shock that he would accuse me of that or if it's seeing him so playful. "I am not jealous of someone you were with twenty years ago. That would be humiliating."

His fingers brush against my cheeks. "I guess that's why you're blushing."

"Maybe we should talk about the men that have touched my body and see how you like it."

His smile fades. His jaw clenches as his eyes burn with a cold, dangerous intensity. "I don't fucking want to hear a word about anyone else touching you."

My body burns with desire. Watching this man rage with jealousy over me makes me feel like this thing between us is something—like we're more—like I'm his. The moment is too tense, I have to look away.

I find a yearbook that looks much older, faded edges and paperback versus a hardback cover. I reach for it, and it opens perfectly to a worn-out page. At first glance, there's nothing out of the ordinary about the page. It's a collage of photos scattered about both sides. The kids in the picture look young, like eleven or so.

Then I notice a picture of two kids smiling at a camera. A boy and a girl. Only the girl is scratched out with a pen, her face barely visible.

"What happened here?" I ask as my finger traces over the pen mark. It's thick, like whoever did it was pressing hard against the paper.

"That is Becca."

I wait for more to come, but he doesn't offer anything. "And why is Becca's face scratched out?"

He sighs. "We were twelve at the time. I didn't handle things in life very gracefully back then."

Is it rude to say I've only known him for a couple weeks, but I don't think he handles things very gracefully today? Probably. I'm just going to keep my mouth shut. I look over at him with raised eyebrows.

He rolls his eyes but continues. "I was in love with her. At least I thought I was," he looks down at the comforter, picking a piece of fabric off of it.

"That was right before my dad's business hit it big, and we were struggling financially. I only wore hand -me -down clothes. I never had the new shoes or hats like the other boys in my class. But Becca and I hung out a lot. I thought there was something there. So, one day I got the nerve to ask her out. While I was asking her out, my friend came up to us and started laughing."

His face looks down, like retelling the story still hurts. I want to tell him he can stop, but I also want to know what happened. This feels like a big moment in his childhood. Something that really left an impact.

"He threw his arm around her. He told her she can do better than a kid like me who couldn't even afford to go to the movies with her. She smiled softly and walked away with him."

I'm filled with anger. Anger for the man sitting in front of me, for the injustice of someone being treated that way at such a young age with no repercussions. For the twelve-year-old Eric who found out how shallow and cold the world can be.

I grab his hand and thread my fingers through his. We both look down where our fingers are laced together. It makes me feel something that I can't describe. Like I've been searching for something my entire life and I've finally found it.

A small tear drips down my cheek. I look up at him. "I'm sorry. I wish I could go back in time and be there. I would punch your friend and tell off the girl for not only letting him get away with it, but for walking away with him."

He smiles. "I can see you doing that, even at a young age. You definitely have this ability to move through life without anybody getting you down."

I wish that were the case. "It may seem that way. I put on a brave face a lot, but I have my own demons. We all do."

He rests his head back against the headboard, still looking at me. "What are your demons?" he asks softly.

I know it hasn't been easy for him to open up to me. As much as I don't want to say any of this out loud, I want him to know me. I trust him despite every action of his telling me that I shouldn't.

"I'm afraid I'll never find someone who will fight for me or love me the way my brothers have fought for their wives," I start, hoping the tears that threaten to come can hold off. "I'm the youngest of the four, but I've always been the one who looks out for them. I've had to talk them through their hiccups in life, been around to make sure they don't do anything stupid or help them pick up the pieces when they inevitably do."

His fingers begin to slide along mine back and forth as I continue. "Whether it was every girl on the block or my own friends, I was always watching everyone around me do anything they could to get to my brothers. I guess I've always just felt—invisible."

A single tear escapes despite me trying to blink it away. He takes his free hand and with the back of his finger, wipes it away. Then grabs my chin and forces me to look at him. His face is serious.

"You're not invisible to me, Mia."

But would you fight for me?

I don't speak those words because I think I know deep down what the answer would be, and I don't think I can handle it

The sound of footsteps running up the stairs breaks the moment. We both jump off the bed just as Layla walks in.

Her eyebrows raise when she walks in. "There you guys are. I've been looking all over for you. Dinners ready."

I walk quickly towards the door, leaving behind the yearbooks spread out on the bed. "I'm sorry. We were just looking at his yearbooks."

"Oh, gosh. Did he show you his awkward years? He was such a dork," she laughs as we all walk downstairs.

I look over at Eric. "No, I didn't see any awkward years. But I'd love to see them after dinner."

"Oh, please. Layla, you had plenty of your own awkward years. Should we pull out the old photo albums?" Eric pushes her shoulder just as we make it to the dining room.

"I've never seen any awkward pictures of Layla. I'll bet that's not possible," Josh says as he gives her a kiss.

"Ha!" Liam laughs. "Trust me, it was possible."

"Stop it," Stella says. "All of my kids were exactly who they were supposed to be. No one was awkward."

"You did dress them awfully odd when they were younger," Dan, their father quips.

"It was the eighties. I dressed them the way every other parent dressed their children back then."

"Aww, Ash has an old box of photos at our house. We went through them a couple months ago," Charlotte says as she rubs her growing belly.

"Did you know that Daddy was a kid?" Brie announces to the table, like it is some huge secret that no one could possibly have been aware of.

Everyone at the table joins in laughter. Brie smiles but clearly doesn't know what she said that was so funny.

"Yes, I remember when your dad was a kid," Stella replies.

Brie's eyes light up. "You do?"

She's so sweet and innocent. I can't help but wonder what it would be like to have my own children one day. I've always dreamed of becoming a mother. I steal a glance at Eric and try to picture him as a father. Judging by the way he seems to adore his niece, he would be a great father.

After dinner is over and dishes are cleaned, Eric and I head back to his house.

"Thanks for inviting me," I tell him in the silence of the car. "I had a great time."

He smirks. "Thanks for coming. I'm glad you were there."

Gosh, I'm so gone for this man. There's nothing special in the words he said, but they make my heart flutter. Probably because him even admitting that he is happy to have me around his family is a big declaration for someone like him.

We both learned more about each other tonight. We are moving quickly past the line of friends who are sleeping together into dangerous territory.

When we climb into bed together, we both turn on our sides and face each other. A soft warmth fills the space between us as we gaze into each other's eyes. His eyes linger on me as a gentle smile plays at the corners of his lips.

I feel the depth of his affection in the way he is looking at me, as if I'm the only person that matters. Time slows down in the quiet of the moment.

His hand gently cups my cheek as his thumb grazes my lower lip. I close my eyes as he leans in, his lips barely brushing mine at first, a soft, teasing touch that sends shivers down my spine.

His mouth moves against mine with a slow, deliberate rhythm, deepening the kiss with a tender intensity. Every movement feels unhurried, each second drawn out, as if he's savoring the taste of me.

The kiss ignites something deeper, more consuming in me.

He rests his warm hand on my thigh and slowly moves it under my t-shirt and onto my back then dips down to my ass. He squeezes lightly, and I moan into his mouth.

He rolls me over and cages me in while his body moves over mine. I feel the evidence of his arousal against my stomach. It only further sparks the intensity of my building desire.

My hand rests on his back then glides into his boxers, the only piece of clothing he has on, and grips his firm cheek. I push his boxers down until they move down to his feet.

His breath accelerates as he moves on top of me. "What are you doing to me?" he whispers. "I can't control myself around you. I need you."

I grab his length and move my panties aside.

"I'm on the pill and I'm clean," I whisper.

With that, he pushes inside and we both gasp into each other's mouths. Why does it feel like the first time every time?

Chapter Twenty-Two

Mia

I wake up in his bed and he is nowhere to be found. I think about how he touched me last night, how he kissed me, and bring the sheets up to my face as a smile spreads across my face.

I throw on my t-shirt and walk downstairs to grab a cup of coffee. I figured Eric got up early to work in his office, but much to my surprise, I walk into the kitchen and he is making breakfast...in his boxer briefs.

It's quite the sight to behold.

"What's happening in here?" I ask.

He turns around and breaks into a big grin. "Morning, beautiful. I thought I would cook you some breakfast then head into the barn and start working on your swing."

"Wow. You're making me breakfast?" I sit down and he pours me a cup of coffee then moves back to the skillet.

"Now, no judging. I can't make fancy pancakes or anything special. It's just eggs, bacon, and toast."

I smile. "Sometimes the classics are the best."

He gets the food on the plates and places them on the island.

"Thank you," I tell him as I grab a fork. "I don't think a man has ever cooked me breakfast before."

"Really?" he asks as his forehead lifts in surprise.

I shrug. "I guess once you show someone that you know how to cook, you just get assigned that task from then on."

"I don't see how that's fair. So, what time is Layla picking you up today?"

"She said nine." I look over at the clock on the microwave. "I guess I don't have much time."

I wish I could spend more time eating breakfast with him, but I need to run upstairs and get ready. I lean in for a kiss and thank him again before darting upstairs.

On my way up, I realize I'm embarking into dangerous territory with Eric. Going to his parents for dinner, being vulnerable with him, and giving small kisses to each other. I'm setting myself up for heartbreak.

We get to the bridal shop and her mom is already there beaming with excitement.

She kisses me on the cheek. "Mia, I'm so happy you could join us. It'll be such a fun girl's day out."

"I'm so happy you guys are letting me be a part of this."

"Hello, is this the Williams group?" a blonde woman, who looks to be in her fifties, greets us in a black blazer and pants.

"It is. I'm Layla."

"Ah, the beautiful bride. Congratulations. My name is Made-lyn. We have your private area set up in the back. You all can follow me."

She brings us to the back where there is a cream couch for me and Stella to sit. There is a fitting stand surrounded by mirrors with lights surrounding it as well as a private changing area off to the right.

"Okay, so the first thing I want to do is get an idea of what you like," Madelyn says. "Then I will pull some dresses for you to try."

Layla goes through what she thinks she wants in her dress while Stella and I listen. When Madelyn leaves to go pull some dresses, we are served champagne.

"Cheers," I say as I raise my glass. "To Layla getting her happi-ly-ever-after. No one deserves it more."

"Aw, you're too sweet. I'm so lucky. I can't believe I'm marrying the first man I ever loved."

"We're thrilled that Josh will be part of the family," Stella says as she pats Layla's leg.

I take a sip of the cool champagne, the bubbles fizz and pop like soft fireworks in my mouth. For a moment, I picture what it would be like to be a part of their family, to marry Eric, and my heart flutters with excitement.

I don't know where it comes from, but it stops me in my tracks. I'm perfectly happy living my life in Cleveland. That's where my family is. Never once did I consider moving away. But would I do it for somebody I love? My brother Marcus did it to be with his wife Lexi. He now lives in Chicago with her. She needed to be close to her sick mother, and he moved to be with her without looking back.

This is crazy. Eric wants nothing to do with a relationship. He has been clear about that.

But things between us have changed. It feels like he's changed. He smiles and laughs now. When I'm with him, it's like his shoulders are relaxed, and he isn't constantly on edge.

"So, how has living with Eric been?" Layla asks, breaking me from my thoughts.

"Oh, it's been good. Not really much to report. Just kind of laying low."

Layla looks at her mother and they both smile.

"What?" I ask suspiciously.

"I don't know. Eric has been different. He smiled like ten times at dinner last night," Layla says.

"And he is awfully protective of you. Installing all of those security cameras and motion detectors," Stella adds before taking a sip of her champagne.

I can feel my cheeks heat at their words. I touch my face, wondering how obvious it is.

Stella smiles. "You don't need to be embarrassed, honey. We think it's great."

"I don't," I start but get cut off.

"Okay. Here we go," Madelyn says as she walks in holding up several dresses. "I'm going to hang these right here on this rack. You tell me which one you want to start with."

Layla puts down her drink and nearly leaps off of her seat.

The rest of the afternoon we spend sipping on champagne while oohing and ahhing over how beautiful Layla looks in each dress. Being the decisive business owner that she is, she was able to nail it down and pick her favorite one with ease.

It was one of those moments when they dim the lights and add accessories like a veil and heels. All of a sudden, it's real and emotions bubble up.

It was beautiful to watch Stella and Layla cry over the perfect dress. I feel honored to have been part of the moment.

But I can't stop thinking about what they said to me earlier. How Eric seems happier and protective of me. I'd be lying if I said I hadn't noticed it myself, but it's dangerous to live in those thoughts for too long. It will only lead to my heart being broken, which I'm pretty sure is something that is inevitable at this point.

Chapter Twenty-Three

Eric

Mia has been with me for five weeks now. Can someone change your life in five weeks? I feel different from the man I was when she first got here.

It's harder to get through a workday now. Everything here feels mundane and monotonous. I keep picturing the swing I'm building for her. It's almost done and I'm itching to get into my barn and finish it.

I didn't even want to go to work today. Mia got a call from her brother last week. Her neighbor said she saw that ex-boyfriend of hers snooping around her house the other night.

I fucking hate this guy. What does he want with her? I don't even like to ask myself that question because I'm terrified of the answer.

At this rate, I don't see how I could ever feel good about her going back home. Not just for her safety, but I'd be a fool not to admit that I feel something for her. Every night on my way home from work, I tell myself to keep a wall around my heart.

Yet the second I walk in the house and see her face, I feel like another piece of that wall falls.

But I still love what I do, right? I mean I've worked my entire life to get to this point. Who throws that all away? Not me.

Yet when it hits five o'clock, I close down my computer and head out to my car. I've left at this time all week, with the promise to myself that I will eat dinner and get back to work in my office for the rest of the night.

Only I don't. Instead, I go to my barn where Mia comes out with some wine and talks to me while I work. We laugh and joke around. I even fucked her up against the wall which was one of the hottest moments of my life.

As soon as I open the door and see her face, there it is. That feeling in my chest that feels tight while the rest of the muscles in my body seem to relax.

I lean down and kiss her lips.

"How was work?" she asks with her perfect smile.

I groan. "It was fine."

She laughs. "You've groaned and said it was fine every night this week."

"What did you do today?" I ask, wanting to steer the conversation away from my work. It makes me tense enough while I'm there.

"I worked on some new marketing ideas," she says, reluctant to make eye contact with me.

I'm not sure what that's about but I shrug it off.

Then we spend the night watching some ridiculous show that I claim to hate but find myself sucked into the drama. Another night that I never thought I would enjoy if you described it to me a year ago, hell even a month ago, but now it feels right.

"What do you think the best type of cheese is?" Mia asks as we snuggle on the couch drinking a glass of her favorite red wine.

Laughter erupts in my chest. "What kind of question is that?"

She swats my stomach. "It is a perfectly valid question. At least coming from someone who is Italian and loves to cook. I'll go first," she offers. "I think pecorino romano is the best. It has a sharpness to it that comes through in your cooking without being too overpowering."

"Does the creamy kind you use in boxed mac and cheese count?"

She tries to sit up, but I pull her back down trying to contain my laugh. "I'm kidding. I really like goat cheese. I've had it in salads and stuffed pork. It always tastes amazing."

"Hmm. That's a good answer. I approve."

"Well, thank you. I guess. I didn't realize my favorite cheese would be so important."

"You can tell a lot about a person by what their favorite cheese is."

I pull her in tighter to my chest. "I suppose you can."

Honestly, I have no idea what she is talking about, but she sounds cute talking about it so I'm going with it.

"Wanna watch a movie?" I ask, not wanting to end the evening just yet. It's so peaceful lying here with her. Once I sleep, the morning will come faster, and I'll be at work.

"Sure. Wanna watch a chick flick?"

"What?" I laugh. "I guess if you want to."

She shrugs. "I just thought maybe you secretly liked them. I opened the drawer to find a remote the other day and there were stacks of chick flicks in there. It's nothing to be ashamed of."

"Oh, that. Those were my exes. She never took them when she moved out, and I keep forgetting to get rid of them."

"Your ex lived here with you? How long ago?"

"Like two years ago. She was my fiancée at the time."

I don't know why I just divulged that information willingly. There's something about being with Mia that makes opening up to her feel easy. Well, easy might be too strong of a word. I wouldn't say talking about my ex is ever easy.

"Fiancée? You were engaged?"

"I was. Didn't work out, obviously."

She tucks her hair behind her ear nervously. "Do you mind if I ask what happened?"

"Not really a big secret. She ended up leaving me for the COO of my company. I believe she said he could provide a better life for her. I'm sure you can read between the lines. She wanted some-one who would spoil her rotten with luxury twenty-four/seven. I didn't make enough in her mind."

She sits up straight. "Are you fucking kidding me?"

I look her up and down, curious as to what her sudden anger is for. "No, I'm serious. She was horrible."

"Where does this bitch live? I think I need to pay her a visit."

"Woah, there baby. No need to get angry. I dodged a bullet with that one."

I say it so quickly, and the best part is, I mean it. My life would be horrible if I ended up marrying Kim. Especially now that I'm seeing what a life with Mia is like.

She takes a deep breath. "I'm sorry. I kind of have a temper. It's the Italian in me."

My lips curl into a slow smile. "I love your temper. It's sexy as hell. Never apologize for it."

She leans her head to the side as her eyes turn soft. "Seriously, Eric. I'm sorry that happened to you. I hope you know that not all women are like that. Your success does not equal how worthy you are of love."

I try to swallow past the lump in my throat. Suddenly, this topic feels suffocating. Maybe because I needed to hear those words, and I'm afraid that she just might be making me believe in love again.

"We don't need to talk about this. I'd much rather take you upstairs and kiss every inch of your perfect body," I whisper as my lips graze hers.

I can feel her reluctance to me changing the subject, but she gives in and wraps her arms around my neck. I scoop her up and head for the stairs.

I don't know what the hell I'm doing. I'm heading for a cliff, but there's no way to stop. Not when everything feels right when she's in my arms. Tonight, I just want to shut the world out. Shut my brain off and get lost in the comfort of her skin against mine.

I know it's not the healthiest way to deal with my past or any negative emotions, but I've never claimed to be a stand-up guy.

Chapter Twenty-Four

Mia

I can watch him work all day long. When he is in the barn, he is in his element. He sweat through his shirt, so he got rid of it. Now he's in my favorite outfit. Jeans and his work boots, and nothing else.

I'm sitting on top of a large wooden work bench as I watch.

"You know how they make those calendars with like firefighters with no shirts on to raise money?" I say as I swing my legs up and down.

"Yeah, I think I know what you're talking about," he replies, not looking away from his project.

The muscles in his arms flex as he measures something with a ruler and marks it with a pencil behind his ear.

"I think I want one of those but of pictures with you working in here. No shirt. I'd like to hang that in my office."

A large smirk spreads across his beautiful face as he uses the pencil and makes a mark on the wood. "Is that what you're thinking about over there while I work on this table?"

"I think about your body a lot."

He looks up at me for a second and winks. That's all it takes to make my heart explode in my chest. I smile like a schoolgirl who's crush just acknowledged her for the first time.

I hear him chuckle and find his eyes on me. "Don't be embarrassed. I think about your body a lot too, babe. In fact, I think I'd like a similar calendar with you in the office wearing nothing but a bra and panties."

"Why does it sound pervy when a guy asks for that?"

He shakes his head and laughs then gets back to work. I take the time to study him. The way he licks his bottom lip when he's concentrating.

His confession to me the other night has been weighing on me ever since. I can't believe he was engaged. Everything about him makes so much more sense. Between his friend selling him out for a chance to look cool in front of a girl when they were twelve to a fiancée leaving him for a man with more money, no wonder he has some trust issues.

It all seems to come back to how much money he has. He's been trained to believe his worth as a man is dependent on the amount of money he makes.

It breaks my heart.

"So, I was thinking," I say as my voice wavers. "Ever since we talked about your ex."

He doesn't look up at me, but I see the muscles in his jaw tense. That should be my warning not to say anything, but I keep going. "Between the story you told me with your first crush and the reasons your fiancée left. I wonder if maybe that contributed to some of your feelings about relationships."

Okay, there may have been a more eloquent way to say that.

A bitter laugh escapes him. "Nice observation."

Ouch. The hint of sarcasm hurts, but I keep going. Seriously, I don't know what my problem is. I just want him to find peace and I hate that those two experiences define love for him.

"I know, but seriously. I hate that you have this impression that all relationships will be like that. There are many women out there that don't need money to be happy. They would love you just for who you are."

He stops working for a second, eyes trained on his work. Then bends down to get eye level with the wood before making a cut. I guess he isn't going to respond. That's fine, but I already started the conversation. I can't just leave it.

"I just hate to see you missing out on life, or love, because you might be scared to..."

His hand comes in contact with the wood, creating a loud boom that echoes in the barn. "Why are you bringing this up? I never asked for your opinion," he screams, eyes dark with anger.

My breath catches in my throat. I try to swallow back my fear. "I'm sorry. I'm just trying to help you."

"Help me? I never asked for help. You know what I think," he says while he leans down on the wood. "I think you're trying to help yourself. You think if you fix me, maybe you have a shot with me. I never promised anything to you, Mia. I was honest with what this was from the beginning."

There it is. The words I've been dreading since the moment I knew I was falling for him. This is all just sex to him. Tears fill my eyes making my vision blurry. It's not worth the effort of trying to blink them away, they already start to run down my cheeks.

I try to open my mouth to respond, but nothing comes out. There's nothing for me to say. He's right. He was honest from the beginning, and here I am doing what every woman probably does to him. Trying to fix him, wanting him to change so they can be together.

I feel so stupid.

I hop off of the work area and wipe my eyes before I race for the door.

"Mia, wait," I hear his soft voice. "I'm sorry."

I don't stick around to hear him out. I can't. My heart feels like someone just sucker punched my chest. This all too familiar feeling that hits. One where I realize I'm more into the guy than he is into me. The story of my damn life.

I take off for the house into a slow jog as tears continue to spill.

"Mia," his voice says from right behind me. Then I feel his warm hand on my elbow. I stop and turn around. He's breathing heavily and has a pained expression on his face. "I'm sorry...I just..." He runs a hand through his hair and looks up at the sky. "Fuck."

His eyes move back to mine. "Look, that came out wrong. I didn't mean to snap at you."

I wrap my arms around myself and look away. "It's fine. You're right. I stuck my nose in your business. You were upfront from the beginning."

I try to step away, but he grabs my hand. "I need you to know. You're not like any other woman I've been with. I have feelings for you. I care about you."

I laugh sharply. "Yeah, I feel like I've heard that one before. I get lots of *I care about you's* in life. I'm easy to care about. Not easy to love apparently."

I pull my hand out of his and run to the house with my all too familiar broken heart.

Chapter Twenty-Five

Eric

I knew this was going to blow up in my face. It was exactly why I tried to stay away from her from the beginning. Nothing about it seemed like a good idea.

But it was impossible to stay away then, and it's impossible now.

I run through the grass with no shirt, the autumn chill reminding me of that fact. I kick off my work boots and run upstairs.

The door to her bedroom is closed. I don't think twice as I whip the door open. She's standing by the window as sobs wrack her body, shoulders shaking. I feel it in my own body. I move towards her until I can wrap my arms around her, pulling her body into mine.

"Mia, I'm so damn sorry. I didn't mean for this to happen."

She doesn't embrace me back and the disappointment is overwhelming. I let her cry on my bare chest, feeling her tears dampen my skin.

I let her cry until I feel her body soften and the tears stop. Then I gently tug her hair, so she is looking up at me. Her face is red and puffy from her tears, but she is still more beautiful than words can express.

"Look, I don't know what is happening between us. I won't deny that you've changed me in the short time that you've been here. I'm sorry I snapped at you. I suck at talking feelings. I used to be good at it. But I'm a different person than I was two years ago. My ex leaving me like that changed me. I wish I was a better man. One that can live up to your expectations."

"It's not my expectations. I was just trying to help you."

"I know. I just—I don't know. I don't have any excuse. I wish I was different for you."

I let my forehead fall to hers and pull her closer to me. "Please, Mia. Don't hate me. I don't think I could handle it if you did."

She reaches up and lightly brushes her lips on mine. I try to inhale a breath, but my chest shakes with emotion. I'm starting to fear the worst. That maybe these feelings I have for her are far beyond caring.

"I couldn't hate you. Ever," she whispers, and I can't help it, I seal my lips to hers.

My hands grab her face and deepen the kiss. I push her back towards the bed as I turn her head to the side to get a better angle. Her lips are molded to mine, moving in perfect sequence with mine. Never have I felt so starved and desperate for someone. I pull her shirt over her head then unsnap her bra and let it fall to the floor. I look down at her, my eyes trying to take in every part of her all at once.

Her eyes on me feel like they're warming each part of my body, even my cold heart.

Her hands are shaky as they unbutton my jeans. I let her delicate hands undress me until I'm naked in front of her.

I scoot her up onto the bed and gently push her until she is lying down. Then I get rid of the rest of her clothes. Her chest rises and falls rapidly as she watches me. I kneel onto the ground and wrap my arms around her thighs then pull them apart with my hands.

My tongue swipes up her center, feeling desperate to somehow show her how I feel about her. I may not be able to do it with words, but my body doesn't need any assistance.

I work her clit with quick flicks of my tongue before I slow it down to draw out the pleasure. Once I feel like she can't take it anymore, I wrap my lips around her clit and alternate between sucking and flicking my tongue until she is screaming my name and pulling my hair as she comes all over me. I softly lick and kiss her until she has completely come down.

As soon as I pull away, I stand up and line my dick at her entrance. I can't wait another second. I need to feel like she's mine, even if she's not.

My head falls back in sweet ecstasy when I bottom out. Dammit, this woman has me in so many ways.

When I look down at her, her eyes still have a hint of sadness in them. I need to be close to her, to be with her. I lean forward and kiss her. My hands splay in her hair as my tongue pushes past her lips.

I start to thrust in and out of her tight pussy, letting the feeling of our closeness wash away any fears of losing her. Something I know is going to happen because I'm not good enough for her.

Just the thought sends panic throughout my body. I respond by kissing her harder and thrusting deeper. She starts to moan into my mouth, and I respond with my own moan that reverberates from my chest.

We are both touching each other anywhere that we can get our hands. I start to feel her walls spasming around my cock as she cries. I swallow her cries with my mouth while I let go myself, spilling my cum into her pussy.

Even after our bodies come down from our orgasms, we still kiss each other. It's like I can't stop. My lips move along hers slowly, trying to etch the feeling into my brain forever.

Chapter Twenty-Six

Mia

The coffee is hot, the morning air is crisp, the view from the porch is incredible, but all I can think about is our fight.

We never really resolved anything. In a moment of pure panic, we made love that felt like something from a romance novel. But I can't let that make me believe that we might actually have a future.

The way he blew up at me for bringing up his past shows that he is not ready to confront any of it. Maybe he never will be.

My phone vibrates in my lap. It's my brother, Gabe.

"Hello," I answer as I hold my coffee in my other hand.

"Hey, sis. I've got some good news."

"Oh, yeah?" I ask, my body tense as I wait for what I think is coming.

"It's been confirmed that Don has been at home now for a couple of weeks. His credit card activity seems clear, and he has been going to work. Your neighbour who thought she saw him the other night must have been mistaken because my buddy happened to be following him that evening and confirmed he was nowhere near your house. We think it's safe for you to come back. You can get your life back and put all of this behind you."

There it is. The good news. Right?

But why doesn't it feel like good news?

"Oh, that's amazing," I manage to muster.

He laughs. "Don't sound so enthused. I might be slightly offended that you don't miss us more."

"No, no I'm excited to come home. I just—I think I'd feel better if we give it another week or so. I mean, maybe more time where he can't find me will put me further out of his mind."

"That's true. I never thought about it like that. Okay, maybe another week to play it safe."

"You should call Ma and tell her. I have no interest in her whining when I let her know her daughter won't be coming home immediately."

I laugh lightly. "I'll give her a call. Thanks again for all of this. I'm sorry I've caused such a headache for everyone."

"Your safety is not a headache for any of us. Stop apologizing. Keep in touch. Let me know when you feel comfortable to move back. We'll make sure we get it all squared away."

"Thanks. I'll let you know."

I hang up the phone and try my best to enjoy the coffee with the bitter taste of my lies. What am I doing to myself? I should just leave now with my heart still partially intact, but I can't make myself do it.

I think I need to get out of this house to clear my head. Knowing that Don is confirmed to be back in Cleveland gives me the freedom to at least go out on my own without any concerns.

Maybe I'll go surprise Layla at her restaurant. I smile at the thought.

Perfect. It'll be exactly the afternoon I need.

I'll pull out my laptop and get some work done right now and then go see her for lunch.

I'm feeling a bit better by the time I walk into her restaurant for lunch. Maybe it's because I'm hungry and walking into a restaurant. I'll never be one of those girls who's too depressed to eat.

I opt to sit at the bar and order a drink when Layla walks by.

"What are you doing here?" She runs over to me with a smile.

"Just figured I'd get out of the house and have some lunch. I was going a bit stir crazy at the house."

She waves at the bartender. "Sorry, Max. You're going to be serving me today because I'm having lunch with my friend."

She hops up on the barstool next to me. Max, a cute bartender with amazing dimples, smiles at her.

"I think I can handle your presence for a little while, boss," he says.

"So, you're out on your own. Is that safe?" she asks.

I smile softly. "It is. My brother told me Don is confirmed to be back in Cleveland and going to work, living his life."

"Oh, that's good." Her voice sounds hesitant and sad. "Does that mean you're leaving?"

"I will be soon. I'm giving it another week or two to try and make sure he stays put."

"Have you told Eric yet?"

"Not yet. I just talked to my brother this morning," I tell her, dreading the conversation with Eric already.

She lets out a troubled sigh. "I wonder how he's going to handle it."

"Why do you say that?" I ask.

Her eyebrows raise at me. "I think we can just be honest with each other at this point. There's definitely something going on between you two."

I look down sadly. Yes, there's something going on. Nothing that means he's going to be crushed when I leave. It might actually be a breath of fresh air for him. He won't have to deal with his own feelings.

My eyes become blurry as tears threaten to spill over. I feel the warmth of Layla's hand on my arm.

"Are you okay, honey?" she asks delicately. "I'm sorry. Did I say something wrong?"

I shake my head back and forth, somehow managing to blink my tears away then take a deep breath before I respond. "No, I'm sorry. You're right, there's something going on between Eric and me. But I don't think he's going to care too much when I'm gone. In fact, he'll probably be relieved."

"I don't believe that for a second. Why would you say that?"

"Because he has basically told me. He's so hot and cold with me. I swear, whenever he feels something real, he freaks out and pulls away."

The corners of her eyes droop, as a soft sheen of moisture appears. "I thought maybe since he was acting different, since he seemed happier, that maybe he had worked through everything. Don't give up on him. I think he's crazy about you."

A soft smile touches my lips. "He has a lot of issues with his past, especially his ex."

Her voice raises slightly. "He told you about her?"

"About his fiancée? Yeah, she was clearly the worst. I mean, to leave him because she wants a man with more money. My gosh, how much money does the woman need? And for the man she married to end up being his boss. Ugh, gross."

Layla's face contorts into pure anger. "That's what happened between the two of them? That bitch left him because of money?"

My body freezes. "He never told you that? Shit. I can't believe I said that. I thought you knew."

I can't believe I just did that. He's going to kill me.

"He never talks about it. With anyone. I'm glad he opened up to you. I told you there's something between you two. He talks to you."

Silence falls between us. I don't know how to respond.

"What do you think about everything? Do you care about him?" she asks softly.

When I look into her eyes, I know I can't lie. Tears blur my vision then spill over my lids. "I love him."

A tear escapes her own eyes as she stares at me. "Don't give up on him."

I nod my head. I won't...if he doesn't give up on me.

Chapter Twenty-Seven

This inability to focus on my work is getting old. I don't know what the hell has changed, but it's starting to piss me off. I like my job. I should be able to focus. I shouldn't be looking at the clock wondering why it's going painstakingly slow.

I wonder what Mia is doing. She's been getting on her laptop more often now as she tries to manage some of her workload from here.

I know she's starting to go a bit stir crazy in the house. It's only a matter of time before she goes home.

My body tenses at the thought of when that day will come. I don't want to think about it. It will just make this shit day even worse. My body is wound so tight from being so damn tense all day as I battle with my own head.

I should check my security cameras again just to make sure Mia is safe. It's become a bit of a habit for me to glance at them throughout the day. It already has me on edge a bit to leave her home alone for so long.

I open up the app on my computer and type in the password. There are cameras in all main rooms and the entire outside perimeter. I sweep through the outside cameras first to clear all points of entry then I click through the rooms.

Everything seems clear. I am about to close out of the last camera that is in the kitchen when Mia comes into the frame. I sit up straight because she is getting herself a glass of water from the fridge—in nothing but a black bra and underwear. Her ass is barely covered by her underwear and it's sexy as fuck.

Is this what she does all day when I'm gone? Anger surges through me as I watch her from afar knowing if I wasn't at this damn job I would be able to be home with her.

I reach for my phone and dial her number. I watch her reach for the phone on the island and pick it up.

"Hey, you," her voice crackles slightly. "Everything okay?"

My hand squeezes the phone as I watch her lean her arms on the island, bending over the counter.

"Not exactly," I bite out.

"What's wrong?" she asks softly.

"There's a lot wrong right now. But I'd say at the top of the list is you."

I watch her stand up straight. "Me?"

"Yes, you. I'm over here at work trying to focus, which is impossible to do when I check in to make sure you're safe and see you standing in my kitchen in next to nothing."

She looks over her shoulder up at the camera and a slow smile spreads across her face.

"Oh, you can see me."

I sigh. "Yes, Mia. I see you. Now, not only can I not focus on work, but I'm hard as a rock."

"How's that my fault?" she replies with a hint of amusement.

"You know I have these cameras. I think you're doing this on purpose. Trying to distract me and get me fired."

"You think I'm doing this on purpose?"

"It seems like it," I growl with annoyance.

She looks up at the camera with a devilish look in her eye. Then she takes me by surprise by reaching behind her back and unhooks her bra. I hold my breath as I wait for it to fall. Her arms remain tight to her sides, holding it up.

"Are you teasing me right now?" I growl. "I'm not in the mood to be messed with."

She giggles in the phone, making it almost impossible to be angry at her anymore. I have to fight not to smirk at how cute she sounds.

"I have to ask," she whispers. "Is there anyone around you?"

"Mia, there is no way in hell I would let anyone but me see you like this."

"Oh," she says as she looks up at the camera, "in that case."

She moves her arms, and the bra falls to the ground. Her perfect breasts appear on the screen—nipples hard and ready for me, but I'm not there.

I stand up and take long, fast steps then lock my door. My blinds are already closed. I can't believe what I'm about to do, but I have zero control when it comes to this woman.

I sit back in my chair. "Touch yourself," I demand, needing to get right to the point.

"Where?" she whispers.

"Start with your breasts, baby. Play with them, give your nipples some attention for me."

"I need to put my phone on speaker," she whispers.

I watch her place the phone on the counter then look back up at the camera. As her hands fill up with her generous breasts, I unzip my pants and pull myself out.

"That's it, baby. Pretend those are my hands. Pinch your nipples for me." She obeys my command, and it makes me want more. "Lose the underwear and get up on that counter."

She slowly pushes her black underwear to the floor and uses both hands to boost her up to the counter. I run my hand up and down my dick as I watch.

"Good girl. Now spread those legs for me. Show me your pink pussy."

I squeeze my dick and jerk it harder when I get a view of her pussy. A bead of precum drips out of my tip. I bring my thumb to my tip and spread it around.

"Now touch yourself. I want to watch you get yourself off while I jerk myself," I demand.

She doesn't miss a beat. Her fingers slide inside of pussy then she moves them up to her clit and starts to rub circles. I almost black out from there as I watch her rub herself to orgasm on my kitchen island then I pump myself hard and fast until I'm spilling into my own hand.

I throw my head back and take several deep breaths, willing myself to get ahold of myself now.

"You're perfect," I whisper into the phone. "I'd love to stay and chat, but I need to clean myself up. See you tonight?"

"Of course," she says heavily, still panting from her release. "I'll see you tonight."

I hang up and throw my phone onto my desk. What the hell am I doing? Jerking off in my office is unacceptable and completely out of character for me.

I grab several tissues off of my desk and clean myself up the best that I can, so I can move to the bathroom.

By the time I get home, I'm exhausted and frustrated with myself. I'm all twisted inside and have no idea how to handle it. The reality of it all is that it has everything to do with Mia.

I've shared more with her than I have with anyone. I've opened up old wounds that I've done everything in my power to forget about.

When I walk through the door, the familiarity of it all starts to feel suffocating this time. The homemade dinner, the smile on her face. How did I let this happen?

Chapter Twenty-Eight

Mia

I'm going to do it. Tonight, after dinner, I'm going to tell him that I can go home. I've been thinking about telling him that I'm in no rush and can stay a little while longer—for safety purposes.

There doesn't seem to be any harm in me staying. I don't know why I'm so nervous to tell him. Perhaps I'm hoping he will be upset at the possibility of me leaving, maybe not want me to go.

I can't deny my feelings for him. In these seven weeks that I've been here, he's somehow managed to burrow his way deep into my heart, grumpiness and all—I love him.

It defies logic or reason. There's just something there, this magnetic pull between us that I can't describe.

I look at him across the dinner table and my heart skips a beat. He seems a bit sad tonight. He's always so tense when he gets home from work. I hate that for him. I wish he could admit how unhappy he is at his job. His true passion is woodworking, and he's so talented.

Maybe I should start with telling him what I've been working on in my free time. I can't bear to see him come home from work another day carrying this load of stress.

"I've been working on something," I tell him from across the table.

"Oh yeah?" he asks as he chews his food. "What's that?"

"I created a logo and a marketing plan for your woodwork," I say, kind of excited now to show him what I've come up with.

His fork falls onto his plate, the contact sending a loud clatter throughout the room. "Why would you do that?"

"You just love it so much. It makes you happy. And I hate how unhappy you are when you're at work. I thought maybe you should consider..."

"Who said I wasn't happy at work? I don't remember saying that," he states.

"It's just that ever since you've been back at work, you come home stressed. And the way you talked about your work, you didn't seem happy about it," I reply, my voice shaky with nerves.

"You know, sometimes a job is just a job. Not everyone gets to do something that they love, but that doesn't give you the right to go around judging others careers. This is typical. Is anything I do ever good enough?"

My body trembles as I try to figure out what I said that is so wrong. I thought he would be excited about this. Maybe I've got it all wrong. Maybe I am overstepping.

"I'm sorry. I guess I misjudged the situation. I didn't mean to offend you," I say softly.

"You didn't mean to offend me when you took it upon yourself to tell me how to live my life when you've known me for all of two months. And what happens when I make the career change and can't afford to live in this house anymore. Would you still find me very appealing?"

He pushes his chair away from the table and storms out of the room. Tears run down my cheeks as I try to register what just happened.

He never did ask me to get involved with his life. I just got so inspired by his passion and skills that I thought he would like what I came up with. Now I feel so stupid.

I stuck my nose in his business when he never asked me to. I suddenly get this strong feeling that I'm just getting in the way. Maybe he doesn't want me here anymore but he feels bad because of my situation.

I stand up from the table and search the house until I find him sitting in his office on the brown leather couch with a glass of whiskey. He seems to be concentrating awfully hard on his whiskey glass as he turns it around and stares at it from different angles.

"Hi," I say hesitantly as I walk into his office.

He looks up at me and sits up straight. "Hi."

Too afraid to come all the way into the room, I opt to lean against the doorframe. I wring my fingers together as my brain spins to come up with what to say.

"So, umm, I talked to my brother the other day," I tell him as butterflies continue to dance in my stomach. "He told me that Don has been home for a couple of weeks now. The guy he hired to follow him has confirmed that he's been going to work, and it should be safe enough for me to come home."

His jaw tenses at my words but he doesn't look at me. "I see."

"Well, I was considering staying another couple of weeks just to give it some more time to see if he makes a move, but I am clear to go home any time now."

"I'm sure you're relieved," he says as he clutches his glass, his eyes dark as they hold mine.

"I guess I was just wondering, since this is your house and all, what you thought about me staying a bit longer or," I trail off, not sure how to finish my sentence.

A bitter laugh escapes him. "You can stay or go. This is your decision."

It's like a knife directly through my heart. I know he's angry, but I didn't think he would be so cruel. "After all we've been through, you don't care whether I stay or go?"

He stands up and walks towards me, each step heavy and deliberate. "I told you from the beginning, I don't do relationships. This was always temporary, so don't talk to me like I'm the bad guy here."

With that, he walks away leaving me stunned and broken in his office.

I pack my bags through the blur of my tears. There's no point in me staying here another minute if that is how he is going to treat our time together. I thought there was something more. Did I make all of that up in my head?

First, I date a guy who turns into a stalker that I have to hide from. Then I move on to someone who is emotionally unavailable, who even warned me that he was, and I still thought there was a chance for us.

I can no longer trust my instincts with men ever again.

Once my suitcases are stuffed to the brim, I close them up and start to take them downstairs one by one to my car.

I don't even care if I'm overreacting. I'm leaving now. An ultimate low point would be to cry myself to sleep in his home like some poor pathetic woman.

As I carry down my last suitcase, he's standing by the front door with his arms crossed. His eyes hold the same distance and anger that I saw the first time we met like nothing has changed. Maybe I did imagine all of those moments where I thought we were connecting on a level that I've never experienced before.

I stop at the door and look up at him knowing my face must look horrific.

"You're going," his deep voice states coldly.

"Like you said, this was always temporary." I throw his words back in his face. "Thank you for keeping me safe these last two months. I appreciate all of the effort you put into that and will always be grateful. Goodbye, Eric."

His hands, which are not at his sides, are balled into fists. The skin is turning red from how hard he seems to be squeezing, but he makes no move towards me. No hug goodbye. He just stays frozen.

A harsh laugh escapes me as I grab my suitcase and walk out the door. Of course, he can't even muster up a simple you're welcome. I throw my suitcases into my trunk and hop in my car without looking back, tears now streaming down my cheeks.

As I drive away, a sudden feeling of emptiness takes up my insides. I've never felt this before. It's like he ripped out my heart as a souvenir, leaving it back at his house while I drive away with nothing but hollowness and regret.

Chapter Twenty-Nine

Eric

I stare down at the numbers on the page but for the life of me I can't focus on them. They might as well be in Japanese. I didn't sleep a minute last night. How can I when I will never know the warmth of her body in my bed again?

I'll never come home from work and see her dancing in my kitchen while cooking dinner. I'll never feel the softness of her lips against mine. I'll never get to watch my favorite shade of red spread from her cheeks down to her chest when she's embarrassed.

But fuck, why was she trying to force me to leave my job? It just hit too close to home. Kim left me because I didn't advance fast enough in my career, and Mia was already trying to get me to switch careers.

It's exactly why I wanted to avoid falling in love ever again. It comes with the other person's expectations and eventually their disappointment in you. I don't need that shit in my life.

I was doing fine before I met Mia. Now look at me. I can't even get a simple task completed at work because she's all I can think about.

My door suddenly flies open, and Layla is standing in my office. She steps closer to me as her finger points at my chest. "What did you do?"

"It's nice to see you too, sis," I say as I throw down my pen.

"Don't give me that shit. What did you do?" she repeats herself, hands now set on her hips.

"Just say what you need to say. I'm busy."

"Don't you dare talk to me like that. I want answers, and I want them now." She closes the door behind her and takes a seat. "Why did I get a message late last night from a crying Mia telling me that she was driving home? What happened that made her hop in her car at night and take off without any warning or saying goodbye?"

"I didn't do a thing. She told me it was safe for her to go home. What did you want me to do?" I reply as my voice rises in anger.

I can't believe this shit is on me. Between her and Mia, they are acting like I was supposed to get on my knees and beg her to stay. She has a whole life in Cleveland. A family and a successful career.

"What did you say to her when she told you she could go home?"

"I told her it was fine," I say through clenched teeth.

"Cut. The. Shit. Tell me exactly what you said," she says as she sits up straight and slams her hands on my desk.

It is suddenly becoming increasingly obvious why they say not to get involved with a sibling's best friend. Here I am, an adult man in my thirties, getting berated by his little sister.

"Fine. I told her I don't care whether she stays here or goes home. Is that what you wanted to hear?" I throw my hands up in the air in frustration.

She throws her head back and laughs. It's creepy and makes my body break out in goosebumps.

"So, you pushed her away. That's exactly what I thought you would do. You're so predictable."

"What the hell did you want me to do, Layla? After eight weeks together, was I supposed to beg her to give up her life and stay with me? And how the fuck did you know there was something between us in the first place? Did she tell you?"

She rolls her eyes so hard I'm surprised they don't get stuck in the back of her head. "Please, everybody knows. It's so obvious how in love you are with her. And no, you idiot, you didn't need to beg her to stay. But how about showing some emotion. I know you're sad that she had to go. You could have asked to keep in touch, try long-distance, or at least be a decent human being and tell her you enjoyed your time together and are sad that it's coming to an end."

I scoff at her words. She doesn't understand the details. She doesn't know about Kim and what that woman put me through. Nor does she know that her perfect friend was trying to change me too.

"Whatever. I thought maybe I was getting my old brother back. The one who smiled and laughed with us. The one who loved freely. I guess that man is long gone."

She stands up and walks out of my office leaving me alone with my thoughts. Maybe that man is long gone. Just because I felt him return in moments with Mia, doesn't mean he's there.

It was only a matter of time before the damaged part of me got in the way. I close my eyes and the same image that haunted me all night appears. Mia's tear-stained face looking up at me with her suitcase in her hand just waiting for me to stop her—and I let her go.

My arm slides across my desk in a fit of rage, sending weeks of work falling to the ground. I push my chair away from my desk and stand up, pacing back and forth. My tie starts to feel like it's strangling me. I feel out of control.

I open my office door and take heavy steps to the bathroom. As soon as I'm there I lean against the counter and splash cold water on my face. I need to get that image out of my damn head, but I can't shake it. I pour water on the back of my neck, anything to distract my brain from these thoughts.

When I feel like I have my breathing back under control, I grab the towels and try to dry myself off. With my hands on the counter, I look at myself in the mirror.

"Get your shit together, man. You can't let another woman do this to you."

Chapter Thirty

Mia

My body feels like it's twisted into knots. Every part of me is heavy with an aching hollowness. My chest thumbs with a dullness to it that feels like someone reached inside and squeezed my heart until it burst.

Every movement feels like I'm trying to run against the wind, like there is a force there stopping me from taking my steps easily.

I sit at the table by the window with my three sisters-in-law, trying to listen as Alexis talks about something my niece said or did. Normally, I can't get enough of the stories of my niece, but right now my brain can't seem to focus on anything.

"Mia, earth to Mia," Lexi says as she waves a hand in front of my face.

I shake my head. "Sorry, what did you say?"

"Alright, that's it," Savannah puts her coffee down. "What's going on with you? Was it too soon to come home?"

"What? No, no. It's nothing like that."

"Then what is it? You've been home for two days and you've been different. Quiet. Something happened," Alexis says softly. "You can tell us."

I will myself not to cry. I've done enough of that since I've left. I think I cried myself to the point of dehydration on the way home.

"It's just Eric, Layla's brother."

"The guy you stayed with?" Lexi asks.

I nod my head. "Yeah."

They all seem to nod their heads with me in understanding. "I see. You two had a little thing, huh?" Savannah asks.

"Well, to him it was a little thing. To me it felt much bigger than that." I wipe the tear that escapes. "Stupid, huh? To fall for a guy in only eight weeks."

"Ha!" Alexis laughs. "I fell for your brother in eight days."

"Really?" I ask hopefully, needing some kind of validation that I'm not some poor, desperate woman who will fall for any man that gives her attention.

"Well, I don't know, I didn't count. But it was pretty damn instant for me. As cheesy as it sounds, sometimes I wonder if it was the day I met him. There was just something that hit different. It was like my body knew before my mind."

"The thing is, he warned me from the beginning that he doesn't want a relationship. It's my fault for thinking something had changed along the way," I admit.

"Oh, please. Every single one of us heard that line from each of your brothers. But let me tell you, the damaged ones are always worth it in the end. They're the ones who feel deeper, that's why they get scared," Lexi says.

"Yes, but there's one difference in all of this," I say as tears are now cascading down my cheeks with no hope of slowing down. "You all got your happy ending. I'm stuck here all alone with a man who told me he doesn't care whether I stay or go."

Even saying those words out loud is like another knife to my heart. My hands shake as I try to lift my coffee to my mouth. The last thing my body needs is caffeine, but I refuse to let his harsh actions stop me from enjoying one of my favorite things.

"Ouch. He said that to you?" Savannah asks. "I feel like we need more context. How did it all happen?"

I go through the entire story. How we started seeing each other, his resistance to intimacy. I tell them about how he got mad at me when I told him I worked on a business proposal for him, and how that kind of steamrolled into him telling me he doesn't care if I stay. I tell them how he told me he never promised me anything and how he just watched me leave without any words, not even a goodbye.

"Mia, I'm so sorry," Lexi replies delicately.

I shrug my shoulders. "Story of my life. I'm the fixer for everyone else's life but can't seem to figure out my own. I was always living in the shadows of my brothers. They were so charismatic. Everyone wanted to be near them, but no one ever noticed me. Maybe I need to accept that I'm just not the type of person someone could possibly fall hard for."

"Mia, that is not true," Alexis says sternly. "You are intimidatingly perfect. If anything, guys don't think they're good enough to be worthy of you. And to be honest, most aren't."

Savannah shakes her head. "Absolutely. I was terrified when I first met you because I thought there's no way someone this put together and perfect will accept someone like me. But then I got to know you, and you are also the kindest, sweetest person I know. You're the total package."

"And if Eric can't pull his head out of his ass enough to see that and work through his issues, he isn't the one for you," Lexi adds.

My head moves up and down in agreement, though their words do nothing to make me feel better.

"Look, I'm not excusing him treating you like this," Alexis says as she rubs a soothing hand on my back. "In fact, I wish I could go down there and kick his ass. But what I will say, is that your brothers were also assholes who pushed us away. We've been here, felt the gut-wrenching pain of loving a man you think is incapable of giving you what you deserve."

She looks at the other girls and they nod their heads in agreement. "So, while I don't know what's going to happen in the end, I do know that you are a very smart woman. You wouldn't fall for a man who didn't show you he deserves it. Now, it's up to him to come to that realization. And if he doesn't...we kick his ass."

"I'm in," Savannah raises her cup.

"Right there with you," Lexi follows suit.

I laugh through my tears, knowing there's no way I would survive this life without these women in my life.

I do my best to put on a happy face for the rest of the brunch. Distracting myself by listening to all the things I missed when I was away.

But everything that brought me joy before seems to feel dull and grey now. I couldn't even enjoy the cannoli I stopped and got for myself on the way home. In all my years, I've never hit rock bottom like this before.

I can't help but think that there seems to be one difference between my sister-in-law's stories and mine. They had a man who loved them enough to fight for them. I saw my brothers when they messed up with them, they were a wreck. They were hollow shells of themselves.

So, while I appreciate them trying to compare our situations and make me feel better, I don't think they understand that Eric is different. Eric let me walk away without a second thought. I'm sure he's happy that I'm gone and out of his space, and that is what hurts the most.

Chapter Thirty-One

Eric

The bitter sting of my whiskey is the only thing that proves to me that I can still feel. I raise the crystal glass in my hand and study the amber liquid. Is this going to be my only companion for the rest of my life?

I take another sip and feel the burn all the way down. The burn isn't intense enough. I deserve more torture for what I did to Mia. It's been a week, and her tears haunt me every minute of every day.

Kim's tears did nothing to me. I actually found myself annoyed when she cried. But with Mia, it's like my body is an extension of hers. When she cries, I feel it down into the pit of my stomach.

I've been playing that evening in my head over and over, wondering what I could've done differently. But the feeling of not being good enough for her still comes barreling back every time. I get angry that she couldn't just leave well enough alone and not try to change me.

Then I sit at work, hating every second of it, and I can't help but wonder if she was right. Maybe I'm not happy. But then what happens when I have to start from scratch and build a business from the ground up and am struggling financially? There's no way she'll want to be with someone like that. Not a smart, successful woman like her.

I open the top drawer in my desk, and something catches my eye. I pull the stapled papers out and read the design on the top page.

The words *Eric's Wood and Grain* are in the middle, and it is surrounded by trees with an ax running through it. It looks like it's pyrographed onto a log.

This is Mia's business proposal for me. The logo in itself is stunning.

I place my drink down on my desk and lean back in my chair. With a shaky hand, I turn the page. As I read through her words, I'm blown away at the amount of detail she has put into it. She captures the essence of what the craft means to me.

Then I get into the marketing strategy which is well researched and thought out. She found my target audience and how to market to them through social media and locally. I flip the page and find a financial projection of the first year. Forecasted revenue, expenses, and cash flow.

She must've spent weeks on this. As I read further, a weird sense of excitement bubbles up in me. Is it really possible to make a living off of this?

Then I think about how I treated her when she brought it up and bile rises in my throat.

A knock on my front door pulls me from my misery. Fuck, I'm not in the mood for visitors. It's probably Layla here to make me feel even more crappy about myself.

When I open the door, I'm surprised to see Asher and Liam staring back at me. They let themselves in before I can say anything.

"We heard you might need a little company," Liam pats my shoulder as I close the door.

We walk into the kitchen as I try to figure out how to get them the hell out of here. I just want to drink my sorrows away on my own.

"Whoever told you that was sorely mistaken," I reply as they take a seat at my island.

"You look like shit, man. Have you gotten any sleep?" Asher asks.

"Is this your idea of trying to make me feel better? Because you suck at it."

I opt to stand across from them on the other side of the island. I'm in no mood to pretend like I want to get cozy and talk.

"Wasn't trying to make you feel better. I'm just telling you like I see it." He rests his elbows on the counter. "So, I hear you sent Mia packing."

Every muscle in my body coils at his words. I want to punch his face for acting so casually about what I'm going through. "Choose your words carefully," I warn.

"Tell us it's not true and we'll leave you alone," Liam counters.

I stand in silence because it's true and I know it. We all know it. Everybody knows what I did, and now I have to deal with the consequences.

"Talk to us. I know we mess with you and all, but we're worried. We know you cared for her, so something happened that made you panic. Tell us what it was."

For the first time in a long time, I don't feel like hiding behind my wall. I'm so confused and torn up about what I want that I just decide to talk. I tell them about how I was already pissed at work because I couldn't focus. Then I come home and she's offering a plan for me to quit my job. I realize through my rambling just how much I've hidden from them because they don't even know about my hobby.

So, I just keep talking. I admit the real reason Kim and I didn't work out. How Mia triggered that fear in me again. So, when she came to me to tell me she could leave, I was already flooded with fear and anger. I tell them that woodworking became my therapy afterwards and has remained the only place that I feel like myself.

Then I admit how I lashed out at Mia and let her walk away in tears.

"Fuck, I'm sorry we didn't' know about any of this. I can't believe that's how you and Kim ended, and you never told us," Asher says as he runs a hand through his hair. "We could've been here to support you."

My eyes look down at a spot on my counter, too embarrassed to make eye contact. "I was humiliated. How could I come to you and tell you she left me because I'm not good enough?"

With my elbows on the counter, I lean my head down as tears threaten to spill over. I can't cry in front of my brothers. That would just add to my humiliation.

"Hey, look at me," Asher demands.

He's my older brother and knows when to take control, and right now he's demanding my full attention. Being the younger one and falling into my role, I obey his command.

I look up through the blur of my tears.

"Kim's greedy desire for more has nothing to do with you being good enough. You were too good for her, and I'm fucking thankful you didn't ruin your life by marrying her. I don't want to hear any of this shit about you not being good enough. You hear me?"

Liam nods along in agreement, but lets our older brother take the reins. I find myself nodding too, letting him know that I hear him.

"I'm sorry we didn't force this out of you earlier. It's my fault for letting you get away with hiding from us. I should've done better," Asher says with a look of guilt on his face.

"It's not your fault. I wasn't ready to talk about it."

"No, I could have made you," he says, and I smirk because he's right. He has a way of turning on the older brother role and putting me in my place. But it doesn't matter.

"There's no point in dwelling about the past, right?" I say.

"How do you feel about how you left things with Mia?" Liam asks, knowing that's a loaded question. I suppose that's the point, he wants me to keep talking.

"I feel like the biggest piece of shit that's ever lived."

"Good. That's a start," Asher replies.

I raise an eyebrow at him, not sure what the hell that means. Has he now switched directions to calling me a piece of shit?

"I'm not going to make excuses for treating the woman you love like shit," he explains.

My eyes open wide at his choice of words. I lean forward. "I'm sorry. The woman I love?" I question.

"Yes, you idiot. The woman you are so obviously in love with."

"What makes you think I'm in love with her?"

That gets a laugh from Liam and Asher. I'm not sure why we are all of a sudden laughing at me. "Because I know you. You were finally smiling again. You were crazy protective of her safety, calling us over and barking orders to make sure every inch of this property was covered with surveillance. You think you'd do that for someone you just kind of liked? You think all of these emotions would come flooding to the surface for a woman you don't really care about?" Asher asks as he raises his eyebrows at me.

"I don't know if I'd call it love. I mean yes, I care about her. But love in that short of time? We barely know each other."

"It sounds to me like she knows you better than we do at this point," Liam points out. "And I know I'm no expert on love, but I don't think it follows a timetable."

"Either way. Love or not. I completely screwed it up with her."

"Are you saying you are giving up?" Asher asks.

"No, I'm not giving up. It's not like there was ever going to be any real possibility of the two of us. Her life is in Cleveland, my life is here. She runs a successful business and probably wants nothing to do with someone like me."

Asher leans back in his chair and sighs. "You're never going to be able to have a relationship unless you figure out how to let your past go. Why would a woman who runs a successful business not want to be with you?"

I open my mouth to answer, thinking I have this amazing response, but no words come out. I've never had to defend my feelings before. Certainly, there's a good reason why I'm feeling this way. I'm just not able to articulate it right now.

"Exactly," Asher says as he points at me. "You are using this as an excuse to not put yourself out there. I'm telling you, women like Mia don't come around very often. Don't take too long to come to your senses."

Just the thought of her moving on with someone else sends red hot lava through my body. I will kill anyone who touches her.

"I think that you have some things to sit and think about. In the meantime, let's say you bring us out to your barn and finally show us the real Eric," Asher says as he stands up.

Liam jumps up eagerly then they both start for the backdoor. I follow behind them reluctantly. Why am I so afraid to show them this part of me? As we walk through the grass out to the barn, my heart accelerates in my chest.

What if they hate my work? What if they think it's stupid but don't want to hurt my feelings? All of these questions are swirling through my brain as we reach the barn door. But we're here now, and I have no reason not to rip off the band aid and show them.

I slide the door open and turn on the light. As we walk in, my eyes remain on my boots as my brothers disperse. I can hear them walk throughout the barn as they take in all that I've hidden from them.

It feels like I'm slicing open my chest for them to see the most vulnerable part of me. Not sure what that says about me and how I think I'm supposed to be viewed in the eyes of others that I find my art to be so exposing.

I'm so lost in my thoughts that I don't realize how much time has gone by. They both stand in front of me with weird looks on their faces. My stomach churns as I wait for their response.

"Mia is right," Liam says as he folds his arms across his chest. "This is clearly your passion, and you're fucking good at it. Let's see that business plan she put together."

They head back for the house leaving me speechless. I follow behind as I try to think of a way out of showing them her proposal. I haven't even finished it yet, and I don't want anyone else's eyes on it but mine right now. It feels intimate. Something she did just for me.

Chapter Thirty-Two

Mia

It's been two weeks since I've been back home. I've gotten into a bit of a routine. Go to work, come home, eat dinner alone, and cry myself to sleep.

I wanted my life to go back to normal. How much did I hope for getting my old life back where I could stop worrying about who was behind me or if I was safe? Now, I have it back and it doesn't feel the same anymore. I don't feel the same anymore.

I'm beginning to wonder if Eric changed me forever. Maybe I'll never be able to get over him.

It was a long day at work as I put on a smile for everyone and pretended to be happy. The last thing I want to do now is shower, but it's been a couple of days. I know I need to force myself. Maybe a hot shower will breathe some life back into me.

I've never experienced depression before. It's exhausting when every little task feels like a marathon. I keep hoping that one of these days I will wake up and the cloud will have lifted. But it never happens. It greets me every morning like an unwelcome house guest. If I could evict it, it'd be gone in an instant. Why can't we evict unwanted feelings from our lives?

I step under the steady stream of water and close my eyes. Waiting for that usual feeling I get of relaxation and relief, but it never comes. In the absence of my usual feelings of contentment, I just feel the crippling feeling of loneliness.

Part of me was hanging on to some kind of hope that he would reach out to me. But after fourteen days of silence, I have to face the facts. He wanted me gone and meant every word he spoke.

I don't know how long I stand under the spray of the hot water. After I get out, I wrap myself in a towel and walk into my bedroom. As I open my dresser drawer, a sound coming from downstairs distracts me.

My hand clutches the top of my towel as the rest of my body freezes. I wait in silence to see if I hear anything else. I'm sure I'm imagining things, but I still find myself tip-toeing to the door of my room.

I lean my head out of the door. I hold my breath as I listen, but I don't hear anything. Still, something feels off. I feel it in my body. I continue to tip toe out of my room to the top of the stairs and peer down to the front door. It's closed.

I breathe a sigh of relief. I'm sure I was just imagining things. I stand up straight and feel a surge of panic when I see Don standing there in my home. My pulse thunders in my ears. I can't believe he's here, inside my safe space. His eyes are fixed on me with an unsettling intensity. My heart races, a frightening blend of fear and disbelief twists in my stomach.

I feel trapped, like every exit is blocked by the weight of his presence. Memories of his control and manipulation flood my mind. I'm forced to confront the reality that he's crossed another line, and now there's nowhere for me to hide.

He looks nervous as he pulls at his neck. "Hi, Mia."

"Don," my voice catches in my throat . "What are you doing in my house?"

He clears his throat like he always did when he was scared. "I just wanted to talk."

"Talk? Don, you don't break into someone's house to talk."

I shouldn't be talking back like this to him. If he has the capability to break into my house then I know it's dangerous to make him mad. I knew my attitude was going to get me in trouble one day.

"I know but," he takes a step towards me.

I take a step back and put my hand up. He stops in his place. I'm on the edge of the top step. I sneak a glance down the stairs wondering if I should just make a run for it now.

"You never listened. You blocked my number," he continues. "What was I supposed to do?"

I look back up at him. "You accept that it's over and move on."

"I can't. Not without understanding what happened. I just wanted to talk it out. I knew that if I got you to listen to my side, you'd change your mind about us We're perfect for each other."

Tears fill my eyes as I listen to this. How am I going to get out of this?

At the end of the day, even if I hear him out, will he give up after I tell him it's still over?

"I can't do this with you," I say as tears roll down my cheeks. "This is not okay, and it has to stop. You can't stalk me, and you can't break into my house. That's against the law. You should be arrested for the fear you've caused in my life."

"Fear?" he asks as his head falls to the side.

It's like he can't even comprehend why I would be afraid of him. It scares me even more that he doesn't see how his behavior in the last several months has been crazy and obsessive.

"Look, I need you to leave. I'm going to go downstairs and grab my phone. If you don't leave, I'm calling the police."

I lift my shaky leg and place my foot on the first step below me, not sure if it's safe to turn my back to him.

He starts towards me as he sees me trying to walk away. "Wait, Mia, no."

I'm in the middle of moving my other foot to the step below when I see him come after me. I try to move my other foot quickly to take another step, but my brain isn't moving fast enough to catch up with my body.

My foot misses the step entirely and I feel the weight of my body start to fall backwards. I reach for the railing but can't get a grip on it. I feel my back hit the stairs first in a crash that sends pain throughout my body.

Then my body rolls and tumbles down the stairs as I feel my head knock against a hard surface. Then everything goes black.

Chapter Thirty-Three

What is that beeping noise? It keeps pulling me from my sleep, and I just want it to go away. My head is killing me. The throbbing feels like I was hit with a baseball bat.

What happened to me?

Did I drink too much last night? I don't remember going out. Alcohol has given me headaches before, but this feels different.

I hear whispering voices around me. I muster the strength to open my eyes, and the light makes my head pound even harder. I look around the room as I spot my brothers and my parents talking in the corner.

Where are we?

I glance down at myself. I'm in a hospital bed with an IV and tubes all around me.

My mother looks my way, and I hear a gasp. "Mia, baby. You're awake," she whispers as she comes to my side. "How are you feeling?"

My voice cracks as I try to speak. "My head hurts."

Her soft, comforting hand strokes my forehead. "That makes sense. You hit your head pretty hard. I'll call the nurse in and see if we can get you some more medicine to make you comfortable."

Ma almost runs out of the room to go find a nurse.

Pa comes up and kisses my cheek. "You scared us, sweetheart."

"What happened?" I ask, looking around at my brothers.

They gather around my bed, hands in their pockets like some kind of synchronized scene.

"You don't remember?" Gabe asks carefully.

I try to think about the last thing I remember. Getting home from work, showering, then it dawns on me. "Don."

They nod their head in agreement.

"I fell down the stairs," I say as I start to recall the evening.

"So, he was telling the truth," Gabe mutters through a tense jaw.

They all look at each other as if speaking in code. I look between them as I try to figure out what they are trying to say to each other.

"What do you mean?" I ask, voice still hoarse.

"He was the one who got you to the hospital," Marcus says as he steps closer. "He claimed it was all an accident. Is that true?"

Was it? I remember him breaking in, begging for me to hear him out. Then I remember starting to go down the stairs and losing my balance when he started to come closer to me.

"I guess so. I mean, I was walking down the stairs and lost my balance when he started coming closer to me. I don't know what he planned on doing, and I just got scared. I lost my footing and…" I say as tears fill my eyes.

"Hey, it's okay," Lucas says softly. "We don't need to rehash all of this right now. All that matters is that he will never be bothering you again."

"How do you know that?" I ask.

"He told us he never intended to hurt you. It wasn't until you were hurt that realized how far he had taken this. He promised he would stay away. Either way, we pressed charges, and the police took him away. Not before I threatened the fucker's life if he so much as thinks about you," Gabe speaks harshly.

Before I can ask any other questions Ma walks in the room with a male and female following her.

The woman, dressed in a white coat, approaches my bed. "Mia, I'm happy to see you're awake. You took quite a spill."

I smile and nod my head in response.

"You suffered a pretty significant head injury. We needed to put thirty stitches in your head to close the wound. How are you feeling?"

My hand rubs my temple. "My head hurts pretty bad."

"That's to be expected. You hit your head pretty hard. All scans show that your brain was not affected. Now that you are awake, we can offer something to manage the pain. You also bruised your back but luckily did not break anything. Your body will feel pretty banged up for a couple weeks."

She turns to the nurse and tells him what to give me for pain management then tells me she'll check back on me soon.

With that, the nurse orders my meds through a tablet. "We'll get you more comfortable soon," he assures me.

"When will I get released?" I ask as he checks the monitors around me.

"The doctors will likely want you here for another day or two to make sure you're healing properly. They are always more cautious with head injuries. You can never be too careful. I'll be back with your meds soon."

I look back at my brothers once he's gone. "I'm sorry about all of this."

Marcus rolls his eyes. "I told you guys she was gonna try to make this her fault."

"I'm not saying it's my fault," I sigh then lay my head back.

The first thing that my brain conjures up is an image of Eric. I wish he were here. Even after everything he said and how he made me feel, I've never felt more protected than I did in his arms.

I wonder what he would do if he found out about this. Would he even care enough to call me?

"Does anybody have my phone?" I ask.

Gabe pulls it out of his pocket. "Layla called a couple of times today. Alex answered and told her what happened. I hope that's okay."

I nod my head as I grab my phone. "That's fine. What did she say?"

"She freaked out. Insisted on coming up here immediately. Alex convinced her to stay put and let you rest. There's enough of us here to make sure you're okay."

"Thanks," I reply.

I want to ask if there were any missed calls or texts from anybody else, but I'm too afraid to hear the answer.

The nurse finally comes back with some medicine to ease my pain. As soon as he puts it into my IV, I can feel it take effect. With the pain beginning to subside, my fatigue starts to set in. My eyelids start to feel like they are being pulled down by weights.

"Alright, let's let Mia get some rest," Ma interrupts the men as they all continue to talk around me. She kisses me gently on my forehead. "I'll be here when you wake up."

I want to tell her to go home and get some rest of her own, but everything starts to fade as sleep takes over.

Chapter Thirty-Four

Eric

"What's up with you lately?" Adam asks across from my desk as I look down at the spreadsheet he brought to me.

"Not a damn thing. Just working like usual," I bite back, frustrated with his pestering.

He leans back in his chair and crosses his arms. "You are behind on your deadline for this acquisition. You're never behind. You leave at five every day now. You never left on time before. You have a permanent scowl on your face and snap at anybody who questions you. Something is up."

"I've been busy. And since when is it a crime to work normal hours around here?" I ask defensively.

"Not a crime," he replies. "But not exactly going to get you in good graces with the higher ups."

"Maybe I don't give a fuck about what they think anymore."

He opens his mouth to reply but my phone rings. I hold up my finger to him and pick up the call.

"Eric Williams."

"Oh, thank god," Layla cries on the other end. "I've called your cell like twenty times."

I sit up straight, my nerves on high alert. "Layla. What's wrong?"

"It's Mia," she chokes.

The air feels heavy, pressing down on me like an invisible weight. My hand clutches the receiver as a sinking feeling washes over me. "What about Mia?"

"She's in the hospital. Her ex, he showed up at her house. I don't know what happened. They just told me she was unconscious, and they were waiting for the doctor to speak to them."

As soon as the words leave her mouth, everything around me seems to blur. My heart slams against my chest. Mia, hurt and unconscious. The words feel wrong as if they can't possibly be real.

My mind scrambles to catch up, to make sense of what she is saying. A wave of nausea hits me as a gnawing feeling of helplessness takes over. I didn't protect her like I should have. I let her walk away from me and straight into danger.

Every worst-case scenario floods my brain. What if she never wakes up? What if the last time I saw her was the last time forever? The thought grips my chest with an unbearable ache.

"I'll call you back," I hear myself choke before I drop the phone to the ground.

"What's going on? Is everything okay?" Adam asks as he watches me stand slowly.

I look around the room, trying to figure out what I need to grab. Fuck it, nothing. I just need to go to her.

"I have to go," I say as I start to take heavy steps towards the elevator.

"What? Where?" he asks as he trails behind me.

"Cleveland."

I press the button several times, willing the elevator to appear. I don't have any time to waste.

"Cleveland? What the hell do you need to go to Cleveland for? You can't just leave. You're already on thin ice with the boss."

A bitter chuckle escapes me. The elevator door opens, and I walk in. I turn around slowly. "Tell him to kiss my ass. I quit," I reply just before they shut completely.

I wait for the panic to set in when I realize I just quit my job, but it never comes. It's clouded by the fear of losing something much more precious and important to me. I was just too fucking stubborn and scared to admit it.

Now she's lying in a hospital bed, and it's all my fault.

I should stay away from her after how I treated her, but I'm not a big enough man to do that. As soon as the elevator reaches the bottom floor, I sprint outside to the parking lot. I don't have time to stop at home and change. I need to get straight to the airport.

On my way, I book the fastest flight that will have me in Cleveland in four hours. Not as fast as I would like but it beats the twelve-hour drive.

I park my car at the airport, race through security with no luggage which seems to make me a target for suspicion. I get pulled aside, searched, and questioned. I want to explode with fury at the TSA agent, but I know that will only land me in jail. Right now, getting to Mia is my top priority.

Once I'm through, I check my watch. Shit, I've got three minutes to make it to the gate. I knew it was going to be a close call, but I'm determined to catch this flight.

By some miracle, I make it to the gate just as the gate agent is closing the door.

"I'm here," I scream as I approach while I wave my phone in my hand with my electronic ticket.

She turns around looking completely unimpressed.

"Scan your ticket," she informs me as she meets me by the machine.

I'm flooded with relief as I walk onto the plane. The only ticket left has me in the last row by the bathroom, but I couldn't care less where I sit.

The entire plane ride, my knees bounce up and down as I try to work out the nervous energy that is overflowing inside of me. I realize I don't even know what hospital she is at.

As soon as I'm off the plane, I turn my phone on and call my sister.

"I need you to tell me what hospital she's at," I demand as I run through the airport.

"Eric. What the hell," she screams. "I tried to call you back, but your phone was off. Why did you hang up on me?"

"Just get me the name of the hospital."

She ignores my demand. "Where are you? Why are you breathing so heavy?"

"I'm in the Cleveland airport. I need to know where to go. Now get me the hospital while I find a ride."

I hang up knowing she's going to ream my ass, but also knowing she'll come through for me.

By the time I get my ride, Layla has already text me which hospital she is at. It's a thirty-minute drive that feels like an eternity. As soon as I'm dropped off, I race inside to the front desk.

"I need the room number and floor for Mia Giannelli," I breathe heavily, not concerned in the slightest with how crazy I might look.

"Are you family?" she asks as she types on her keyboard.

"Yes, I'm her...brother," I state, knowing it's kind of gross but likely the easiest lie I can manage without being suspicious. If I say husband and her file is marked single, that won't go over well.

"Okay, sir. She is in room 425. Fourth floor on those elevators to your right."

I thank her and run towards the elevators. On my way up, I try to think about what I want to say to her. My brain is fried from all of the traveling and has decided to stop functioning. Fuck it, I'll think of it on the spot. I just need to know she's okay.

What if she's not okay?

The doors open and I take off walking as fast as I can. The sound of beeping all around me from all the machines just adds to the growing fear taking up residence in my stomach.

I find the room and enter without knocking or checking to see if anyone else is in there. The sterile scent of disinfectant floods my senses and fills me with dread. Then I see her lying in the hospital bed with her eyes closed. The sight of her hit s me like a punch to the gut. She looks so fragile lying there in the blue hospital gown surrounded by machines.

My chest tightens with an overwhelming mix of relief and heartbreak. Relief that she is alive, that I can see it with my own eyes, but the sight of her hooked up to all of these machines is almost too much to take.

My legs feel shaky as they take me to her bedside. I swallow hard. This isn't my Mia. I want her to open her eyes, to smile at me, to laugh. I fall into the seat beside her and gently reach for her hand. I don't want to hurt her, but I need to feel her skin against mine.

I close my eyes and press my lips to her hand. Is she in a coma? I couldn't bear it. It feels like I hold my lips to her hand for an eternity, too afraid to back away.

"Eric?" a whisper pulls me from my thoughts.

I open my eyes, and her perfect green eyes are staring back at me. "Mia. Thank God. You're awake."

"What are you doing here?" she asks softly.

I stand up, keeping her hand in mine as I sit at the edge of her bed. "Layla told me you were hurt. I came right away. I'm so sorry."

Her head turns to the side as she looks up at me. "Why are you sorry?"

"Because this is all my fault. If I hadn't been so stupid and pushed you away," I say as my voice wavers with emotion.

"Your decision has nothing to do with what happened," she replies coldly.

The warm Mia that I fell in love with is not the one lying in front of me. I broke her trust. I can feel it, and it may be the worst feeling I've ever experienced.

"When I get my hands on that motherfucker," I say through clenched teeth.

I can't believe he thought he could lay a finger on her without any repercussions. Just thinking about him has me seething. I should've found him first and beat him to a pulp.

"He didn't hurt me," she replies.

"How can you say that? You're lying in a hospital bed."

"I mean...yes, he broke into my house and scared me," she says and every muscle in my body tenses. "But he didn't lay a finger on me. I tried to back away when he stepped closer to me and lost my footing and fell down the stairs."

I should feel better that he didn't do this on purpose, but there is no relief. He still scared her enough to back away which led to this.

"Mia. He did this. Don't make excuses for him."

She closes her eyes and takes a deep breath. I don't want to stress her out, so I don't press her on it. But this conversation is not over.

"Why did you come here?" she whispers, eyes still closed.

"I didn't even think about it. The second Layla told me, it was the only decision that I could've made. It made me see things clearly for the first time. It's like everything fell into place."

It's the truth. I just went on instinct without my head getting in the way. I don't usually believe in fate, but something about this feels like it happened for a reason. I hate that I needed such a kick in the ass to wake up. To think all of this is my fault makes my stomach churn.

"So, you felt guilty like it was your fault, so you came," she says as her eyes open and meet mine.

"What? No," I reply defensively. "That's not the reason."

"You said it yourself. You feel like it's your fault. So, you came here out of guilt."

"Mia, I did not come here out of guilt. I came here because...because I love you."

Her lips curve inside her mouth as tears threaten to spill over her lids. "Don't do that. Don't say something you don't mean."

"Don't mean? Of course I mean it. I'm so sorry about how I behaved. I was just scared of my feelings for you. But I do, I love you."

She shakes her head back and forth. "No. Maybe you think you love me, but it's just the guilt you're feeling right now."

"Dammit, Mia. That's not true," I reply desperately.

"How can I be sure?" she asks as a tear slides down her cheek. "I don't want someone to confess their love for me out of guilt. That's not love."

"This is not about guilt."

"But I don't know how I can trust that. I'm sorry, Eric. I know you're trying, and you're a good guy. I appreciate you coming here, but I can't put my heart on the line if I don't trust the person that I'm giving it to."

The idea that she doesn't trust me makes my heart ache, raw and exposed. The quiet that follows creates a hollowness that takes residence in my chest. I just quit my job for her, just declared my love, and she's rejecting it.

Coming here, I feared I lost her in the worst possible way, but this is much worse. This is losing her by her choice, and it kills me. But if it's what she wants, I have to accept that.

She's been through enough, and has had one crazy ex to deal with. She doesn't need the stress of another.

Tears threaten to come, but I hold them back. I don't want her to feel any worse than she does right now. Just because I fucked up my chance with her, doesn't mean she needs to feel the brunt of my pain.

I lift her hand to my lips and give it a kiss. Her lips tremble as tears fall down her cheeks.

"I'm sorry I let you down. You'll never know how much I will regret losing my chance with you." I let her hand go and stand up. "Goodbye, Mia."

It takes everything in me to get myself out of her room without turning around and begging for forgiveness. I want to fight for her, but I also don't want to be her next Don. I love her too much to put her through dealing with another man who won't let her go.

I just have to accept that I fucked up. I had my chance with her, and I let my stupid past   get in the way.

As I walk outside, I hesitate.

Why am I giving up? So, I pushed her away when I was scared. That doesn't mean I don't love her. That doesn't mean she can't trust me ever again. All that should matter is that she loves me, and I swear she does.

I can feel it when I'm with her.

I'm about to take a step back inside the hospital, but I can't. I ball my fists at my sides as I picture her trying to rest and having to deal with someone kicking me out. It makes me sick. No, I was right to leave. She asked me to go, and I'm going to respect her wishes.

Before I head back home, there's something I need to do. I pull out my phone and text Layla. There's one more piece of information I need her to get for me.

This one comes with a bit of confusion and refusal on her part until I demand that I get the address. It takes her an hour to get it for me, but at least I'm in the car and on my way.

If I can't have Mia or be here to protect her, then I'll be damned if I don't take care of business before I leave.

The entire drive my body shakes with rage as I think about Mia falling down the stairs. She could have been seriously hurt or even killed. I don't understand how her ex isn't in jail. Layla says according to Mia's brother, he was questioned by the police with the restraining order reinforced. That's not enough.

The car slowly comes to a stop in front of a large house. I look up at it through my window.

"I need you to stay here," I tell the driver. "This will only take a minute."

I don't wait for his response. Stepping out of the car, I pull down each sleeve of my shirt as I take calculated steps towards the front door.

The house is in a cookie cutter wealthy neighborhood with no personality whatsoever. A Rolls-Royce sits in the driveway. It all screams insecurity to me, but then again, who am I to talk? It's amazing what money does to all of us.

I get to the front door and pound on it with my fist. As I wait, I adjust the collar on my shirt, wishing I didn't feel so constrained in it.

When the door opens, I have to refrain from rolling my eyes. Of course, the dude is dressed in a polo and has perfectly gelled hair.

He looks me up and down. "Who are you?" he asks with a sense of discomfort.

I take a step forward and slam my fist into his face. He falls forward and moans as his hands rest on his knees. Before he can recover, I grip his shoulders and knee his stomach. He falls back onto the ground with a howl that echoes the foyer.

With his hands over his face, he screams. "Who the fuck are you?"

I grab him by the collar of his shirt and lift his head off of the ground. "I'll be your worst fucking nightmare if you so much as look at Mia ever again. Do you hear me?" I growl.

He looks up at me in silence.

I shake his collar. "Answer me," I yell.

"Yes," he stutters. "Yes, I hear you."

"Good," I bite. I release my grip on his collar and let him fall back to the ground. "Just remember," I say as I back away, "touch her, and you'll die."

With that, I turn on my heel and walk out the door. I open and close my fist as the pain sears through my knuckles and fingers. I'll have to check and see if it's broken when I get home, but it was worth it.

That motherfucker better never be anywhere in the same vicinity as her or I'll come back here to take care of him myself.

I get back into the car and tell him to take me to the airport. As I lie my head back on the seat, I close my eyes and all I see is Mia's face when I told her I loved her. She didn't believe me. How could she not believe me?

I wouldn't drop everything, quit my job, and run to someone if I didn't love them. I wouldn't feel like my entire world was going to be over if something happened to them and I wasn't there to protect them.

How was she supposed to know you felt any of this if you didn't stay to explain, you idiot?

But she asked me to leave. She didn't want me to explain. There was nothing left for me to do but give her what she wanted. I lost her the second I pushed her away from me. I don't deserve another chance.

It's a good thing her brothers weren't there at the time. They probably would've kicked my ass for hurting her in the first place or making her cry while she was lying in a damn hospital bed. I would've done the same thing to anyone making Layla feel like that.

The driver comes to a stop and lets me know it's my time to get out. I take a deep breath and open the door. This isn't how I pictured coming back home.

I don't know what the answer for us would've been, but I was willing to fight for it and figure it out. Maybe I could've opened my open wood crafting shop in Cleveland. Although, what I make is more geared to southern living. Plus, the weather in Ohio wouldn't be great for a barn during the winter.

Whatever, the point is we could have figured it out. Now, I'll never know what could have been because I was too afraid to take that leap when it really mattered. I'll have to live the rest of my life knowing I fucked up.

Chapter Thirty-Five

Mia

Everything hurts. My head, my back, my shoulders, but most of all—my heart. The pain of watching Eric leave was far greater than any of the pain from my fall.

My sisters-in-law came to visit me just after Eric left my hospital room. They could tell that I was a mess, and I didn't have the energy to deny, so they know everything.

It didn't take long for me to spill my guts about how conflicted I was. I know I told him to go, and in some sense, I wanted him to. But when he did, I felt angry. Why did he fly all the way out here to give up so easily?

What the hell was that about? He didn't fight even a little bit for me. Of course I was going to struggle with my trust. I had every right to be weary.

Now, I'm sitting here on my couch as my brothers and their wives clean my house and stash my fridge and freezer with all the food my Ma prepared for me. It's like I just had a baby, only I'm sitting here all alone with nothing to show for it but a massive head injury and a banged up body.

Just the thought of it brings more tears to my eyes. Despite all of this, I miss him. I miss him so much I feel it in my bones.

I'm staring out my backdoor as I sit on my white, fluffy couch as Alexis approaches. She hands me a coffee cup filled with my favorite brew.

"Thanks," I smile softly as I take it from her.

She joins me on the couch. I can feel her eyes on me as I take a sip of my coffee.

"Got something you want to say?" I ask as I turn my head her way.

She laughs to herself. "Sorry, I guess I'm being pretty obvious right now. I'm just worried about you."

"I'll be okay," I say unconvincingly.

"You should call him," she says as wraps her arms around her legs.

A bitter laugh escapes. "I can't do that. I asked him to leave."

"Can I ask why you did that if it's not what you really wanted?" she asks gently.

Tears start to run down my cheeks. God, I am not a crier, and I've cried more times in the last month than I have in the last decade. "I guess I just wanted to see him fight for me. And it's not like I was lying. It's hard to believe he truly does love me. I was scared to just jump in and get hurt again."

"But...you didn't expect him to give up so easily?"

I nod my head as my chest rises unevenly, each breath more of a struggle as the tears cascade down my cheeks. I bite my lip, a futile effort to hold back the waves of emotion.

I don't realize my brothers have joined until I dry my tears. They all sit on the couches and chairs around me as they watch me. I watch Marcus swallow his emotions down as he watches me breakdown.

He's the youngest boy and the most emotional.

"Mia," Gabe says. "He won't be back. We made sure of it. He's learned his lesson. He will stay far, far away from you. You're safe."

I look at Alexis with wide eyes. I don't know if I even want to go down this road with my brothers to tell them the real reason that I'm in this state.

"What's going on, Mia?" Lucas asks as his eyes bounce from me to Alexis. "Is there something we need to know?"

"It's nothing," I say through the thick of my emotions.

His head turns to the side as I see the concern written all over his face. "It doesn't look like nothing. This isn't like you. Something else is going on."

"Mia?" Gabe asks. "Is there something else going on?"

Ugh, I can't lie to them. Not when they are looking so concerned for me. My eyes remain on the coffee floating around inside my cup as I work to gather the courage to talk.

"You're right. I'm not upset about Don. It's about Eric."

When I look up, Lucas seems confused. "Eric, the guy you stayed with in Savannah?"

My head moves up and down. "Yeah."

They seem to understand instantly what I'm referring to. I can't believe that I'm sitting here broken hearted over a man who walked away when I didn't want him to, while recovering physically from one that refused to walk away when I begged him to? The embarrassment that I feel right now is making me want to hide under my covers and never come out.

"Do you want me to continue?" Savannah asks, knowing I can't explain it all over again to anyone right now.

I nod my head, thankful that she knows me enough.

I remain seated as I listen to another person tell the story which sounds so much more pathetic as I hear someone else talk about it. Was I really that ignorant that I saw it going any other way with Eric? He told me from the beginning what his intentions were. Maybe I was right to tell him to leave.

After she's done, we all sit in silence as I wait for them to tell me I need to grow up and start making better choices.

I look from Gabe, to Lucas, to Marcus as they all wear solemn faces. The silence of the room feels deafening. I tuck a non-existent piece of hair behind my ear just to do something with my hand.

"You love him?" Marcus asks.

My head moves up and down as I fight back the tears that want to continue. I refuse to let out any more tears in front of anyone.

"I wish you told us," Lucas adds.

"I guess in the beginning, there was no reason to say it out loud because there were no promises being made between us. Then when I knew I was falling in love, I was afraid to admit it. When it blew up from there, I was embarrassed to admit it. Between Don and this, I feel incapable of making a decent decision to save my life."

"But then he came to the hospital?" Gabe asks with his elbows on his knees, his hands under his chin.

"Yes," I answer.

"And told you he loved you?" he continues.

"Mmm hmm," I reply reluctantly.

"Then you told him to leave?" he questions.

"Yes," I cry.

"Good," he says as he sits up straight.

My head jerks up at him. Did I hear him correctly? "Why is that good?"

"Because he fucked up. It's going to take a hell of a lot more for him to win you back after how he made you feel. He can't just fly here when he thought the worst had happened   to you and declare his love. That's not fair for him to put you in that position when you were trying to recover."

"You think so?" I ask, wondering if maybe I'm not crazy after all.

"Of course," he replies quickly.

"But he's not that type," I tell him. "If I ask him to leave, he's not going to come back and try harder. I don't think he loves me that hard. I don't think I'm worthy of that kind of love."

Everyone's face seems to fall.

"Are you serious?" Marcus answers loudly. "Mia, you are worthy of that kind of love and more. No one is more kind and giving than you. How could you think that?"

I shrug my shoulders. "No man has ever treated me like that. Like I was worth the world, and they would do anything to have me. Minus Don, but he doesn't count. He wasn't all there in the head, and he doesn't really love me. He just thinks he does. But growing up, it was you guys who had girls fawning over you. I was just the invisible sister that never grabbed anyone's attention."

"That means men are fucking idiots, not that you're not worth it," Lucas replies. "And our idiot friends all wanted a chance with you, but we threatened their lives if they ever thought about touching you."

You would think that would make me feel better, but I don't care anymore. I only want Eric, and I'm afraid that I've lost him.

"I just wonder if maybe I should've listened more when he was making that effort. I'm sure it took a lot for him to come say all that to me," I admit as I pick a piece of lint off of my yoga pants.

"Why did you ask him to leave?" Lucas asks.

Savannah smacks him behind the head for his question which makes me laugh.

"It's ok," I say with a smile. "I guess I was scared to believe it. It seemed too good to be true. The thought still scares me. What if he's confusing caring for me with being in love with me? I get that he cares about me, and it was scary to hear something had happened to me. But that's not the same as love."

"So, you need more proof before you put yourself out there again?" Marcus reiterates for me.

I nod my head. "Does that sound stupid? Like I'm the reason for my own misery right now?"

"Not at all," he replies. "I get it. From everything he told you from the beginning, how much he hates relationships, to letting you go the way he did. You're right to be cautious with your heart."

I don't know what to think or feel anymore. I think what I need right now is a nap. Everything that has happened since I've been home is catching up with me, and all I want to do is pretend my reality doesn't exist.

"Hey, thank you guys so much for stopping over, but I think I need to get some rest. I just took that pain medication not too long ago, so I should rest while I'm most comfortable."

"Are you sure?" Lexi asks gently. "I can hang out for a bit while you sleep just so there's someone here when you wake up."

I smile at her sweet offer, but I know her and Marcus need to get back to Chicago. Her mom must miss her.

"You don't have to do that. You guys really should get back to Chicago. I promise I'll be okay. It'll take time, but I'll move on from all of this."

I let them all look at each other around the room to see if someone is going to object or honor my request. Gabe, being the oldest, nods his head and makes the final decision.

"If you want to be alone, we can go. But we are stopping over tomorrow, no questions asked," he says.

I nod my head in agreement. "Deal."

After they leave, I make sure all of my doors are locked, including the additional deadbolts my brothers installed on every door, and then settle back onto my couch. I wrap my fuzzy blanket around me and lie down.

I wonder what Eric is doing back in Savannah. Is he in his barn making another masterpiece to get out all of his pent-up energy? I grab my phone and look at the time.

What am I thinking? It's ten in the morning on a Thursday. He's at work.

I wonder what he does when he comes home these days. Does he order himself some takeout and go straight to the barn, pretending like the stress from his work is worth it?

I shake my head. It's not my business. I can't keep doing this to myself. I have to accept that it's just not meant to be between the two of us.

I close my eyes and let sleep take over. At least when I'm sleeping, I don't have to pay attention to the ache in my heart.

Chapter Thirty-Six

Eric

I look at the large logo that I made to hang on the outside of my barn and compare it to the picture on the page. Mia did a great job designing this. Looking down at it, I get a tingle of excitement for what's to come. I don't remember the last time I felt this way about my career. Come to think of it, I don't think I've ever felt this way. It's a new and welcome feeling to have a sense of thrill at the possibilities that lie ahead of me.

As great as it feels, the joy is dampened by the permanent cloud that hangs over me. It's been a week since I came back from Cleveland, and everyday feels just as depressing as the last. No matter what I do, I think about how much better it would be with Mia there.

After another hour of working on some projects in my barn, I decide to head inside for lunch. Just as I'm making myself a sandwich, my front door opens, and I hear my brothers shuffle inside.

Asher and Liam walk ahead of three other men that I've never seen before. I'm really not in the mood to entertain them and their friends at the moment. They know all about what happened when I went to Cleveland. They should know I just want to be alone right now.

"Hey, bro." Liam smiles as he takes a seat at my island. "We ran into some strangers in your driveway. They say they're Mia's brothers."

I drop the piece of bread in my hand. I look up and can definitely see a striking resemblance between Mia and the three strangers standing in my kitchen. They all have dark hair and olive skin, but more importantly—they are scowling at me.

I can instantly tell who the leader of the pack is as he stands slightly in front of the other two with his arms crossed over his chest. He is looking at me like he is trying to figure out the best way to end me with the most amount of pain and torture involved. I swallow down my anxiety as I stare back.

"Well, this is awkward," Liam laughs. "Would you like to join me? I'm guessing you have a few things to say to my brother, and I for one would love to witness it."

I roll my eyes. "Liam, shut up." I look over at the man standing closest to me. "Would you like to take a seat outside on the patio?"

It's a little cold out there but it's feeling a bit squished in here. I never had that feeling before in this house. It's very spacious, but it feels like there are six large personalities in here, and my house can't contain all of them.

Plus, I'll be closer to the tools in my barn if I need them for self-defense.

"Outside is fine," he says deeply.

I lead them outside, disregarding my lunch which doesn't matter since my appetite has vanished. We all sit around my large table. As I wait for everyone to take a seat, my annoying brothers included, I try to think of why they could be here.

Could they be pissed that while I was supposed to protect their sister from harm, I couldn't keep my hands to myself. Not only that but ended up hurting her. Maybe they want to scare me and make me suffer before they kick my ass.

It's a little extreme to fly all the way out here to kick my ass.

After we all sit in silence, everyone refusing to speak first, I decide I'm not in the mood for this powerplay bullshit.

"I take it you didn't travel all the way down here to sit in silence," I say directly to the guy who seems to be leading this.

"Eric," Asher says, giving me a look of warning.

I nod my head to him like I know what I'm doing, although I don't. I don't even care. If they want to beat me up, go for it. I doubt I'll feel much of anything since everything has felt numb since I've been back.

"We'll talk when we're ready to talk," one of the other brothers bites at me.

The other one gives him a look that I know well. It means shut the hell up. Then he turns his head towards me. "We did come here to get a couple of things straight. I'm Gabe, Mia's oldest brother."

Oldest brother. Makes sense. Then he points to the man on his left. "This is Lucas and that's Marcus."

I respond with a nod of my head. They all look at me with blank stares now. It's hard to tell if they are mad or just have great poker faces.

"So, what things do we need to get straight?" I ask as I lean forward and fold my arms over the table.

"We came here to talk to you about our sister," Gabe starts. "She's been pretty upset ever since she came back from Savannah, even before the incident that landed her in the hospital."

My eyes close as shame washes over me. I hate to think that I'm the reason for that incident even occurring.

"I'm sorry," I reply, no other words come to me.

Should I explain? How much do they know?

"Well, since it's your fault that she's miserable, I imagine you should be sorry," Gabe replies, jaw set tight. "The question we came here for is what are you going to do about it?"

My eyebrows raise, mouth falls slightly. "What am I going to do about it?" I repeat.

"Yes," Lucas, her other brother, replies. "What are you going to do about it?"

"Well, I don't think she wants me to do anything. Did she tell you that I came to see her in the hospital?"

"Yes," Marcus answers me. "She told us that. You told her you loved her."

"Yes, but she told me to leave. She doesn't trust me, doesn't believe that I love her."

"So, that's it?" Gabe answers loudly. "You're just going to give up? If she's that easy to give up, then I don't think you actually love her."

That pisses me off. I slam my hand down on the table. "That's bullshit. I gave her up *because* I love her. I've spent every miserable minute in this place since she left trying to keep myself away. Once I finally realized my feelings, I got on the plane, quit my job so I could leave, and got to her as soon as I could. But I couldn't fight her on it. She was lying in a hospital bed because of a man who didn't know when to stop fighting for her. I couldn't do that to her again," I say, as my throat constricts from emotion.

Everyone at the table sits in silence as my words hang in the air. I don't fucking care who knows how much I love her or if they judge me for the reasons I left her alone, but I'll be damned if I'm going to put her through anything else that she doesn't want.

"Look, I respect that decision. I appreciate you looking out for our sister, but that's our job," Lucas declares. "But through all of this, did you ever think about the difference between what you mean to her versus what Don meant to her?"

My forehead turns down as I try to figure out what he means.

"I take it by your reaction that you haven't considered it," Lucas replies.

"I'm not sure what you're getting at," I reply.

Liam rolls his head back and moans. "Dude, open your eyes! Do you need them to spell it out for you?"

Gabe lets a small smirk break free at Liam's attitude towards me. Apparently, I'm missing a little detail that they all seem to know.

"The difference is that my sister is in love with you," Gabe says. "She didn't love Don. Didn't even like him. The difference is that she's been crying daily since you left."

The words hit me like a jolt. I'm momentarily stunned as time stands still. Could that mean I haven't lost her yet? A smile threatens to break free at the idea that this thing between us might not be over.

"Are you...are you saying that she still loves me? That she still *wants* me?" I whisper.

"Of course," Marcus replies. "She's just scared. She wants to be sure that you really mean it when you say you love her. You need to fight for her. You need to *show* her that you love her."

I sit up straighter as ideas start to bounce around my head. I nod. "I can do that."

"Now...before you get all kinds of ideas," Gabe states. "I need to know that you are one hundred percent ready to do whatever it takes to be with her. I mean anything. Would you move to Cleveland to be with her? Because if you're not willing to work with her on how you two can be together, I don't want you getting her hopes up for nothing."

That's the easiest decision I've ever made in my life. "Of course, I'm willing to do absolutely anything to be with her."

"Can I ask you a question?" I say as I look at her brothers. They all nod their heads. "Why don't you hate me more? I've been such a dumbass throughout all of this."

They all share in a little chuckle which makes me feel oddly self-conscious. Not something I'm used to feeling around a bunch of guys.

"It would be easy to hate you for hurting our sister, but we've all made these stupid mistakes with our women," Lucas replies. "Mia has opened up to our wives about how she feels like she was always the one helping us out during our stupid moments and making it right. This is our way of returning the favor to her. She deserves all the happiness in the world, and if being with you would make her happy, then it's a no-brainer for us. We trust our sister and her instincts. If she's in love with you, there's probably good reason to be."

I hate the idea that she felt like she did all the fighting for her brothers without anyone doing the same for her.

After I promise to them that I will be taking the time to make sure I know what I'm doing when I do it, they all stand up and head back inside. When we get to my front door, Marcus turns to me.

"One more thing," he starts. "Next time an Italian visits your house, offer food, wine...something. You're a shitty host."

That makes me laugh. I can see these guys becoming extended brothers. I clap him on the shoulder. "Noted, man. I'll work on my hosting skills."

After I close the door, Asher and Liam stand there with their arms crossed.

"So," Liam states deeply.

"Sooo," I draw out, not sure what he's looking for.

He rolls his eyes. "What's your plan?"

I throw my arms up in the air. "They just left two seconds ago. You think I've had time to come up with my plan?"

"Well, don't take too long," Asher replies. "Come to think of it, make sure you tell us the plan when you come up with it."

"Why would I do that?" I ask.

His eyes open wide like I should know. "So, we make sure you don't do anything stupid."

I chuckle. "Get the fuck out of my house. I need to be alone and think."

As they walk out, Asher turns. "And when were you going to tell me that you quit your job?"

"Stop distracting me. I don't have time for that right now."

I close the door and for the first time since I left Cleveland, I feel a glimmer of hope.

"Dude, this is so weird," Liam whines as he holds the camera. "Why the fuck did I agree to do this for you?"

I stand straight in my barn with my hands on my hips. "I already told you. Mia said it was something she would love. I'm grasping at straws here. I just want to put a smile on her face. To remind her that despite the drama of the last couple of weeks, we need to remember our time together and how good it was. I want her to remember why she fell in love with me."

"Yeah, I didn't think it would be this weird until now," he whines.

I roll my eyes and adjust my low hanging jeans. "Just take the fucking picture, asshole."

He bitches and moans the entire way through, but eventually we get all of the shots that I need. I look around my barn to make sure I have everything. I plan to leave in two days when I have everything that I need to make the trip. I don't know how long I'll be gone or if I'll be returning to pack my stuff up and move, but I'm ready for whatever it takes to win her back.

To say that my mom was happy when I told her what my plans are is an understatement. She's on cloud nine and so relieved that I've opened my heart up to love again. I didn't realize how much stress my misery was causing her.

I also never thought I'd go through such lengths to be with someone. It's amazing how much clicked when I heard she was hurt. I'll forever feel shame when I think about what it took to open my eyes to my feelings, but I can't dwell on that right now.

Chapter Thirty-Seven

Mia

Being back in the office is helping a bit. Throwing myself into my work helps keep my mind off of Eric. If I'm not thinking about him, then I'm not kicking myself for pushing him away. I don't know how many times I've picked up my phone and almost called him, begging for him to forgive me for pushing him away.

I'm so miserable that I wonder if I even care if he doesn't love me the way I love him. I'd rather feel the relief of talking to him right now than worry about if I lose him down the road.

If that sounds desperate, then that shows exactly where I am emotionally right now.

A voice startles me from my thoughts. "How are you doing?"

I look up and see my brother Lucas standing at my door. "I'm fine. You don't need to ask me every single day how I'm doing with that look on your face."

"What look?" he asks defensively.

My shoulders fall as I sigh. "The look that says that you are worried about me, wondering if I'm going to break."

"Is it so wrong for me to be worried?" he asks as he leans against my door frame.

"No, of course not. I appreciate you worrying about me. But constantly watching me like I'm a sad little puppy isn't going to help me get over this any faster. All it does is make me feel worse."

I see a look of guilt cross his face. "I'm sorry. I don't want to do that to you. I promise I'll try to stop asking. Did you see the new account Marcus locked in?"

A smile breaks out on my face. "I did. He's doing such a great job out there in Chicago. That's a big client. I'm so excited to start working on how to promote their wines."

"They said one of the reasons they wanted to work with us was seeing your portfolio. They're excited to work with you."

That makes me feel so proud. I love what I do. It's so rewarding when you can make someone else's dreams come true through creating their brand and helping them show it to the world.

After work is done, I'm so exhausted I feel like crawling to my front door. My body is still kind of banged up and definitely needs more rest than I am used to. But sitting at my house alone all day is just not an option for my mental health.

I get to my front porch and the fall cold, which in Cleveland is basically winter, makes my body shiver as it begs for warmth. Something catches my eye at the end of my porch. I turn my head and see a swing hanging at the end.

My breath catches in my throat. It's the swing Eric made for me.

How did it get here?

I take shaky steps all the way to the end of the porch until I'm standing right in front of it.

Did he bring this here? Is he back in Cleveland?

My heart flutters at the thought. I crane my neck to see if there's anyone around, but there's nobody in sight. Then I see something odd installed around the roof of my porch with a cord going down to my outlet. There's a button attached to the cord. I press it and the thing comes to life as it turns orange all around.

It's a heater. So, I can stay warm out here in the fall and winter while still using the swing. It's amazing. I feel it warming me up already.

I don't know what to do. Am I supposed to text him back? But if he wanted to talk to me, wouldn't he have called and told me about this. I don't think he would have snuck in and installed it while I was at work if he wanted to see me.

My vision clouds with emotion. That's what kind of man he is. He arranged to have this set up for me or did it himself all because he knows how much I wanted it. Even after I pushed him away from me and asked him to leave.

I bet he hates me right now.

How did we both manage to hurt each other while claiming to love each other?

I guess that's why we are both single. We clearly both have issues.

I walk into my house and instantly change into comfy clothes before I reheat some food, take pain medication, and fall asleep with my phone in my hand as I tried to think of what to text him.

The next morning when I get into my office, I get a weird feeling. Something seems different but I don't quite know what it is. I look around but don't immediately spot anything different.

I don't know how many times I've grabbed my phone to text him before lunch, but it's borderline driving me insane. There's always something stopping me. This nagging voice in my head telling me that if he wanted to see or talk to me, he would have done it by now.

I throw my phone down on my desk. With my elbow on my desk, I plop my head in my hand. Then I spot it, a picture hanging on my wall across the room.

My vision sucks. I can see it's a man in jeans with no shirt on, but I can't really make out any details. Is this some prank from my brothers? Kind of weird if you ask me.

Maybe one of my sisters-in-law thinks I needed a little pick me up.

I stand up from my desk and as I get closer to it, my jaw hits the floor. I grab it off of the wall and try to process what I'm holding.

It's a calendar. Not just any calendar. One with Eric on the front posing without a shirt on in his barn. He's bending over his workspace as he cuts a piece of wood.

I recall what I said to him one time when I was watching him work in his barn. I told him how much I would enjoy a calendar of just sexy pictures of him in his barn with no shirt on. A smile spreads across my face when I realize what he did.

I walk over to my desk and take a seat then I flip it open. The January picture is of him cutting a log in his backyard. The muscles in his arms are bulging from the strength of him holding his ax over his shoulder.

My body instantly reacts to the picture. I almost forgot just how insanely gorgeous this man is. I flip the page to February where he seems to be cutting out a piece of wood in the shape of a heart.

He's wearing a red and black button-down shirt with the shirt opened for me to have the perfect view of his abs. Each page that I flip to makes me laugh with delight. I can't believe he did this. I wonder who he talked into taking these pictures.

I wish it was me.

A sting of jealousy hits me with who got to be behind that lens. What if he hired a woman?

When I get to December, the thought of who was behind the lens is gone, replaced with sheer joy. He is in his classic jeans, low cut with no shirt but wearing a Santa hat. This time he is in the woods cutting down a tree, but the sexy look he gives the camera makes me shiver.

The rest of the day, I'm a mess. I can't figure out what all of this means. First the swing, now this calendar. The swing was sweet, the calendar hilarious, but there's no notes or anything along with them for me to understand what they mean.

It's driving me crazy and I'm about at my breaking point. I want to call him and scream at him! It's not fair. I'm not strong enough to feel so close to him throughout these gestures and yet so far away.

The entire drive home I'm convincing myself that if I do call him, I need to be calm and rational. I can't go off on him for being so damn confusing even though that's exactly what I want to do. But when I pull into my driveway, my heart sinks into my stomach.

There's a rental car sitting in my driveway. I park my car behind it and slowly get out of my car. As I walk past the car, I peek through the window but no one is inside. Then I hear someone clear their throat.

I turn my head and spot him sitting on my new swing. His eyes remain glued to me as I walk up the driveway. My body hums with excitement and shakes with nerves. It's an odd combination.

When I approach, the warmth of the heaters actually makes it bearable to stay outside. He's in dark jeans and a hoodie with a backwards hat on. I think it's my new obsession seeing him dressed like this. My heart flutters at just how handsome he is.

I open my mouth to say something, but nothing comes out. I don't know what to say.

A small smirk crosses his face, like he can tell I'm at a loss for words. "Hi, Mia."

Well, I guess I could have started with a hello. But I'm too startled to think clearly. "Hi," I say as my voice breaks.

"How are you?" he asks like this is just a casual conversation. Like this is normal. Nothing about this is normal.

"Umm, I'm fine."

His head falls to the side. "Aren't you going to ask how I'm doing?"

I take a deep breath, willing myself to say what I want. "Actually, I'm more curious as to what you're doing here."

He nods his head. "That's fair. Care to take this conversation inside?"

"Oh, yeah, sorry," I say as I realize I haven't invited him in yet. "Come on in."

I reach for my key, hoping he doesn't notice my shaky hand as I open my front door. I take a step inside and turn on my lights then kick off my shoes and take off my coat. I lead him into the family room and take a seat on my couch.

I expect him to sit on the other couch or one of the chairs, but he takes a seat right next to me like it's the most natural thing in the world. The suspense of all of this is killing me. He rests one arm on the back of the couch, and I have to remind myself not to fall into the crook of his arm like I used to. But the physical urge to do so is powerful.

"Where do I start?" he says as he looks at me softly.

I tuck a hair behind my ear nervously. "I don't know, Eric," I say as my voice cracks with emotion. "I just…"

"Hey," he says gently as he places his hand on top of mine, which is resting on my thigh. "I'm sorry. Let me just start from the beginning." He takes a deep breath, and only then do I recognize his own nerves.

"That night that you left," he starts.

"I'm sorry," I blurt out, but he holds up his hand.

"Please, don't apologize for a single thing. I'm the one who owes the apology. That night, I had just gotten back from work and was already on edge because I had just realized how much I hated my job. It was an effort to get through the workday when all I wanted to do was come home to you. That scared me. I knew deep down I was already in love with you, and I felt out of control. So, when I came home, and you were there to give me that business proposal, I was already in a terrible headspace."

Well, that sounds like shitty timing. I wish I had known that.

"It's no excuse as to how I acted," he continues. "But I just wanted you to have some context. I was jealous of how much you loved your job, but I kept telling myself that not everyone gets to do what they love. For the longest time, I've contributed money to being worthy. But the second I thought something could have happened to you. It was like everything fell into place. I realized it didn't matter the amount of money I had sitting in the bank if the woman I loved was gone."

I inhale a shaky breath. Hearing him say he loves me again when I'm not lying in a hospital bed feels different. Can this be real? It's everything I want to hear.

Why do I still feel so scared?

"But I was a fool. I came to you and unloaded all of this on you when you were weak and hurt. And I expected you to believe it after just one moment of declaration. For that, I'm sorry."

He lifts his hand and glides his thumb across my cheek. Only now do I realize that I'm crying.

"When you told me to leave, I shouldn't have taken that as an ending to our story. But I was scared," he says as I see emotion cloud his eyes as well. "You were in that hospital because of an ex who didn't listen to your demand to leave you alone. I didn't want to be another ex who didn't honor your request."

I can't believe I never thought about it like that. I stare back at this man. This amazing man who just wanted to make sure I never felt pressured again, and I suddenly can't stay away. I throw myself into his arms, wrapping my arms around his neck as I cry into his shoulder.

"I'm so sorry. I'm sorry I made you feel that way. I was just so scared of getting hurt," I cry.

His arms snake around my waist and he pulls me into him. Everything already feels exactly like it should again. I'm so crazy for this man.

When I pull away, I sit back down but this time our bodies are touching. I don't want to feel any distance between us again.

"I understand, Mia. But I owe you the apology. None of this would have happened if I was just able to pull my head out of my ass for a second to realize that I was the one afraid of getting hurt again. But I should have known from the moment I met you that you were different."

He pauses and smiles down at me. "I quit my job."

"What?" I gasp. "You quit? When?"

"The second Layla called to tell me you were in the hospital. I was already being told that my bosses thought I was slacking off when I started working normal hours. Then when I knew I had to get to you, explaining why I needed to leave just pissed me off. So, I quit."

"And...how do you feel about that now?" I ask cautiously.

I hope he doesn't regret it. I would feel awful.

He smiles. "I feel great about it. You know the crazy part? I told my colleague to tell them I quit, and they haven't even called me since I left. They never gave a shit about me. But then I found your business proposal for my company. Mia, it was amazing."

"You think so?"

He cups my cheek tenderly. "I have already bought the LLC and worked with a bank to get it all setup. I even made a sign for my barn. Do you want to see it?" he asks.

"Of course I do," I say with excitement.

He pulls out his phone and shows me a picture. The sign has the logo that I designed burned into it. "Eric, it's stunning. I love it. I can't believe this. I'm so proud of you."

I look up into his eyes and the way he is looking at me has my heart skipping a beat. "You saw me, Mia. The real me. The one who always dreamed of this but never knew it was possible. I'm so crazy about you. I...I love you."

"You do?" I ask as my heart thunders in my chest.

He nods his head. "Of course I do. And I'm willing to do anything to be with you. Have you move to South Carolina and live with me or move up here to be with you. Whatever it takes. You are my forever. I've never been more certain of anything in my entire life."

"You would move here for me?"

His finger runs along my jaw as I swallow heavily. "I would do anything for you, Mia. The only time I have ever felt loved and accepted for who I am, has been with you. You are my world now, and nothing will stop me from making sure we are together."

All these years I've wondered if there was someone out there who would go to the ends of the earth to be with me. I never thought it would happen. Even when I thought I was running away from the scariest time of my life, it was leading me to my happy ever after.

"Eric," I say through a cloud of emotion. "I love you too."

He smiles as he leans down and presses his lips to mine. Every worry, every fear that I've had melts away as he deepens the kiss. When we pull away, I'm panting with desire, and my brain conjures up all the pictures on my calendar, and I laugh.

"What's so funny?" he asks.

"I'm just thinking about the calendar you made," I laugh.

He chuckles to himself. "I just wanted you to laugh. You have Liam to thank for that. He told me to tell you that he is personally scarred for life and will never be the same."

I throw my head back and laugh. This man. I don't know how I got so lucky, but I'm going to soak up all of the love and laughter that I know he has inside of him. He just needed to feel safe enough to give it to someone. I will never take for granted that I am the lucky recipient of it all.

Life has been crazy up to this point. But I have a feeling that the only time I will look back at my past, is to see how far I have come.

The End

Epilogue

Mia

One Year Later

"You look beautiful, Bella Mia," Ma says as she stands behind me while we gaze into the mirror. She wipes away a tear. I turn around and grab her hand.

"Ma, don't make me cry," I say through thick emotions.

She waves a hand in the air. "I'm sorry. It's just my beautiful girl, my only girl, is getting married today."

I smile, loving the sound of those words. I can't believe I'm getting *married* today. I'm standing in the front room of the church in Little Italy that my grandparents were married in as I wait for the signal that everyone is set.

Layla and my sisters-in-law all stand in front of me in their brown bridesmaid dresses. I realize how lucky I am to have so many amazing women in my life. Growing up without a sister was rough, but I've certainly won the lottery with these women.

Pa peeks his head inside. "We're ready," he says with a smile.

I nod my head and take a deep breath. I'm not one for being center of attention, so my nerves are through the roof. I hear the music start as my Ma gives me a kiss than walks out of the room. I wish I got to see everybody walk down the aisle. Once all of my bridesmaids have gone, Pa comes over to me and walks me behind the large church doors.

He turns to me. "I'm so happy for you, Bella Mia. I'll always remember you as my little girl, but I know it's time to watch you start your own family."

"Pa, nothing is going to change. Sunday dinners, our secret late night desserts. We can still have it all."

Before he can answer, the music stops and changes. I place my hand on his arm and the doors open. I think I'm going to pass out as everybody stands and turns to look at me. Then my eyes find Eric, and everything else melts away. It's just him and me in this room, and I suddenly can't wait to get to him. My steps become hurried as Pa tugs at my arm.

"Remember, walk slow," he whispers.

I keep a smile on my face and do what we rehearsed, but everything in me just wants to be by Eric's side. When I finally reach him, his smile makes my heart skip a beat. I still can't believe he wants to marry me. I'm the luckiest woman alive.

Hours later, Eric and I are standing in the corner at our reception. He pulled me behind a large pillar in the building to steal a kiss. Now, he has his arm wrapped around my waist while we look out at the dance floor.

His chin rests on my shoulder. "Look at those fools," he says with amusement.

Our siblings are all out on the dance floor having a great time together. Even Asher and Gabriel are out there busting some moves. I chuckle as I watch them dance and get along like family already.

"I'm so happy they all get along," I tell him as I spin around and wrap my arms around his neck.

He leans down and kisses me soft and slowly. I can tell what kind of mood he is tonight. He's going to take his time in the bedroom when this is all done. I squeeze my thighs together in anticipation.

"I've been thinking about taking this dress off of you all day," he whispers over my mouth.

I smile then kiss him. "Oh, how romantic."

He pulls away. "Hey, I think being insanely attractive to your wife and wanting to worship her body is romantic."

"Yeah. I don't know if it's wedding day romantic."

He wraps his arm back around my waist. "Okay, how about this? I was a nervous wreck standing at the altar today. My body felt like it was on fire. But the moment I saw you, everything in me settled. That's what your presence does to me. It instantly tells my body that everything will be okay as long as you're by my side."

Tears border my eyes. "That's amazing. That's exactly what happened to me too. I hated everyone looking at me, hated the attention, but the moment I saw you...it all went away."

He leans down and kisses me lips. "Now that's romantic."

That *is* romantic. It's amazing how in tune our bodies are with each other. I can't wait to spend the rest of my life with this man.

We have done so much traveling in the last year that we decided a romantic stay at our house in Isle of Hope is just what we need for our honeymoon.

He claims he is going to get me pregnant this week. While I know that's a long shot, I can't wait for it to happen.

I can't wait for all of our firsts together. I know I'm in for a lifetime of surprises with this man, and I couldn't be more ready.

Also by Nicole Baker

Follow Me On Social Media

To have access to my bonus scenes– visit my website and subscribe to my newsletter. You will be directed to a special page on my website with ALL bonus scenes.

www.nicolebakerauthor.com

Follow me for exclusive news on releases, signings, and giveaways.

Facebook @nicolebakerauthor

Instagram @nicolebaker_author

TikTok @authornicolebaker

www.ingramcontent.com/pod-product-compliance
Lightning Source LLC
Chambersburg PA
CBHW021340150726
47989CB00005B/2051